JANICE WHITEAKER

Cowboy Seeking a Wedding Date, Book 3 of the Cowboy Classifieds series

www.janicemwhiteaker.com

First printing, 2021
Cover design by Robin Harper at Wicked by Design.

CHAPTER ONE

"WHAT DO YOU think?" Maryann held up the newest impulse buy she wanted worked into the decor of The Inn at Red Cedar Ranch. "I saw it and I just knew it would look perfect in here."

Nora stared at the tapestry, trying to come up with the right words.

It was beautiful, that wasn't the problem.

The problem was the huge floral pattern stitched in deep gem tones that didn't remotely match anything else in the building.

"Um," she took a deep breath, using it to buy time, "I'm not sure it really fits in with the rest of what you have going on."

Maryann actually had very good taste, which was more than she could say for most of the client's she'd worked with. Unfortunately it was also varied as hell, and without constant intervention The Inn would look like a *Better Homes and Gardens* magazine day-drank too much wine and barfed everywhere.

Which honestly didn't sound like a terrible idea most days.

Maryann tucked her chin, looking down at the wall hanging draped across the front of her body. "Well," she glanced up at Nora, "shit." The older woman immediately started cackling, and Nora couldn't help but laugh right along with her.

This was why she didn't mind Maryann's constant curveballs.

Because while Maryann made sure she was involved in every step of the design process, The Pace family's matriarch was as good at taking rejection as she was at throwing out the ideas that resulted in it.

Nora reached out to finger the well-made decoration. "It really is beautiful, though. I hate to see it go to waste."

Maryann pushed it her way. "You take it." She smiled. "I'm sure you have someplace where it will look just perfect."

"I definitely don't have a place for it." She didn't just not have a place to hang the tapestry, she didn't have a place at all. Currently, her home was a long-term hotel room about thirty minutes away in a town only slightly larger than Moss Creek.

Unless you wanted to count the storage unit in Seattle holding all her stuff.

"But you will." Maryann pushed it closer. "You are going to have a beautiful place all your own soon."

Nora sighed.

Maryann was as stubborn as she was generous.

She took the tapestry. "I will hold onto it in case we find a spot for it here."

"Or," Maryann lifted her brows, "you can pack it up for your new home."

Nora shook her head. "You are a pain in the butt sometimes."

"But I make really good cobbler." Maryann crossed to the set of double ovens in the kitchen of the main house at Red Cedar Ranch. "I still can't believe you hadn't had cobbler before you came here."

"My parents aren't big cooks." Nora carefully draped the tapestry over one arm and slowly began backing toward the door. "I should get out of the way before everyone comes in for dinner."

As the only child of two workaholic parents, she grew up spending most of her time alone. Happily.

Getting caught in the middle of a Pace family dinner was her worst nightmare.

Outside of the cows that seemed to be everywhere around here. Mooing and crapping like it was their job.

"You should stay for dinner." Maryann lifted out the tray of dessert making the kitchen smell divine. "I made your favorite."

Nora continued her slow backwards retreat. "You can't call it my favorite if it's the only kind I've ever had."

Maryann managed to talk her into staying for dinner once, back when she first took the job and felt guilty saying no, and she'd been gunning for another stay ever since.

It wasn't going to happen.

"All the more reason for you to have dinner here more often." Maryann gave her a grin. "I figure eventually you'll get tired of me hounding you and just give in."

Nora sighed again. She did that a lot here.

Maryann's face softened as she set the hot dish down and came her way. "I'm sorry, Honey. I'm not trying to pressure you. It just makes me crazy to think about you eating dinner all alone."

"I eat dinner alone all the time." Always had.

Maryann's hand went to cover the spot over her heart. "That's just not right."

Nora laughed. "It's not a big deal." She moved a little faster, ready to escape before the crowd infiltrated the house, filling it with noise and commotion and chaos. "It's what I'm used to."

"That's even worse." Maryann's lips turned down in a frown. "It breaks my heart."

"Everything breaks your heart." Nora took another step back. "I keep trying to tell you everyone else's happiness is not your responsibility."

Definitely not hers.

"It should be." Maryann's frown softened and she let out a huff of air. "Fine. If you don't want beef stroganoff and warm cherry cobbler then you're beyond help."

Nora grinned. "We've already established I'm beyond help." She blew Maryann a kiss. "I'll see you tomorrow."

Maryann gave her a single wave. "Go eat your lonesome dinner."

Nora turned and hustled out the front door before Maryann could come up with some other reason to try to suck her back in.

And she most definitely would try. Not a day passed that Maryann didn't do her very best to lure Nora closer to the all-encompassing family she'd built and continued to expand at every opportunity.

But Maryann's dedication wasn't necessarily a bad thing. It made it easier to forget what was waiting back home. What she had to eventually face.

She'd come to Moss Creek needing a distraction from the recent events that had upended her life.

It worked, but now that the end of her time here was closing in, it was becoming harder to ignore what was coming.

What she had to do.

Nora rushed to her car and jumped inside, ready to make her escape. She pressed the button to turn over the engine on the long-term rental.

Nothing happened.

She pressed it again, this time harder, just in case that would help.

Still nothing.

Her finger switched to the window control, planning to let out some of the hot air already making her sweat.

Nothing there either.

"For the love of Go—" Nora shoved her door open and the seventy-five-degree outside air rushed in, feeling like a wave of air-conditioning.

"Car troubles?"

She jumped so high it knocked the cell phone perched on her thigh to the floorboards.

Brooks Pace smiled at her as he leaned down to peer inside the car, resting one tanned arm along the roof. "Doesn't seem to be starting, does it?"

Nora poked the ignition again, stabbing it with every bit of strength she had in that single finger, each jab more frantic than the last.

Because Maryann wasn't the only Pace she needed to escape.

Brooks tipped his hat back as he straightened. "Pop the hood."

Nora blinked. "What now?"

Brooks' easy smile held. "I got it."

Suddenly he was very close, toned body crowding her space in a way she'd worked hard to avoid in the month she'd been here.

But now she was trapped. Forced to sit there while he brushed closer, his nearness teasing her as he reached under the dash and pulled a little lever.

Something popped and she jumped again.

Brooks looked at her over one wide shoulder, a single brow lifted in question. "You okay?"

"Yes—" Her voice was squeaky and sharp. She cleared her throat and tried again. "What was that noise?"

Brooks' blue eyes went to the front of the car. "That was the hood unlatching." He lingered, staying long enough his scent filled the inside of her car.

She always thought he might smell like sweat and dirt. At the very least straw. Hay.

Whatever it was they fed horses.

But the smell clinging to his worn shirt and jeans was something more akin to spice and sunshine. Deep and fresh at the same time. Warm and rich.

It was the most awful thing she could imagine.

Outside of being trapped at Red Cedar Ranch.

Brooks' lips curved in a slow smile. "I'll be right back."

As he left a slow breath of relief escaped the confines of her lungs. She'd worked hard to stay the hell away from Maryann's sons.

Primarily the eligible ones. Brody and Boone were harmless little kittens. Completely smitten with the women they had.

But Brooks and Brett? Those boys were dangerous.

It was there in the way they walked. The way they talked.

The way they smiled and said 'yes ma'am'.

They were the kind of men that girls make stupid decisions over.

And she was done making stupid decisions because of a man.

Brooks reached under the hood of the car and moved his hand along the gap. Something clicked and he lifted the whole thing up, blocking out her view of his painfully perfect body.

She *would* end up taking the one job in the world populated by rugged cowboys.

Too bad she was probably the only woman not looking to be swept off her feet by a cowboy.

By anyone really.

She had shit to deal with.

A lot of it. Unfortunately.

"Try to start it again."

Nora leaned out the open door. "With you right there?" No way was that safe. Engines had to be dangerous. Combustion. Chemicals. Moving parts. He might lose a finger.

Burn that horrible face he had.

Brooks leaned to peek at her around the edge of the hood. "What's the worst that could happen?"

Neither the loss of an appendage or the incineration of a handsome man was at the top of her list, and that showed just how bad off she really was right now.

The *worst* that could happen was that she might end up stuck at Red Cedar Ranch for dinner with the whole extended Pace family instead of enjoying a quiet dinner in her hotel room.

Away from them and all they were.

Nora jammed her finger into the ignition button.

Nothing.

The hood blocking her view of Brooks suddenly dropped, leaving her staring right at his ruggedly handsome face.

Into his clear blue eyes.

"I think you need a new battery."

"That's impossible. This car is practically new." She hit the button again.

"Probably just a faulty unit." Brooks was back at her open door, blocking out most of the evening sun baking into her clothes and skin. "I'm sure the rental place will give you another car."

That didn't help her right now.

Nora dropped her head to the headrest and closed her eyes. Partly so she could think.

Partly so she could pretend Brooks wasn't standing so close to her.

Which turned out to be impossible. He was unignorable.

Which is why she always resorted to avoidance.

"I rented it at the airport." She huffed out a frustrated breath. "It's an hour and a half away from here."

"Maybe they have a place closer."

"Nothing is close to here." It was her main complaint about Moss Creek, Montana. There was nothing around. Nothing but cows and the cowboys who wrangled them.

No distractions to steal her focus and keep it somewhere safe.

Nora fished her cell phone from the floorboard and pulled up the number for the car rental company. She tapped her fingers against the steering wheel while waiting for someone to answer. The phone rang.

And rang.

And rang.

"Somethin' wrong?"

She let the phone fall to her lap. "Nope. Everything is just fine." Nora stared out the windshield.

What in the hell was she going to do?

"I know how to get a battery changed, Miss Nora." Brooks leaned down. "We can head out of here and have a fresh one put in before the sun goes down."

The thought of a new battery to fuel her escape from Red Cedar Ranch was tempting. The idea of spending an evening alone with Brooks Pace was not.

"I'll just call an Uber to come get me."

Brooks chuckled, low and deep. "Uber doesn't come out here. And even if they did, it'd be dark before they pulled up."

She knew that. No one came out here.

She definitely shouldn't have.

"I'd be happy to replace it while you stay here and have dinner."

Shit.

Nora risked a peek at Brooks. "How long would it take to do this?"

Brooks' smile was slow and steady. "Travel time included? A few hours."

Nora glanced at the time on her phone. Dinner would start in less than fifteen minutes, and if she was here when it started she would be trapped. "Okay. Let's go."

"Yes, ma'am." Brooks straightened and took a step back.

Make that a half-step.

Nora edged out of the car, doing her best to keep as much distance between her and Brooks as possible. "How are we getting the car to the shop?"

Brooks lifted a brow. "We aren't taking it to a shop." He fished a set of keys from the pocket of his well-worn blue jeans. "I know how to do more than ride a horse, Miss Nora."

Her mind immediately tried to take a detour. One she couldn't allow.

"*You're* going to replace the battery?" She'd never met a man capable of doing anything besides dropping a car off to have work done. Heck, her own dad probably didn't even know how to open the hood on his car.

Brooks tapped the front brim of his hat, knocking it up so his clear blue eyes were easier to see. They barely crinkled at the edges with an unseen smile. "I can replace more than your battery."

This time the detour was impossible to avoid.

She was screwed.

Going with Brooks was a very bad idea. Her eyes went to the house that would soon be filled to capacity. It was suddenly seeming like the lesser of two evils.

Almost.

But ultimately, the company of one Pace won out over a swarm of Paces.

Nora glanced at the driveway, expecting to see more people rolling in any second. "We should go, otherwise we'll be up half the night."

Brooks slowly headed toward one of the large red trucks occupying the driveway. "There's worse ways I can think of spending half the night."

"There's also better ways." The words were out of her mouth before she realized how they sounded.

What they suggested.

It was because of that damn detour her mind couldn't help but take. The split second her brain managed to consider what it might be like to spend time close to the cowboy wreaking havoc on her evening.

The smile on Brooks' face turned to a shit-eating grin. "You took the words right out of my mouth."

Hell.

This was why she tried to stay away from them. These men were impossible to ignore. Impossible to avoid. And impossible not to find attractive.

It was ridiculous.

And now she was stuck spending a few hours with one while he fixed her car in dusty boots, dusty jeans, and that damn cowboy hat.

Her time in Moss Creek was turning out to be a distraction all right.

Just not in the right sort of way.

Brooks pulled open the passenger door of the truck, holding it wide as she climbed in. Nora settled into the seat and looked around the space.

"Somethin' wrong?"

"No." The truck was remarkably well-kept. Clean. Organized. No sign of the haze that seemed to coat everything around here. "Just looking."

"Look all you want."

Nora fixed her eyes on the dash instead of doing exactly as he offered and looking all she wanted.

Looking was a terrible idea. Looking led to liking and liking led to wanting and wanting led to—

"Watch yourself." Brooks' voice was close. Very close.

"Watch myself what?" She was trying not to watch him, not herself.

"Watch your *feet*." The low tone of his voice held a hint of amusement. Like he might realize exactly what she was trying not to watch.

Nora's eyes rolled down to where her feet sat just outside the scope of safety. She slowly tucked them into the spotless floorboard.

"Thank you." Brooks closed the door and ambled around the back end of his truck, clearly in no hurry.

It was strange.

None of the Pace men ever seemed in a hurry to do anything, yet they still got more shit done than anyone she'd ever known.

Including, apparently, changing car batteries.

Nora watched from the corner of her eye as Brooks settled into the driver's seat, slinging one calloused hand across the top of the wheel. He looked relaxed and calm and perfectly at ease with their current situation.

She gripped the leather of her handbag tighter as he backed out of his spot at the ranch and eased the truck onto the gravel drive leading to the unmarked road that went to downtown Moss Creek.

Brooks was silent as he drove. The only sound in the cab came from the air blowing through the vents and onto the hot skin of her cheeks.

Nora made it twenty minutes, counting each one as it passed, before she couldn't stand it anymore. "I'm sorry you're missing dinner."

"I'm not missing dinner."

"I know your mom will save you dinner, but it won't be hot and I feel bad." He was doing her a favor, and the least she could do was be appreciative.

It wasn't his fault she was such a mess.

"I'm not eating dinner at the ranch." Brooks' blue eyes came her way as he waited on the single traffic light in Moss Creek to turn green. "We're picking up dinner while we're out." He turned to face forward as the light turned green. "I'm not making you wait three hours for your dinner."

Double shit.

Dinner at the ranch with the whole family was one thing. Dinner alone with one single member of the family was another.

Especially this single member.

"You don't have to do that. I'll be fine." She was already hungry. She'd skipped lunch, instead using the time trying to get everything in order for the upcoming grand opening of The Inn. "I'll just grab something on my way to the hotel."

"Must be a nice hotel."

That was another thing about these cowboys. They were never in a hurry but still got shit done, and they didn't say many words but always managed to say a lot.

"It's nothing personal."

"Didn't say it was." His head barely tipped her way. "You're just putting an awful lot of work into a place you don't want to stay at."

"It's not that I don't want to stay there." How could she possibly explain things to Brooks without offending him?

Making it seem like she didn't enjoy his family's company.

Because it wasn't that.

They were just not something she could handle right now.

"I can't say as I blame you." Brooks almost looked like he was going to smile. The dimple in one cheek peeked out for a second before disappearing. "My mother can be quite overwhelming."

"I like your mother." It was a truth she was willing to admit. She liked Maryann. As a person. As an employer. Even on a friendly basis.

"I'm just not used to a family like yours."

"I'm not sure anyone is used to a family like mine." Brooks did smile this time, his dimple on full display. "And my mother keeps trying to make it bigger."

"She just likes to take care of people." It was one of the many qualities Maryann had that she tried not to think too hard about. "She can't handle when someone isn't getting the love she thinks they deserve."

"And she wants to give it to them, whether they like it or not."

Nora tried to press down the smile Brooks' accurate assessment brought on. "It comes from a good place."

"Usually she gets away with it." Brooks eyed her from across the cab. "Not with you, though."

"It's nothing personal."

"You keep saying that, and it makes me think it might be personal." His head barely tipped. "Just not towards us."

The smile she'd been fighting flattened immediately, dragging her back to the reality of her situation.

She needed to get the hell out of Moss Creek, Montana.

Actually, what she needed was to get the hell out of this truck before Brooks Pace managed to get her talking about things she had no intention of talking about.

"I wouldn't worry too much about it. I won't be here long enough for it to be a problem." She glanced out the window as they passed the last building of downtown Moss Creek. Soon this little town and all the people who lived in it would be a part of the past she had to leave behind.

Nora pressed two fingers against her breastbone, pushing on an odd ache. One she hadn't felt before.

Certainly not when she left Seattle. Not even when she left Dean.

Which meant maybe she had more problems in Moss Creek than she realized.

CHAPTER TWO

IT MAY HAVE taken over a month, but he finally had Nora Levitt all to himself.

The woman was skittish as hell and after biding his time for almost a month he'd been considering leaving well enough alone.

But then he caught a few of the cautious glances that kept coming his way. Saw the way her dark eyes moved over him when she didn't realize he was watching.

Whether she was what he was looking for was still anyone's guess, but at least now he was close enough to have a chance to figure it out.

As long as Nora didn't decide to take full advantage of her new battery and never come back to Red Cedar Ranch again which, from the sound of it, might be exactly what she intended to do.

Brooks kept his eyes on the road instead of letting them wander her way like they wanted to do. "Sounds like you're planning to hightail it out of here."

Nora lifted a shoulder and let it drop. "I have to get back to my life." Her voice was flat and hollow, her words clipped and short.

And it pulled him in a little more. "You don't sound too thrilled about that."

Her gaze moved to sit squarely out the side window. "It is what it is."

That was a telling statement. Meant she'd come to terms with a situation.

But wasn't happy about it.

"Some people might say it is what you make it be." Brooks watched her as he drove toward the next town over, taking advantage of the fact that Nora refused to so much as peek his direction. Her purse sat on her lap, hands planted on top of the large leather bag. Both feet were flat on the floorboard of his truck, and her back was stiff and straight, chin tipped up just the tiniest bit.

This was what drew him to her. The way she carried herself. The way she handled everything that came her way with calm composure.

Even when it was clear she was pissed as hell.

And he wanted to know why.

"Some people might not realize what I'm dealing with." Her lips pressed together as her face turned even more toward the side window. Once again she fell silent.

He was used to being the one with short answers. The one with less to say.

His mother was as long-winded as it came. She said about twenty words for every one that came out of his dad's mouth. It led him to assume that's how all relationships would be.

How all women would act. So far he'd been right.

But this city girl was making him reconsider all sorts of things. Making him wonder just how much might end up being different from what he always thought.

"That sounds interesting." He wanted her to open up to him. Wanted to know why Nora was in such a rush to get out of town and go back to something she clearly wasn't in a hurry to deal with.

Especially when the alternative was staying in Moss Creek.

"Interesting is definitely the wrong word." Her lips sealed together, ending yet another short sentence. Stopping her words before he managed to get enough of them.

And it left him trying to figure out how to get more.

"What would the right word be?"

Nora's lips pinched to one side as she considered his question. "Complicated."

Yet another reason he was shocked she would be so ready to go back to Seattle. Things weren't complicated here. Life was simple and steady. "Then why rush back?"

He wasn't really playing it as cool as he'd planned, but after waiting a month just to get a second alone with her, it was difficult to keep his cards close to his chest.

"Just because it's complicated doesn't mean I don't still have to deal with it."

She wasn't giving him much, but it was still enough to narrow down the possibility of what exactly happened. "That sounds an awful lot like a bad breakup."

Nora's eyes slowly came his way. "Why would you think that?"

"Aren't many things more complicated than a bad breakup."

"Is that something you know from experience?"

It was the opening he'd been waiting for. The opportunity to share some of himself in the hopes Nora would return the favor.

"Course. Doesn't everybody?"

Nora shrugged again. "I guess I figured Boone was the only one with a bad breakup in your family." She paused. What she said next surprised him. "You guys just all seem so perfect."

"I'm gonna take that as a compliment." He continued as she scoffed. "But I definitely wouldn't call my family perfect."

"Then you're delirious." Her shoulders seemed to ease down a little. "You work together. You run businesses together. You freaking eat dinner together every night." Nora sounded almost aggravated by the last bit. "You guys are like the Brady Bunch."

"The Brady Bunch didn't live on a ranch."

"You know what I mean."

"I'm not sure I do." Now they were getting somewhere. "You seem to think we're something we're not." Brooks turned into the automotive supply store. "And you seem a little offended by it."

"I'm not offended by anything. Like I said, I enjoy your family."

"You didn't say that." He wanted to get to the bottom of what was hanging Nora up. Most people loved ranch life. They loved the horses. They loved the views. They loved the peace that could be found far from the rest of the world.

Nora did not appear to be most people, and he wanted to know why.

"Then I'll say it now. I enjoy your family." She crossed her arms. "And I'm positive that I already said I like your mother."

He stopped her before she could continue on. "Which doesn't make any sense." Brooks pulled into a parking space and put the truck in park. "Because my mother is usually the issue."

"There is no issue. I had a life before I came here and I have a life I need to go back and figure out." This time Nora's sigh was louder and longer. "Why is everyone so shocked that I'm going to go back to my regular life?"

"Maybe because you don't seem that thrilled with your regular life." That's what bothered him the most about this whole thing. Nora seemed dead set on going back to something that clearly made her unhappy.

And she did a hell of a job of staying away from him, which made it impossible for him to figure out why.

"Just because it doesn't thrill me doesn't mean I don't have to go back and make it work." The last word stalled out in the middle, trailing off to nothing. The slope of her shoulders dipped even more. "Can we just fix my car so I can go back to my hotel?"

She suddenly seemed almost defeated.

And it bothered the hell out of him.

"I'm sorry. I didn't mean to upset you."

Her eyes came his way, confusion lining the edges as they skimmed his face before pulling away. "You didn't upset me." She opened her door and climbed out onto the blacktop, not looking back as she walked toward the front of the store.

Brooks jumped out of the truck and hustled after her. "My mother would kick my ass if she knew I didn't get the door for you."

"Then we probably shouldn't tell her." Nora grabbed the door to the shop, opened it and walked inside like she came here all the time.

Every eye in the place came her way.

He couldn't blame a single one of them. Nora was beautiful. Long dark hair. A body that was lush curves and soft slopes. She was stunning and carried herself like she knew it. The woman was confident.

And there was nothing sexier than a confident woman.

"Is there something I can help you with, Miss?" One of the Baker boys practically tripped over his own feet trying to get out from behind the counter to chase Nora down as she marched through the store like she knew exactly where she was going.

She stopped suddenly, eyes moving along the aisles for a second. She pointed up towards the sign stationed at the end of the next row. "Nope. I got it."

She went straight down the line of batteries. Her steps started to slow about halfway down and her eyes started to glaze over. She stalled to a stop and slowly turned his way.

"You ever shopped for a car battery before?" Brooks made his way to her side.

"I've never actually seen a car battery before." Nora leaned toward the rack lined with the heavy cases. "They're smaller than I was expecting."

Brooks eyed the racks as he passed, searching for the one her rental required. Luckily, what he was looking for happened to be right in front of Nora. "Well you have good taste." He reached out to pull a battery from the rack. "You found exactly what we need."

Nora's shoulders barely squared. "Good." Her attention moved down the racks. "There are different kinds of car batteries?"

"Sure are." He tipped his head toward the front registers and started to walk their way.

"Interesting." Nora followed along behind him continuing to look around.

"Some people would call it that." Brooks set the battery on the counter, relaxing against the edge as Josh Baker made his way to the register, looking more than a little disappointed that Brooks was the man helping Nora with her battery problem. He scooted the new unit Josh's way. "I'll bring the dead one down tomorrow."

Nora's eyes went from the new battery to Josh to Brooks. "Why would you bring him the dead one?"

"That's the way it works. You bring the old one back and you get credit towards the new one."

"Hopefully they reimburse me for this." She pulled her wallet from her purse.

"We'll get you a letter from a certified mechanic, says they're the ones that replaced that battery for you." Living in a small town certainly had its perks. Everyone might know every stupid thing you've ever done, but you could also pull a few strings when you needed to.

Get letters about dead batteries. Tires repaired and replaced. Buildings reconstructed. Almost anything a man might need to take care of the things that mattered to him.

Nora flipped a credit card Josh's way, keeping it pinched between two of her fingers as Josh rattled off the cost. Her brows lifted. "That's it?"

"Being able to do for yourself has its perks, Miss Nora."

Nora peeked his way from under her lashes as she tucked the credit card back in place. "Thank you for doing this."

Initially he hadn't intended to try to get close to the interior decorator his mother hired to help with The Inn.

Partly because his mother wouldn't appreciate it.

At least he hadn't expected her to.

But that was when Maryann Pace assumed she could woo Nora into their world with good food and good company.

Except Nora was turning out to be immune to his mother's charms.

And it made him want to see if her immunity covered his charms too.

"Do the perks outweigh the convenience of being able to drop it off and have someone else handle it?" Nora grabbed the handle of the battery and tried to heft it off the counter.

Brooks snagged it, taking the weight as it dropped toward the ground. "Looks to me like you're getting the perks and the convenience."

"Aren't I a lucky girl?"

"Seems like I also offered you dinner." Brooks managed to get ahead of her this time and opened the door, holding it as Nora passed him and walked out into the parking lot.

"And I told you that you don't have to do that."

"It's not about having to. It's about being a gentleman." Brooks set the new battery in the bed of his truck as he rounded to the passenger's side. "And I think you know my mama would kick my ass if she found out I wasn't being a gentleman." He shot her a wink. "Especially to her best friend."

"Your father is your mother's best friend."

Her observation stopped him in his tracks. "That's because my dad's been at her side since she was nineteen."

It was the same thing he'd been searching for. A woman to be his best friend. His partner. His everything.

It was a tall order. One he was starting to worry might never be filled.

Nora's eyes widened a little as she followed him to her side of the truck. "That's insane."

Brooks opened the door and waited while Nora climbed into the seat. "Not something you see much anymore, is it?"

He knew Bill and Maryann Pace were the exception to almost every rule. In some ways growing up with parents who were desperately in love was a good thing.

In other ways it was hugely problematic.

"Not something that happens *ever*." Nora tucked her feet into the floorboards without having to be asked. When he didn't immediately shut her door she reached out, grabbed the handle, and closed it herself. Leaving him standing alone.

Wondering if he was chasing yet another dead end.

Because that's what having parents like his got you. Standards that could never be met.

Brooks had a little less pep in his step as he went back to the driver's side and eased into his seat. "What kind of food do you like to eat, Miss Nora?"

"Simple things."

Her short answers were going to drive him bat shit crazy. "I'm gonna need a little more explanation than that."

"Cheese and crackers. Yogurt. Nuts."

"So you're a grazer." Weren't many of those around here. Wasn't enough time in the day to graze. Not for anybody besides the cattle.

"I guess you could call it that."

One more short non-answer, and it was one too many.

He wanted someone who would talk to him about everything. Someone who shared her hopes and dreams with him.

So he could make them a reality.

"All right then." Nora might not be the girl for him, but that didn't mean he wouldn't still do his best to be the kind of man his mama raised him to be.

Brooks turned into the small grocery store just across the street from the automotive shop. "Let's go grab some stuff for you to graze on then."

This time Nora didn't argue.

Brooks parked the truck in a spot near the entrance and got out. Once again Nora got out on her own, robbing him of the chance to prove he was raised right.

To prove he knew how to take care of the people around him.

"You aren't used to men opening doors for you are you, Miss Nora?"

"Guess not." Nora walked through the automatic doors of the small, but upscale, store, snagging a basket from the stack as she passed.

"If a month on a ranch can't get you used to it then nothing will." Brooks tried to take the basket from her hand.

Nora gripped it tight and yanked it out of his reach, dark brows drawing together. "What are you doing?"

"Same thing I've been trying to do all night." Brooks made another grab for the basket, this time managing to get it away from her. "I am attempting to be nice to you."

"You *are* being nice to me." Nora lunged, snatching the basket back, her soft body bumping against his in the process. Her eyes widened and the skin on her cheeks pinked as she put another step's worth of distance between them. "I don't expect you to do everything for me. I can carry a basket."

"I'm not trying to do *everything* for you." Brooks watched as she snagged a tray of mixed berries and set it in the basket. "I'm just trying to do *one* thing for you."

Nora bent down to examine a row of snacks lined across a shelf just above the floor. Her purse dropped from her shoulder and banged into the basket in her hand. She shoved it back in place only to have it fall back down again.

"Let me hold your purse then."

Nora's gaze lifted to his. "You want to carry my purse?"

"It's not about wanting to." Brooks managed to get the leather bag away from her. "It's about splitting the bill."

Nora was quiet for a minute, dark eyes holding his for a second before she turned back to the snacks. Finally, she chose a pack of crunchy chickpeas and added them to her basket before straightening to face him. "It's not splitting the bill if you try to do everything."

"I didn't pay for your battery." He'd thought about it. Then decided against it, figuring Nora would give him hell right there in front of Josh Baker.

And Josh Baker would've taken full advantage, figuring Nora was up for grabs.

Not that she wasn't. He just didn't like the idea of every single man in town bothering her.

Like he was.

"Why would you pay for the battery? It's not even my car." Nora headed for the cheese counter.

She definitely wasn't from here, and every minute that passed showed more and more of the divide between her way of thinking and his. "Because that's just how things are handled around here."

"Well I'm not from *around here*." She picked up a plastic container of pre-cut cubes of cheddar cheese, looking it over before putting it back in favor of a matching container of pepper jack.

"Clearly." Their differences were becoming more and more obvious.

He wanted what his parents had. Wanted to take care of a woman the way she deserved.

For some reason that didn't appear to appeal to Nora.

Which meant she shouldn't appeal to him.

Nora dropped the pepper jack into the basket and meandered to the side of the deli where full dinners could be bought, hot and ready to eat.

She scanned the offerings as the older man behind the counter waited patiently for her to decide what she wanted. Finally she leaned toward the glass separating them and lifted one finger toward the middle item. "Can I please have the meatloaf with mashed potatoes and gravy?"

Brooks stepped closer to her. "Thought you liked to graze."

"I do." She gave the man filling the foam tray a dazzling smile. "And can you add in some corn and a roll?"

"Yes, ma'am." He filled the tray to the brim before closing the lid, printing a sticker for the side, and passing it off to her. Nora took it and immediately held it out.

"Here." The smile she gave him was smaller. Softer. "The least I can do is buy you dinner."

CHAPTER THREE

"WHY ARE YOU looking at me like that?" She was trying to be nice to him.

As nice as she could safely be. Being around Brooks was a delicate balancing act.

One she was clearly terrible at.

"I just figured we'd be grazing tonight."

She'd seen him and his brothers eat. The men could put away some food. "You're not a grazer."

"How do you know that?"

This time she couldn't avoid the dip of her eyes down Brooks' broad, toned frame. "By looking at you."

If you looked up *corn fed* in the dictionary it would have a picture of Brooks Pace. He was a perfect example of what manual labor and home cooking could create.

And it was really making her already difficult situation even more of a struggle.

"Didn't think you looked at me."

Was there a touch of hurt in his tone?

"I'm looking at you right now." And it was a terrible idea.

She should stop. And she would.

In just a minute.

"That you are."

Nora's eyes snapped up to Brooks' face, abandoning the flat plane of his stomach. "Shut up." She turned away from his smug smile and distracting form and marched toward the cracker aisle.

"Don't be embarrassed." Brooks was moving fast trying to keep up with her.

"I am not embarrassed. I'm just in a hurry." That was a huge understatement.

She knew damn well being around Brooks was a bad idea, and yet here she was. Stuck trying to hold her own until she could get this battery thing done and over with and get as far from him as possible. The sooner that happened, the better off she'd be.

Nora snagged the first box of crackers she saw and headed straight for the wine aisle.

Because getting through this unscathed was going to take a little wine.

Unfortunately the options were pretty slim if she didn't want to risk guzzling an entire bottle on her own.

Not that the day didn't warrant it.

The week.

The month.

Months plural.

She grabbed a four-pack of tiny individual bottles and added them to her basket then headed straight for the checkout. It was time to get this show on the road and put this day behind her.

She grabbed the foam box from Brooks' hands, scanning the barcode before adding it to a bag and passing it back his way. She scanned her remaining items, swiped her card, and tore off the receipt, adding it to the plastic bag with all her snacks. "Let's go, cowboy."

Brooks was oddly quiet as he followed behind. He'd been giving her a hard time most of the evening, which she was appreciative of. The last thing she needed was to get along with him. Add one more problem to her never-ending list.

She should be glad he wasn't talking to her now. That was even better than him giving her a hard time.

But it still felt odd.

This time Brooks didn't try to race her to the truck door. He let her go by herself. Open it by herself. Get in by herself.

Which was fine. The way she should prefer it.

By the time Nora was loaded into the truck Brooks was already in his seat, staring down into the bag at the container of food she bought for him.

It hadn't occurred to her that maybe the food here wasn't great. It smelled good. It looked good.

But looks could be deceiving.

"Would you rather have something else?"

Brooks reached into the bag and pulled out the container, along with the plastic-packed utensils the man had stacked on top. "Nope. This will be just fine."

He flipped the lid open and stared at the food inside.

An odd ache tugged at her belly and loosened her lips. "I just saw the meatloaf and I knew it was your favorite, so I thought—"

Brooks' head snapped her way. "You knew this was my favorite?"

Shit.

"I mean, I just assumed." Her mind scrambled for a way to backtrack. "It's what your mom made the night I stayed for dinner, and it seemed like you ate a lot of it, so I thought you liked it."

It was a half-truth. Her knowledge of Brooks' likes and dislikes went far beyond a single dinner's worth. Any time his name came up in conversation her brain hung on to the information, stowing it away like a squirrel hoarding nuts before winter.

Brooks stared at her for a moment, those clear blue eyes working their way over her face in a slow pass that made her feel exposed.

Made her wonder if he could see all that she fought to hide from everyone.

Including herself.

Nora pulled the plastic bag of food on her lap a little closer, using it like a shield.

Not that a little bit of plastic could protect her from Brooks Pace.

From the potential he had to upend her already spilled life.

Finally his gaze pulled from her face. "I do like meatloaf." Brooks pushed the fork through the plastic and stabbed the tines into the loaf, cutting off a chunk and putting it in his mouth. "And this place makes damn good one."

"Good then." She struggled to look away from his face as he continued to watch her.

With that same strange expression.

No. Strange was the wrong word.

He looked.

Thoughtful.

Nora opened the container of pepper jack cheese and a sleeve of crackers. She held the cheese container Brooks' way. He eyed her for a second before taking a chunk and popping it into his mouth.

"Do you like spicy food?" She shouldn't be asking him personal questions. It didn't matter what he liked. Who he was.

But this was just small talk. It was fine.

"I love spicy food." He scooped up some potatoes. "Don't get to eat it much though since my mom and dad don't really care for it."

"Bill doesn't like spicy food?" Now that she was thinking about it, Maryann never seemed to be making anything spicy as Nora rushed away in the evenings.

And she knew Maryann well enough to know that Bill was her number one consideration when it came to meal planning.

Because while it might seem to most of the world like Bill doted on Maryann, she knew Maryann doted on him right back.

It just looked different.

Brooks shook his head. "Not anymore. Gives him heartburn."

"That sucks." Food that made you sweat was one of the greatest pleasures in life. "Hopefully that doesn't happen to me one day."

Brooks dug around in the well of corn. "What's your favorite spicy food?"

"Hmm. I'm going to have to think about that." Nora tapped one finger against the container of cheese in her hand. "I really like hot wings. But I also really like Indian food."

"That's two different kinds of hot." Brooks shook his head. "Didn't expect you to be a spice lover."

A scoff jumped free, chased by a smile she didn't mean to give him. "I'm a little offended by that."

"No reason to be offended."

"You just basically called me boring." She might be a solitary creature, but she definitely wasn't boring.

"I don't know that I'd say boring." Brooks grinned at her. "Specifically."

She sucked in a mock gasp. "Ouch."

Brooks laughed. "Fine. I take it back."

"It's too late now." Nora hid her smile behind a cracker.

"It's never too late." Brooks popped the lid back in place on his half-eaten dinner and set it on the console between them. "Unless I sit here for twenty minutes eating my dinner and end up replacing your battery in the dark."

Getting caught alone with Brooks Pace in the dark sounded horribly interesting. Like the beginning of a fantasy she absolutely could not entertain.

Nora eyed the pack of wine in her bag.

Damn open container laws.

Luckily the drive back to the ranch went relatively fast thanks to light, easy conversation. Mostly about spicy food.

Nothing too deep. Nothing that dug beneath the surface she worked hard to keep intact.

By the time they pulled into Brooks' spot at the main house it was well after dinner. Long enough there was no sign of the crowd she'd once again managed to avoid.

"You can go in the house while I do this." Brooks' blue eyes came her way, resting on her face in a way that felt oddly comfortable.

She'd spent the whole day with Maryann, working on the last of the details for the grand opening. And while she enjoyed Maryann's company, it was frequently exhausting.

And she was already a little exhausted.

"Or you can just stay out here, kick your feet up, and enjoy your wine and cheese while I do all the hard work." He didn't sound upset about it, but it still made her feel bad.

"I could probably help." It couldn't be that hard. Nora snagged one of the bottles of wine and cracked the screw cap. "Let's do this."

It might be nice to learn a new skill. Something that proved she was capable of making a life of her own.

Finding success that no one else could question or claim.

Brooks' brows lifted like she'd surprised him. "All right then."

Nora jumped out of the truck to hide another smile and headed right to the front of her car. She stuck one hand in the gap like she'd watched Brooks do.

"Is there a button or something?"

Brooks pulled open the driver's door and reached under the dash. "You gotta release it first."

Nora jumped a little as the hood popped loose.

Brooks slowly came her way. "Now try."

She set her plastic bottle of single-serve wine on the ground at her feet, making sure to put it far enough away she wouldn't accidentally kick it over. Then she stuck her fingers back in the crack that was a little bigger now and felt around.

There was nothing there.

"What am I looking for?"

"Here." Brooks came closer, his wide frame crowding close as his hand came to hers, warm and rough.

Her heart immediately picked up speed, racing along like a brakeless train. She held very still as Brooks moved her hand to a spot towards the front right corner of the hood. His fingers slid between hers, dragging along the gap. "There." He seemed to come a little closer, the brush of his body making her light-headed from lack of oxygen. "Do you feel that?"

She felt things.

None of them had to do with opening the hood of a car.

Nora tried to suck in a little air. "Maybe."

"Here." Brooks leaned in until the front of his body barely rested against the back of hers. He flipped the lever and slowly lifted the hood. "You see this?" He thumbed across the latch that released the hood. "That lever fully releases the catch. Once you press it you can lift the hood up."

"Got it." Nora edged away from the heat of his body, snagging her bottle of wine from the gravel and chugging a few gulps as she put a safer distance between them.

Brooks reached deeper into the open space, lifting out a bar that hinged at the front. "Then you lift up your prop bar, and hook it into place." He settled the end of the bar into a hole on the underside of the hood and stepped back.

"That doesn't seem secure." Nora leaned in to peek at the spot. "All that's keeping that from falling on your head is a metal stick stuck in a hole."

"As long as you don't bump it everything will be just fine."

Nora stepped away from the prop bar and a little closer to where Brooks was. "Now I'm nervous." She drank a little more of her wine, hoping it would relax at least one set of the nerves running amok through her insides.

"Don't be nervous. It's my head on the line." Brooks leaned in and went to work unhooking the dead battery.

"I don't want you to lose your head either." While she might not be interested in cowboys, she could still admit the loss of Brooks Pace's head would be a travesty. There weren't too many handsome heads to go around, and it would be a shame to lose one.

"I have no intention of losing my head, Miss Nora." Brooks rested both hands on the front of the car and leaned in. "I haven't lost it yet, and I don't seem to be losing it anytime soon."

Nora took another drink of wine. "That's good then."

She watched as Brooks continued unhooking the battery. Once it was separated he lifted it up and out of the car, carefully setting it on the ground at her feet.

"That's it?" She was expecting it to be some long, involved, complicated process.

"You sound unimpressed." Brooks made his way to the back of his truck and she followed, making a stop at the passenger's side to grab a second tiny bottle of wine. "It's not that I'm unimpressed. I just expected it to be more than unhooking one and putting a new one in."

"Any man you know ever done it?"

That was an unnecessary attack. One that clearly held an accusation she couldn't quite put her finger on.

So instead she opened the second bottle of wine and took a few sips before taking a deep breath as her eyes wandered the fields around them. "I'm sure men aren't the only ones capable of changing a battery."

Brooks propped the battery into the void left by the previous one. He turned her way. "Then maybe you should be the one who finishes our little project."

Nora drank down the last few gulps of wine before recapping the empty bottle and setting it at her feet. "Fine."

She could do this. She watched Brooks pull one out in under five minutes. It couldn't be that hard to put it back in.

Nora leaned under the hood, giving the prop a once-over to make sure it was still fixed in place. "So I just stick these things back on the new one?"

Brooks chuckled. "Maybe it's going to be more of a guided process." He pointed to one of the wires. "Take that one and screw it in right here."

Nora picked up the piece he indicated and twisted it into the spot where he was pointing.

"All right. Now do the same thing with this one but put it here."

Nora followed his instructions, hooking the other wire in place. Once everything was together she stepped back and dusted her hands off. "There. I told you I could do it."

"That you did."

Nora tossed her empty bottle into the grocery bag, only hesitating a second before grabbing another one.

She took a deep breath.

The air smelled clean and fresh.

And a little like cow, but not in a bad way.

Brooks reached for the prop.

"I can get that." Nora grabbed the stick of metal and started to yank.

"Woah." Brooks grabbed her hand and the hood just as it started to drop. "You're getting a little ahead of yourself here." He carefully put the prop back in place and lowered the lid. "I thought you said you didn't want to lose your head."

"I said I didn't want *you* to lose *your* head." Nora tipped back the mini bottle of wine as she made her way to Brooks' truck. The stuff was surprisingly good. Smooth. A little sweet.

She collected all her stuff, packing it into the plastic bag from the grocery store. She grabbed the final bottle of wine and started to drop it in.

"You made friends with any of our horses yet?" Brooks was suddenly very close. Close enough she could reach out and touch him if she wanted.

Her fingers held tighter to the bottle of wine as her eyes spent too much time inspecting the stretch of his cotton t-shirt. "I'm not so sure horses and I get along."

"Why's that?"

Nora chewed her lower lip. “I’m not really an animal person.”

She’d never had a pet. Her parents didn’t have time to commit to her let alone a dog or cat.

And now he had that odd look on his face again. “Not even puppies?”

“I’ve never been around puppies.”

“Cats?”

Nora shook her head, swallowing down a little of the wine in her hand.

“I’m gonna guess you’ve never been around horses then either.”

“No.” She’d never had any interest. Horses weren’t a part of her everyday life.

Until recently.

His gaze lingered on her on a second longer before he turned away. “So you can’t officially say you’re not an animal person.” Brooks slowly sauntered toward the barn.

Nora slowly followed after him, doing her damndest to keep her eyes away from his ass. “Is that something that needs to be official?”

“Of course.” Brooks continued toward the barn door.

Nora continued following him, taking little sips of her wine as she went. She paused just outside the wide door, her stomach flipping with what might be excitement if she thought about it too long.

But thinking about things wasn’t something she’d been doing recently and now seemed like a terrible time to start.

She stepped through the doorway and into the barn.

And stopped immediately.

At least three giant horse heads stared at her from behind wooden gates.

“Why are they looking at me like that?”

"Probably because Clara has them tricked into thinking pretty women give them treats." Brooks reached into a giant tub and pulled out a few hard nuggets. "Here."

Nora held her hand out and Brooks dropped the nuggets into her palm. She stared down at them. "These don't look extremely appetizing."

Brooks' chuckle was low and deep. "They're definitely not chicken wings."

"That's for sure."

He backed deeper into the barn, watching her intently as he went.

Following him seemed like a bad idea.

Not as bad as normal though.

"Whose horses are these?" Nora took a few steps, edging closer to the first horse, who was watching her with giant brown eyeballs.

"That one there used to be my mother's horse but he recently decided he preferred Clara's company. His name's Edgar and he wants to be your best friend."

"I thought he was Clara's horse?"

"He is. But he'll be your best friend if you give him a snack." Brooks reached out and took one of the treats from her hand, his fingers dragging across her skin slowly. "Hold it out like this." He flattened his palm, keeping his fingers tight together as he held the treat under the horse's snout.

Is that what they called a horse nose?

Nora skipped the large brown horse Brooks was feeding and walked to the next horse in line. It was a pale gray color but had the same big brown eyes lined with long lashes that Edgar had. She flattened her palm and placed one of the hard little nuggets right in the middle before holding it out.

She was feeding a horse.

She'd lost her mind.

The horse's lips were velvety soft as they searched her palm for the snack, whispering across her skin with a surprisingly light touch.

"That's Shadow."

Nora watched the horse as he carefully chewed the treat, taking a lot longer to eat it than Edgar had. "Thank you for not biting me, Shadow."

"Shadow wouldn't hurt a fly." Brooks reached out to scratch along the horse's cheek. "He's a sweetheart."

"Whose horse is he?" Nora lifted her hand.

Was she considering petting a horse?

Maybe.

She hesitated just a little as Shadow's eyes came to hers, but the horse went very still.

Like he knew this wasn't her thing.

Or maybe like he knew she had more snacks.

The tips of her fingers barely brushed across his cheek.

"Give him a good scratch." Brooks ran one hand down Shadow's neck, demonstrating with vigorous sweeps.

"I don't want to hurt him." Nora flattened her hand and rested it against Shadow's cheek.

"He's a thousand pounds. You're not going to hurt him."

"But you said he's sweet." She patted Shadow with a delicate touch. "I want to be sweet back to him."

"I said he wouldn't hurt a fly."

"Same thing." Nora gently stroked along the horse's face, leaning a little closer as she dropped her voice. "*Tell Brooks to be sweet to you.*"

"Are you trying to turn my horse against me?" Brooks leaned against the gate blocking Shadow in.

"It's a conspiracy." Nora held out another snack for Shadow.

Brooks chuckled. "You might be right about that."

Nora jumped a little as Shadow huffed out a breath of air and stomped on the dirt floor of his stall. "Is he mad?"

"He wants out." Brooks gave Shadow a pat on the neck. "But he's got a long day of work ahead of him tomorrow, so he's not going to get what he wants."

"*Does he make you work?*" Nora focused on Shadow. He was beautiful. Calm. A gentle giant.

She'd never had a pet outside of a few goldfish. Her parents were the practical type who didn't see the need for animals.

She always thought she was just like them.

"*You're a very handsome boy.*" She gave the horse a final pat before turning back toward the front of the barn.

It was a slow spin but it felt insanely fast.

And a little wonky.

Nora lifted the tiny bottle in her hand, shaking it as she stared through the plastic.

It was empty.

Had she accidentally drunk all four of the tiny wines?

She counted on her fingers.

"Shit."

CHAPTER FOUR

"SOMETHIN' WRONG?"

Nora had a strange look on her face as she stared down at the bottle in her hand.

"Huh." She pursed her lips. "I don't remember how many of these I drank."

"If you don't know then I'd say there's a pretty good chance you drank too many." He hadn't noticed her get any of the other bottles from his truck. He was too busy trying to keep his eyes to himself after an evening of contradictions that had him wanting to consider a possibility he'd all but given up on.

"Shit." Nora pressed the empty bottle to the center of her chest as she rushed out the front door of the barn.

Almost.

The toe of her shoe caught on the barely-there lip of the threshold and she immediately started to nosedive toward the gravel outside.

Brooks lunged for her, grabbing whatever he could to stop her forward trajectory.

He pulled her up by her middle, settling her back on both feet.

Nora's head tipped forward, eyes dropping as her chin tucked to her chest. "Your hand is on my boob."

Brooks yanked both hands off her body and immediately shoved them into his pockets, taking a step back as he did. "You okay?"

Her cheeks were a little flushed and her dark eyes seemed a little unfocused. Her lips pressed downward in a frown. "I think I might be drunkish." She blinked a few times.

There weren't many things he was scared of.

But this scenario right here was one of them.

Nora's glassy eyes moved to her car. "I can just wait it out."

"You can't just sit in your car." He didn't like the thought of her sitting all alone in the driveway, waiting to sober up.

He'd spent his fair share of nights in his truck, sleeping off a few too many beers.

It wasn't fun.

"Let me take you back to The Inn. You can sleep there."

Nora's eyes slowly moved from her car to rest on him.

Then they did a slow drop, raking down his front in the most obvious perusal she'd ever given him.

So far all the peeks she took were short. Snuck when she thought he wasn't paying attention.

But this one was blatant. Obvious enough that it made him stand a little taller. Push his shoulders back a little more.

"What happens when I'm ready to go back to my hotel?" Her words were slow but still clear.

"Then you can call me. I'll come get you and bring you back up to your car."

She didn't immediately respond.

"Nora?" He moved closer. Maybe she was more inebriated than he realized.

She shook her head a little. “Sorry.” She blinked a few times, each one coming slower than the last. “I guess The Inn is fine.”

It better be. There was no way he was standing by while she slept in a damn car.

Brooks pulled his keys out and ushered Nora toward his truck, using a hand on her back to keep her feet moving.

This time she let him open her door.

She even let him help her get in the truck.

It would figure drunk Nora would be more in-line with what he’d been looking for.

“Aren’t you gonna tell me to watch my feet?” This time her words were a little messier, but the smile that accompanied them was anything but.

Brooks leaned against the edge of the opening. “Are you flirting with me, Miss Nora?”

“Nooooooooo. That would be a terrible idea.” Her head tipped back to rest against the seat.

“Would it now?” He reached down to move the feet she’d clearly forgotten were in the way, carefully placing them in the floorboard. “Why would that be such a terrible thing?”

He knew exactly why it would be a terrible thing.

It would be terrible because, aside from the fact that Nora made it clear she had no intention of staying in Moss Creek, this woman was not what he was looking for.

Nora would be going back to Seattle and he would be staying here, left to continue his search for the woman meant to be at his side.

Nora sighed. “It just would be.” Her head rolled his way and her dark eyes barely opened. “I wish you were at least a little ugly.”

It sounded like a compliment but it didn't seem like one.

"Sorry to disappoint you."

Nora snorted. "I don't think you're sorry at all." Her eyes closed and her head rolled back to the center of the rest.

Brooks studied her a second before closing the door.

It was something he'd been doing all night.

Studying her.

He thought he had at least a basic idea of what Nora was like, but she kept throwing him off. Like maybe some of what she showed him was an act.

A façade.

He did a quick scan of the items Nora bought at the store. Sure enough she'd emptied all the bottles.

And none of the snacks.

No wonder she was struggling.

"Damn woman." He closed the door. Grazing wasn't eating.

She'd barely gotten anything in her stomach, and now she was suffering for it.

Nora didn't move a muscle as he climbed in and started the truck, backing out to head down the driveway, deeper into Pace land.

But he didn't head to The Inn. Camille had enough on her plate. She'd stay up all night making sure Nora was okay, and the last thing that woman needed was another sleepless night.

Instead, Brooks turned down the lane leading to the cabin he shared with Brett. Luckily his younger brother was out of town picking up a set of new bulls they purchased to add to their stock. That meant there would be no one to witness Nora's appearance at their place. No one to ask questions he didn't want to answer.

Probably couldn't even if he tried.

He parked his truck and killed the engine. Nora barely stirred beside him, her soft body wiggling the tiniest bit before she let out a soft sigh.

He swore under his breath before shoving open his door and sucking in a long draw of the cooling night air.

This was nothing more than him taking care of a friend. That's all.

He counted the steps around the truck to keep his mind idling in safe waters. By the time he opened her door the sound of that soft sigh was almost a distant memory.

Almost.

He reached out, gently taking her by one shoulder and shaking. "Miss Nora, let's get you inside."

She sucked in a loud breath. "I'm fine."

Then she started to snore.

"Nora." He waited.

She didn't move.

"*Nora.*" This time he said her name louder.

She still didn't move.

"Hell." Brooks wiped one hand down his face before glancing up at the front door to the cabin.

He was just helping a friend.

He picked up her right arm and slung it over his shoulders before scooping her up from the truck, kicking the door shut behind them.

"You are a right pain in the ass." He was looking for calm and easy-going. Someone to easily settle into his simple world.

But so far nothing about Nora was easy or simple.

Brooks jostled the door open and carried her in, intending to put her on the couch.

He paused, eyeing the aged piece of furniture.

How many dirty cowboy asses had sat on that couch?

More than a few.

"Hell." He stomped his way down the hall to his bedroom.

The covers on his bed were tucked neatly into place and that's how they were going to stay. Just the thought of seeing Nora wound up in his blankets threatened to plant all sorts of bad ideas in his head.

Ideas he'd sworn off long ago.

He wasn't out for a fling. He was looking for the real thing.

Brooks laid her across the made bed then straightened.

"Hell." He leaned back down to work her shoes off her feet, letting them drop to the floor.

Nora immediately sighed, rolling to curl on her side, tucking one hand under the pillow he slept on every night.

Maybe he'd been wrong drinking beer all these years. Might be worth it to switch to wine.

Looked like it gave you a hell of a night's sleep.

He turned, stopping at the door to glance back at where she was tucked into a tight ball.

Like she might be cold.

"Dammit." Brooks yanked open the hall closet and grabbed one of the extra blankets they kept on hand in case a night of beer and cards ended with farmhands crashing on the couches. He pulled out the softest of the lot and carried it to his room, shaking it out and dropping it over Nora's sleeping form.

This time when he walked out Brooks pulled the door shut behind him.

It was a barrier he shouldn't need.

If nothing else tonight showed him Nora wasn't the woman he'd been searching for.

It didn't matter that she somehow knew he loved meatloaf. It didn't matter that they shared an affinity for fiery foods. And it didn't matter that she stepped up and helped change the battery of her car.

Because at the end of the day she was still a city girl who 'wasn't an animal person'. Making friends with one horse didn't change that. Especially since it might have been due to nearly a bottle of wine.

Brooks forced his feet down the hall, resisting the urge to check one more time to make sure she was okay. He collapsed into his recliner and switched on the television, hoping it could distract him from the woman sleeping soundly down the hall.

In his bed.

How long had it been since there was a woman in his bed?

Too long.

His brothers claimed he was too picky. Too choosy when it came to the women he dated.

It was because he wasn't looking to date. He was looking to get married. Find a partner to be at his side.

Looking for a woman he could take care of the way his dad took care of his mom.

And the woman in his bed now was definitely not that woman.

He kicked off his boots and flipped the recliner back, eyes glued to the television.

Because all he saw when he closed them was her soft body stretched across his sheets.

****

"HEY." THE SOUND was soft enough it almost didn't wake him.

"Brooks."

He lifted the lid of one eye.

Nora was bent at the waist, dark eyes fixed on his face. Her hair was a little tousled and her cheeks were a little flushed.

Like she'd been taken to bed.

Technically she had been. Just not in a way that satisfied either of them.

Not that he was looking to satisfy Nora Levitt.

"You ready for me to take you back to your car?" He sucked in a deep breath and stretched his arms over his head, trying to work out the tension bunching his shoulders.

It was just from sleeping in the recliner while his bed was otherwise occupied.

But the deep breath he took didn't seem right.

It didn't smell like a house inhabited by cowboys who worked long days in the heat.

It smelled like breakfast.

Nora straightened, holding out the plate in her hand. "I accidentally slept the whole night, and since you didn't eat all your dinner yesterday I made you breakfast."

"*You* made *me* breakfast." It was about as ass backwards as it could get. When a woman spends the night, a man should make her breakfast in the morning.

Not that Nora really spent the night, but still.

"I feel bad." She shoved the plate closer. "I ruined your whole night."

Brooks took the plate before it ended up impaled in his body. "I'm not sure your night was any better."

"Well," Nora took a few steps back, "I slept in a bed, so I would say I came out with the better end of the deal."

"Recliners aren't too bad." Brooks glanced down at the plate in his hand.

"I went through your fridge." Nora cringed. "I hope you don't mind."

"Too late now, isn't it?"

Her eyes barely narrowed. "You're not a morning person, are you?" She slowly lowered to sit in the recliner opposite him.

Brooks picked up the fork tucked into the food on the plate. "You could say that."

It was one more thing his brothers gave him a hard time about. Being a night-owl cowboy was rough. Bedtime was something he'd always struggled with, but there was no room for sleeping in on a ranch.

"That probably sucks."

"It's not always easy." Brooks eyed Nora. "Where's your breakfast?"

"Oh." She shook her head a little, reminding him her hair looked like she'd had a much more interesting night than she actually had. "I'm fine."

"So you even graze at breakfast?" He didn't like thinking she never had a full belly.

Nora gave him a half-smile. "My stomach isn't feeling the best it's ever felt this morning."

"Makes sense." Brooks stood, taking his plate with him as he went to the kitchen. "You did a fair bit of damage on that wine last night."

"Please don't judge me based on last night." Nora stood, one hand lifting to press into the side of her head. "I'm actually not much of a drinker."

He pulled the bag of bread from above the fridge. "I figured that out when you passed out in my truck."

"I thought you said you weren't going to judge me?"

"No. *You* said I wasn't going to judge you." He dropped two slices of bread into the toaster then glanced over his shoulder in her direction. "I fully intend to judge you."

She scoffed, a smile working across her lips. "You're a jerk."

"I've been called worse." Recently, as a matter of fact.

He and his brothers' reputations around town hadn't had much updating since their high school days and it continued to bleed into their adult lives. To this day, most women expected the Pace boys to chase them. When they didn't, feelings got hurt.

And he was gettin' good at hurting feelings.

It wasn't personal. They just weren't what he was looking for.

"I have a hard time believing that." Nora came closer, leaning against the counter beside him.

"Why's that?" He caught the toast as it popped up and went to work smearing each piece with a little butter.

"You put a new battery in my car. You didn't get mad when your horse liked me better than you. And you let me sleep off a wine miscalculation in your bed while you slept in a recliner." She shrugged. "That all seems pretty nice to me."

Nice. Not something most men got excited about being called, but he'd take it from this woman. "Thank you." He held the plate of toast Nora's way. "Here."

She looked from the plate to his face, hesitating just a second before taking it. "Thank you."

"Just trying to prove I'm as nice as you say I am."

She smiled around the small bite of toast in her mouth. "What time does everyone else get up around here?"

Brooks checked the clock on the wall. "You've got about thirty minutes to escape."

"Okay." Nora fell silent as she slowly chewed through the breakfast he made her.

When they were each done with their food Brooks stacked their dishes in the sink before grabbing his keys and heading out to the truck. The short drive was quiet with Nora silently staring out her window. They were almost at the turn to the main house when she finally spoke.

"It's peaceful out here in the morning, isn't it?"

Brooks turned to study her.

It was easy to get caught up in Nora's looks. She was beautiful. Dark hair. The kind of body a man wanted to get lost in. Full lips. A beautiful smile.

All that could keep you from looking closer.

But that's *all* he wanted. A closer look.

And now that he was getting it he noticed something.

Nora looked relaxed.

The set of her jaw seemed softer. The slope of her shoulders lower.

Normally she was all business. Completely focused on the job his mother hired her to do.

But not right now.

And it was like seeing her for the first time.

Not the woman his mother hired.

Not the city girl intent on going back to a life she didn't seem excited about.

And not the woman with short answers and clipped comments.

"It's very peaceful in the morning." Brooks forced his eyes away from her. "As long as you don't mind the smell of cow shit."

A bark of laughter jumped from her lips. One hand immediately went to her head and she groaned. "Don't make me laugh. It hurts."

"You almost had me sold on drinking a little wine before bedtime." Brooks couldn't help but smile as she continued to laugh and groan. "Now I'm rethinking it."

Nora wiped the corner of one eye, her lips holding a wide smile. "Well I'm pretty sure I can't carry your big ass to bed, so if you try it you'll be on your own."

CHAPTER FIVE

"ARE YOU READY for the grand opening?" Mae sat across the booth from Nora, her forkful of food hovering in front of her mouth as she waited for an answer.

"We are as ready as we are ever going to be." She'd been busting her ass to get everything together for the celebration this weekend. Unfortunately, Maryann had been busting her own ass coming up with new ideas at least three times a day.

"Maryann keep changing things?" Clara grinned from her spot next to Mae.

Nora poked at her own lunch. "I think she has so many ideas it's difficult to choose just one."

Maryann would actually make a great collaborator. She could always come up with ten different options for how to do something. Which was great for brainstorming.

Not so great when you were actually trying to get shit done.

"I think she spent too many years raising four rowdy boys and is finally getting to do something that interests her." Liza bit off a hunk of warm bread and chewed as she continued to speak. "I can't say that I blame her. She gave up a lot to marry Bill and live in the middle of nowhere with stinky men."

Mae eyed her best friend across the table. "Didn't you do the same thing?"

Liza's lips pressed into a tight frown. "Unfortunately I didn't get a Bill out of the deal."

The table fell silent.

There was something Nora was missing. If she planned to stay in Moss Creek then she might be interested in finding out what it was.

But she was not staying. She was going back to Seattle.

"Speaking of Maryann's rowdy boys." Clara rested her elbows on the table and leaned against her hands, eyes bright as they settled on Nora. "How's Brooks?"

The question came as a surprise. One that left Nora momentarily speechless.

A fact her friends didn't miss.

Liza leaned away, her head turning toward Nora. A slow grin crept across her lips. "Is there something we need to know?"

"No." Nora shoved a bite of tuna salad into her mouth, using it as a way to avoid the conversation.

It didn't work.

"Brooks?" Mae's brows crept up her forehead. "Brooks Pace?"

Nora ignored them, choosing to continue to eat her lunch instead of indulging the women around her.

"I just thought when I saw him drive you back to your car yesterday morning that there had been a little something going on." Clara shrugged. "Maybe I was wrong."

"I am pretty sure if a Pace man drives you back to your car early in the morning it's because something went on." Mae wiggled her lifted brows. "What I don't understand, is why a woman wouldn't claim it."

Clearly there was no ignoring this conversation. "Nothing happened."

"Well that's disappointing." Liza turned back to her lunch.

"So, your argument is that you were with Brooks Pace all night and nothing happened?" Mae shook her head. "I don't believe that for a second." She pointed a finger Nora's direction. "Look at you. You're freaking gorgeous."

Clara nodded. "And super smart."

Liza bumped her with a shoulder. "And you're funny."

Nora tipped her head Liza's way. "I am definitely not funny."

Liza snorted. "It's pretty funny when you freak out over snakes."

"Nothing happened because I'm going home soon." She was leaving very soon.

Within days soon. She had pressing issues to deal with.

Whether she liked it or not.

Clara was still nodding. "That's why I was so surprised when I saw Brooks driving you back to your car."

She shouldn't want to know what was surprising about it.

It didn't matter.

But the question still seemed to pop free. "Why is that surprising?"

"Because Brooks is the picky brother." Mae answered for Clara. "He doesn't date around. Like at all."

"Well he's still not dating around. Nothing happened." It was the truth, but explaining the full scope of her evening with Brooks would only lead her friends to believe that something had happened.

Technically she slept in his bed.

Technically he made her breakfast.

And she was moderately suspicious that he'd actually carried her from his truck to his bed.

And while their evening together hadn't been terrible in spite of the pounding headache it left her with, it also had not been what her friends were trying to make it out to be.

And it would never be that.

She had no interest in cowboys and no interest in staying in Moss Creek.

It didn't matter how considerate the cowboy in question may be. It didn't matter how nice the women of Moss Creek were.

She couldn't stay here and pretending like she could would only make it that much harder to go back.

Which she had to do.

She had a whole life in Seattle.

Past Tense.

But she would rebuild. Find a new job. A new apartment.

New friends.

And no one would be able to claim she didn't deserve it this time.

No one would be able to take it away in the blink of an eye.

And it's not like she had all those things here. Just the friends part.

"Brooks has been single pretty much since he stopped chasing every skirt that walked past." Mae's brows slowly came together. "Which might have been a while ago now that I'm thinking about it."

"He's going to be single for a while longer, because nothing happened."

"You keep saying that. It's starting to make me suspicious." Liza's grin held. "If you're disappointed nothing happened you can just say that. None of us would judge you for being sad a cowboy didn't try to get in your pants."

"I don't want a cowboy in my pants." Her pants were currently off-limits to cowboys.

Honestly they were pretty much off-limits to the entire male species. She had to have the contents of her pants thoroughly inspected because of one of them and wasn't in a hurry to have to do it again.

"I need to be focused on finding another job." Nora held firm. "That's all."

Her job with Maryann was the only one she had in the pipeline after parting ways with her previous employer.

Who was also the mother of her previous boyfriend. Also known as the man who caused the full inspection of her lady parts.

"There aren't too many interior decorating jobs around here." Clara pushed out her lower lip. "Are you sure you don't want to try something new?"

"Like what? Shoveling manure?" Moss Creek, Montana was not the place to start a new career unless you were interested in working on a ranch.

"We don't *just* shovel cow shit around here." Liza took a long drink of the flavored tea Mae made especially for their lunches.

"You see how you said *just*? You don't *just* shovel cow shit. That's still too much shoveling for me." She liked to make things pretty. Liked the challenge of taking her client's vision and bringing it to fruition.

De-cow-shitting a barn was not her idea of fruition.

"What are we going to do when you leave us?" Clara seemed to be the one most upset by her impending departure. "You're one of us now."

An odd tightness formed in her chest.

How long had it been since she really felt like she was a part of something?

A while.

She'd worked for the same company since graduating college, but even after five years she still didn't feel like she was part of the team.

She always assumed it was because she was dating the boss's son. That everyone assumed she was getting preferential treatment.

Not that there should have been any confusion.

Nora was always assigned the most difficult clients with the worst taste and the most horrible rooms that needed redone.

And every time she busted her ass to make it perfect. To prove she could do anything.

It got her nowhere.

Actually it got her worse than nowhere.

It got her cheated on and terminated. Kicked out of her apartment with nothing but the few items she could claim as her own.

"You guys will be just fine when I leave. Soon it will be like I was never here at all."

Mae snorted. "If you think that's how it will be then you clearly don't know how shit works around here."

****

"OH HONEY, THIS is beautiful." Maryann Pace came Nora's way, her arms already out and ready for a hug.

And today Nora didn't feel like dodging it. She was on the home stretch and might just make it out of Moss Creek relatively unscathed. Tonight's grand opening party at The Inn was her final commitment here.

Then it was back to the reality she tried hard not to forget was hers.

"I'm glad you're happy." Nora let Maryann scoop her into a tight embrace.

"I'm not happy." Maryann didn't let her go. "But I'm happy with everything you've done. Besides the leaving part."

"I haven't left yet." Nora patted Maryann's back, waiting for the older woman to release her.

It didn't happen.

"But you're going to." Maryann sucked in a breath. "And I'm heartbroken."

"Mom. Let her go."

The deep voice behind her was more problematic than Maryann's never-ending hug. Suddenly being trapped in Maryann's grip didn't seem so terrible.

Unfortunately, Maryann immediately released her and stepped back, her eyes moving off to one side. She smiled across the crowded space, looking at someone in the distance. "I'll be right there."

And then she was gone, rushing off toward whoever called her away at the worst time possible.

Leaving Nora alone with the man she'd hoped to avoid for the rest of her days in Moss Creek.

Nora turned to face him, plastering on a smile that immediately froze in place at the sight of him.

Brooks had on a pair of jeans that didn't look like they'd seen a single day of work and a crisp button-up shirt with the top button open, letting out a peek of the tanned skin underneath. His ever-present cowboy hat was traded out for a light camel version that was just as clean and neat as the rest of him was.

"Don't you look nice." Admitting anything more was useless. Possibly worse than useless.

"I've been told I don't clean up bad."

"I'm sure you have." The Pace brothers were not hard on the eyes. In another time and place she might have given spending time with Brooks a long, hard consideration.

But given the recent events in her life, the only option was to smile and walk away.

Which was exactly what she was going to do now.

"You've done an amazing job here." Brooks came a little closer, blocking the exit path she had in mind. "I'm not sure anyone else could have done any better."

She was a little speechless. "Thank you." She'd gone a very long time without having anyone appreciate her. Especially anyone from the male species.

"It wasn't hard to do. It really is beautiful out here." When she let herself really look around it wasn't difficult to see why so many people enjoyed this area. The skies seemed bluer. The breeze seemed softer. The mountains served as a stunning backdrop for landscapes that could fill a gallery.

But it was not where her life had to be.

Brooks gave her a slow smile. "Even with all the animals around?"

"I thought I made friends with one of the animals." She hated leaving him thinking she didn't like it here. Didn't see the beauty in the place he was lucky enough to call home. "It's nothing against Moss Creek. Things are just..." Nora fished around for a word to describe her current situation. "Tricky."

"Don't hear many people call life in Montana tricky." Brooks eased in a little closer as the music from the live band grew louder. "Usually they call it boring."

"Well my life isn't really in Moss Creek." If it was, she might not be where she was now. Homeless. Jobless. Friendless.

With a point to prove.

Brooks tipped his head in a slow nod. "That's right. You're a city girl."

She was a city girl. Always had been. Her parents lived in downtown Seattle. Her apartment was in downtown Seattle.

No. That wasn't true anymore.

Her former apartment was in downtown Seattle. Now it belonged to her ex and her replacement.

Nora looked out across the open fields surrounding The Inn. "The first time I ever saw a cow in real life was when I drove to the ranch."

"I can see how ranch life might come as a shock to you then." Brooks leaned against the railing that surrounded the in-ground pool that spanned the back of the building she'd been brought here to decorate. "All these open fields and mountains instead of skyscrapers and traffic."

Nora had to tip a little closer to hear the last bit as the band's volume picked up even more. "It's just strange. I think I'm used to more noise."

Brooks glanced toward the band enjoying the hell out of their performance. "Well you're getting plenty of noise now."

Nora couldn't stop the laugh that bubbled up and out of her mouth "It's not easy to find a band out here."

Brooks suddenly seemed closer. "If this is the best you could find then I'm sure this is the best there is."

Was that another compliment?

Nora cleared her throat and shifted in her heels. Finding Brooks Pace attractive was not a struggle.

But finding him charming could set her up for disaster. "I should probably get back to work."

Brooks' long body was almost against her as he leaned into her ear. "I thought your job was done here, Miss Nora."

Technically he was correct. Her contract with Maryann was fulfilled and paid for. Tonight was simply a professional courtesy.

The tempo of the music blaring across the outdoor patio suddenly shifted, flowing into an easy rhythm.

Brooks slid the glass of soda she'd been nursing from her hand and set it on the rail. "How about I teach you to two-step before you go back to your fancy life."

Nora glanced down at the hand he held her way, calloused palm up.

What could one dance hurt?

"Are your boots steel-toed?"

A slow smile lifted the corner of his mouth. "Not much of a dancer?"

"Just what happens at high school dances, and I'm not sure many people would call that dancing." Her heart picked up speed as his palm came closer.

"I'm sure we'll be just fine."

She took a deep breath, holding it as she put her hand in his. Brooks immediately tucked it into the crook of his arm, keeping his hand on hers as he led her toward the small dance floor.

Maryann and Bill were already at the center of it, with Bill spinning his glamorously-dressed wife all around the parquet flooring, a wide smile on his tanned face.

Nora was so distracted watching them, she almost forgot why she was there in the middle of it all.

Until suddenly she was spinning too.

Right when she was positive her face was going to end up on the floor one strong arm banded around her waist, steadying the whole world.

Nora blinked a few times, trying to figure out where she ended up.

Besides dangerously close to Brooks Pace.

"You ready?" His voice was low in her ear. The warmth of his words sent a shiver snaking down her spine.

"For what?"

"To learn the two-step." He took her hand and spun her until she faced him. His hand stayed in hers while the other rested in the perfectly decent spot just below her shoulder blade. "Other hand on my shoulder."

Her eyes dragged across the broad band of muscle pulling his shirt tight.

If that's how the dance went then who was she to complain?

Nora did as he instructed, forcing her fingers not to flex.

"We're gonna take sets of two steps at a time. Two quick. Two slow. You're going to go backwards, right foot first. Ready?"

He didn't wait for her to answer.

She immediately stepped on his foot.

"Shit." Nora stopped moving, her eyes going to the couples moving around the dance floor, all of them following the pattern Brooks laid out. "Does everyone around here know this dance?"

"Everyone around here grew up doing this dance." He eased a little closer. "Ready to try again?"

She blew out a breath. "It's your toes on the line."

"I've got ten. I can stand to lose a few." He started the steps and she did her best to follow along, eyes glued to her feet as she counted to two over and over again.

"Eyes up here, Miss Nora."

"If I stop looking at my feet you're going to end up with a heel through your boot."

"You let me worry about that." Brooks' voice was calm and relaxed. Like he was perfectly fine with whatever fate his feet faced.

She huffed out another breath and lifted her eyes to his.

It was an unfortunate change of events.

She'd spent so much time working to keep her eyes off him, which left her unprepared for what it would actually be like to look at Brooks Pace and have him looking back at you.

He pulled her a little closer as they fell in step with the other couples, everyone moving counterclockwise around the small space. As more people crowded around them his body inched in, moving closer and closer until she was tucked tight against him.

Brooks dipped his head to her ear. "You're a pretty good dancer."

"I'm just doing what you told me to do." She tried to ignore the slide of his thigh between her legs as they took longer steps, working their way toward the outside of the circle.

"Dancing is a team sport." Brooks' steps slowed once they reached the outskirts. "But somebody's got to be the captain."

"I'm assuming you like to be the captain?"

"Not always." As his steps slowed the way he held her shifted, his hand sliding lower to rest on the small of her back. "Life requires a partnership. Not a team."

"I don't really watch sports." The closeness of his body forced her hand up to the back of his neck.

"I won't hold that against you."

Suddenly she was spinning again.

But this time as she circled she watched everyone around her. Listened to the women as they laughed like they were having the time of their lives being spun around by the men they were with.

It was impossible to imagine what it would be like to trust someone enough to let them spin you through life, knowing they would catch you when you started to fall flat on your face, instead of letting you hit the ground.

The music slowed as the song came to an end. Brooks stayed close as the melody moved into a faster beat.

"With a little practice you could be one of the best two-steppers out here, Miss Nora."

Once again she was a little befuddled by his compliment. She'd gone forever without one and now he'd given her three in one night.

Nora tucked her hair behind one ear, forcing her eyes from the gaze she'd gotten a little lost in. "I guess we'll never know. I'm heading out first thing Monday morning."

Her flight was booked. Her reservation at the hotel complete. Her rental car set to be returned.

"That doesn't leave much time to see what you could do."

"I guess not." Nora offered him a little smile as she eased out of his arms. "Thank you for the dance."

Brooks tipped his hat. "The pleasure was mine."

Nora watched as Brooks moved through the crowd, leaving her standing on her own.

"Hey." Clara stood so close the sound of her voice made Nora jump.

Her head snapped Clara's way as one hand rested over her racing heart. "You scared the shit out of me."

"That's because you were staring at Brooks' ass."

"I was not doing that. It's just weird to see him in clothes that don't look like they've been dragged all across the pasture."

Clara's dark brows lifted. "Look at you. Learning all the words."

"Cow yard takes too long to say." Nora crossed her arms, doing her best to keep her eyes as far from Brooks as she could manage. "What do you think of the party?"

"I love it." Clara's eyes went to the band Nora spent hours hunting down as a favor to Maryann. "I think I'm going to see if they'll come back for my wedding."

"I'm pretty sure they will for the right price." The band was only willing to drive so far because almost all of Moss Creek would be attending the party and they knew it was a good chance to get some word-of-mouth interest. "Or if you crank up the invite list."

"Nah." Clara watched as Brody took his twin daughters out onto the dance floor, one hand in each of theirs as he twirled them in their fluffy dresses. "Maybe I'll just get a DJ."

"A DJ would be good too." Clara wanted to keep her wedding small and Nora couldn't blame her. At the end of the day it was about who you married, not what the wedding was like. Should be anyway. "You'll have to send me some pictures."

"Or." Clara turned to face her. "You could come back and see it first-hand."

Guilt tugged at her stomach. "If I have a new job I'm not sure I would be able to get away."

"What if you don't have a new job?"

"I have to find a place to live. I have to get all my stuff out of storage." Her list of excuses for not wanting to come back to Moss Creek was never-ending.

Reasons. Not excuses.

They were reasons. Real. Valid. Important reasons.

And one of them was the cowboy watching her from across the pool with an intensity that made her stomach clench and her lungs stall out.

No matter what happened she had to get the hell out of here.

Before she did something stupid.

Like wonder what it might be like to stay.

CHAPTER SIX

THE PLACE LOOKED just as bad as he remembered it looking.

Brooks stood in the center of the lawn that was still littered with the random shit Junior threw out in a fit of rage. Clara, Mae, Liza, and Nora had done their best to clear the place out, thinking Camille would eventually want to move back in, but Camille decided she had no interest in going back to a place that held so many terrible memories.

So, he'd taken it off her hands, intent on giving the house a new life too.

It was something he'd considered getting into for years, but always found a reason to put off.

But now that Boone was back and taking on some of the work at the ranch, Brooks had more time to dabble in a hobby that would also make him a little cash.

He made his way up the rickety steps and across the worn planks of the porch. The padlock on the door kept the inside from suffering any more damage from teenagers or angry raccoons.

But the place still needed a lot of work.

And he was almost looking forward to it. The opportunities it presented.

"Oh." Nora stood at the open door, one hand resting on the casing. Her eyes moved from side to side, scanning the small space. "Is Camille here?"

Brooks turned, wanting to face Nora head-on when he admitted the truth. "Camille isn't coming."

Nora stared at him. "Okay." The hand on the door dropped. "Your mom asked if I could come here. I assumed it was to meet Camille."

That was what he wanted her to think. He was pretty sure Nora would never have come if she knew it was him she would find.

For some reason he made her skittish.

And he couldn't help but wonder why.

"Not Camille." Brooks slowly crossed what used to be a tidy living room as he made his way toward Nora. "Me."

"You?" Her dark eyes moved around the house. "Why would you want me to meet you here?"

"I want to hire you."

She stared at him again, her lips locked together. He'd been around her enough to know it was what Nora did when she wasn't sure what to say.

And it seemed like that happened a lot when he was involved.

"What do you want to hire me for?"

"I bought this house." Brooks forced his feet to stop instead of moving closer like they wanted. "I'd like to renovate it and sell it for a profit."

"I thought Camille might want to move back in?"

"So did I." He'd been prepared to help Camille fix the place up so she and Calvin could enjoy it. "But when it came down to it, she decided it would never feel like a home to her."

The line of Nora's lips tipped down. "That makes me want to hit someone with something heavy."

"Mae already did that."

"He deserves to be hit again."

If he didn't already like her that comment would have sealed the deal. "We could stand here and talk all day about the shit Junior deserves, but I'd rather talk about how to turn this house into a home for someone new." Nora was supposed to be leaving tomorrow. That gave him less than a day to convince her to stay and help him on this.

He'd seen what she could do. The Inn turned out better than any of them thought it could be. And she'd done that in spite of his mother's meddling.

He could only imagine what Nora could accomplish without someone buffering her talent.

"I'll give you free rein. Whatever you want. I just want it to look like a home someone would want to live in." He knew how to do the work involved with renovating. He could build walls and hang drywall. He could install countertops and sinks and showers.

But his taste was what could best be described as *single man.*

"So you want me to help you design this house?"

"No." Brooks let himself ease a little closer. "I want you to design the house. I'll just follow your instructions."

It was the thing that held him back from doing this before. It didn't do you any good to have a house no one liked the looks of.

Nora was silent.

Again.

He was used to his mother. Every thought she had came right out of her mouth. You never wondered what was on her mind.

But Nora held back more than she said, and that made conversing with her a little more complicated.

"I'm supposed to fly back to Seattle tomorrow." She fell silent again, but this time she began to slowly work her way deeper into the house. Nora paused in front of the nonworking fireplace and gave it a long look.

"I'm not sure I can get that running again." Brooks stepped in behind her as she walked past the room's centerpiece.

"They make nice inserts." Nora kept walking, slow steps taking her down the hall and into the first of the two bedrooms. She paused in the doorway and looked over the messy jumble of broken toys and discarded clothes. "This house makes me sad."

"Me too. That's why I want to give it a new life." Most people thought it was strange to give a house a feeling, but he always thought they had them. Felt them when he walked inside.

And this house definitely had a feeling.

"Have you redone a whole house before?"

Brooks shook his head. "No. Have you?"

Nora peeked his way over one shoulder. "No."

"Seems like we might be a good match then."

That didn't come out exactly the way he meant it.

It also didn't come out exactly wrong either.

He and Nora might actually be compatible. Maybe not in the way he initially hoped, but in a way that could still benefit both of them.

"My mom said you didn't have another job lined up and I thought maybe..."

"I'll remember not to tell your mother any more of my secrets." The teasing line of her lips was the only indication Nora wasn't upset that his mother betrayed her confidence.

"She'll just pry it out of you anyway." Brooks followed as Nora moved to the second bedroom. "It's her MO."

Nora spun slowly, her eyes narrowing slightly as they scanned the space. "What are you thinking of doing here? Are you keeping it the same size?"

"Hadn't really thought about it." Brooks edged closer to the sweet smell that teased him every time she passed. Was it vanilla? Honeysuckle? "I was kind of hoping you'd do that."

Nora crossed one arm over her chest and rested the second on top, one finger coming to tap against her chin. "I'm not sure I can stay very long."

It wasn't an outright yes, but it also wasn't the immediate rejection he'd been worried he might get. "I'd be happy with any time you had to offer."

"I might not be able to extend my hotel or car rental." She sounded dangerously close to talking herself out of this.

"There's always room at The Inn." The thought of Nora being closer made him feel oddly comfortable. It was a long drive to the city where she'd been staying. "And if you stayed at The Inn you would be closer and we could make the most of the time you're here."

"I thought you said you'd be happy with whatever time I had to offer?" Another tease of a smile across her lips.

"I never said I wouldn't try to get more." Her help would benefit him immensely. That's why he was offering her this job.

"I could maybe stay a week and help you figure out what you want to do." Nora's eyes moved across the master bedroom. "Are you sure you don't have anything in mind?"

"Just making money and giving this house the life it deserves." That's all this was about. Righting a wrong the only way he could. Fixing at least one part of Camille's life. Helping her and Calvin get the fresh start they deserved.

"Okay." Nora didn't sound as excited as he'd hoped she would.

"I appreciate it."

Nora tipped her head in a nod. "Sure." She ducked past him. "I guess I'll go see if I can stay in my hotel room another week."

****

"I THOUGHT NORA was going back to Seattle." Boone stood just outside the barn that housed the family's horses.

"Oh." Explaining that he was the reason Nora was still in Moss Creek would only end with his brothers giving him hell. "Maybe she stayed to help Mom with a few more things."

"That would make sense if she was in the house talking to Mom." Boone turned and shot Brooks a shit-eating grin. "But it looks like she's headed this way for some reason."

Brooks straightened from where he'd been passing out hay to the stalls. He quickly swiped down the front of his shirt and jeans, knocking as much dirt and debris off as he could.

"Fancy meeting you here." Boone tipped his hat as Nora came into view. "I thought you were heading out?"

Nora held a file of papers tight to her chest. "I decided to stay another week and help Brooks with his house renovation."

Shit.

"That's awful nice of you. I'm sure Brooks is grateful as hell to have you on his team." Boone tipped the front of his hat up as he backed out of the barn. "You two enjoy your evening."

Nora gave him a tight smile. "Thanks."

Brooks took another swipe at the bits of hay clinging to the front of his shirt. Normally they wouldn't bother him, but he knew Nora wasn't a fan of ranch life and since she was doing him a favor by helping him, the least he could do was try to make her more comfortable.

"Hey." Nora's eyes moved to where he was still working a stubborn bit of hay free of the fabric of his shirt.

She reached out and snagged it, her fingers brushing against his stomach as she pulled the thistly clump of roughage free.

Her touch had him sucking in a breath he didn't know he needed.

"Sorry." The hand she touched him with tucked tight into her armpit as she wrapped her arm back across her chest. "I thought maybe that was poking you."

"Just a little." He pointed to the papers in her arms. "What's all that?"

"Um." Her eyes dropped from where they were still fixed on his chest to the pile. "It's just some ideas I have about the house."

"That's a lot of ideas."

"You said you didn't have any sort of plan so I wanted to give you options."

"And I said I'd do whatever you thought was best."

She frowned, the dark line of her brows coming together. "I don't think that's a good idea."

"Why not? You're the professional."

"But I'm not the only one involved in this project." She straightened. "As much as I would enjoy getting to do anything I wanted, I don't know enough about life in this area to do it justice."

"Then let's fix that." Brooks snagged the pile of papers and set them on the shelf just inside the door, right above the buckets of equine treats they kept on hand for Clara to spoil the horses. "Come on." He turned and walked deeper into the barn.

Nora stayed exactly where she was. "Where are you going?"

"I'm going to saddle up a horse for you to ride."

"I'm not riding a horse." She shook her head. "It's not happening."

"Why not?" Brooks pulled his horse from the stall. "I thought you liked Shadow." He lifted his brows. "You're gonna hurt his feelings."

"I doubt that." Nora held one foot out and pointed to the slip-on shoe covering it. "And I'm positive I'm not dressed for horse riding."

"I've ridden barefoot before." Now that the idea was planted, he was determined to show Nora her ideas and notions about ranch life were all wrong. "Nut up, Buttercup."

"This has nothing to do with *nutting up*." Nora propped her hands on her hips. "This has to do with the fact that I'm not the kind of girl who rides horses." She waved one hand around the barn. "This isn't my thing."

"You haven't given it a chance." He'd initially thought Nora was right. That she wasn't the kind of woman who could ever enjoy anything besides big buildings and city lights.

Then she accidentally got a little wine drunk and made him wonder.

Then she accidentally learned the two-step, quickly taking the spot of best dance partner he'd ever shared the floor with.

And now she was still doing her damndest to prove she wasn't cut out to be here.

But maybe she wasn't trying to prove it to him.

Maybe Miss Nora was trying to prove that to herself.

"I've got a whole slew of city girls coming out here in a couple weeks. If I can't even get you on a horse then I'm in trouble."

Nora eyed him. "What are they coming here for?"

"Bachelorette party." Brooks brought Shadow to the front of the barn where Nora stood. The horse immediately leaned down, expecting her to be the same as she was the night they met.

Nora didn't disappoint him.

She lifted one hand to scratch along the horse's cheek. "I feel like you're using him against me."

"I'm not above it." Brooks shot her a wink.

He never winked. Definitely not at women under the age of eighty-five.

"Just one ride. So you can get in the country girl mindset."

"How do you know it's a woman who will buy the house?"

Brooks backed toward the tack room, leaving Shadow with Nora. His horse would do a better job of convincing her than he could ever do on his own. "Women are always the ones who pick the house. Men don't care what a place looks like, as long as they have a spot to hang their hat."

The confused look was back on her face. "That's not been my experience."

"That's why you need to wrap your head around how things are here." Brooks snagged the double saddle they used when friends brought their kids over. It was a way to know an inexperienced rider would be safe no matter what happened. He hefted the saddle onto Shadow's back. "Things are different here."

"I've noticed."

He tried to ignore Nora's eyes as they fixed on him. "Have you? Because it seems like you work really hard not to notice a lot here."

"It's nothing personal."

"So I've heard." He tightened the strap that ran under Shadow's belly. "But I won't hold it against you if you get up in this saddle."

"I didn't come here to ride a horse. I came here to do what you hired me to do." Nora snagged the folder of papers from the shelf and held them up. "We're working on borrowed time here. I don't have forever to help you."

He didn't need forever. All he needed was one week.

One week to see if maybe Nora Levitt might be more than she was showing him.

Might be more than she was willing to show herself.

"Bring it all with you." Brooks rested one arm across Shadow's rump. "We can talk about it as we ride."

"I'm not presenting this on the back of a horse."

"It's your only option right now." Brooks grabbed Shadow's reins and got him moving, hoping it might get Nora moving too. "Because I'm not done workin' for the day. You can either come with me or you can wait here until I'm done."

Nora glanced toward the house that would be bustling with the dinner crowd in under fifteen minutes. "When will you be done?"

"I'm not done until the sun goes down."

"You work from the time the sun comes up until it goes down?" She didn't sound completely shocked.

She sounded more... interested.

"Sometimes." Brooks didn't turn as she started to follow him. "There's times where there's more work than there are hours in a day."

"Don't you get tired?" Nora edged a little closer to him as Shadow's wide body swayed with each step.

"Course." Brooks glanced her way as he stopped. "But the work doesn't go away. It's got to be done." He double-checked the fit of the saddle. "That's why men out here don't care what the house looks like. They don't spend a lot of time in it."

"Bill seems to be home quite a bit." Nora squinted toward the main house. "So does Brody."

She'd caught him in a technicality. "Do they seem to care what the house looks like?"

He knew for a fact Brody wasn't making a single decision in the house he was building for his family. Everything was up to Clara.

And Nora knew it too. She'd helped Clara with more than a few decisions when it came to the finishings.

"Brody lets Clara pick because he wants her to be happy, not because he doesn't care." Nora's eyes narrowed. "Actually, he cares a lot what the house looks like."

"He cares because he wants to be sure it's exactly how Clara wants it." Brooks knew his older brother well. Had watched with no small amount of envy as Brody landed what Brooks chased, easily finding a woman perfect for him.

A woman to be at his side. To be on his team.

To warm more than his bed.

"That's different from not caring at all." Nora's head tipped. "I'd say Bill is the same way."

"We still get to the same point. Women buy houses." Brooks patted the saddle. "So let's get to talking about how to make our house one a woman wants to buy."

Nora's gaze was wary as she eyed the saddle. "There's no way I can get up there."

"Sure there is." Like Nora said, he was working on borrowed time and waiting for her to find her own way into the saddle clearly wasn't an option. So Brooks grabbed her around the waist and hefted her up. She let out a half-scream, half-shriek as she flailed around with the arm not clinging to her papers.

Luckily her free hand missed his head, instead only managing to clip the brim of his hat, knocking it to the dirt as her butt settled into the saddle.

"Have you lost your mind?" Her voice was shrill and loud as she clung to the edge of the saddle, dark eyes wide.

"Nope." Brooks settled his hat back on his head before pulling up behind her.

"What are you doing?" Nora tried to turn his way, but the move shifted her side-saddle position and sent her free hand back his way. She grabbed him tight, fingers fisting in the front of his shirt.

"I'm tryin' to get you situated." Brooks banded one arm around her waist, hoping it would ease the panic making her breath come faster and faster. "Face forward and swing your leg to the other side."

"I can't believe you're making me do this."

"Someone's got to make you do things. Otherwise you won't have any fun."

"I have fun." Nora kicked her foot out, easily swinging it around Shadow's head and down to the other side.

"Do you?" Brooks used his hold to get her centered in the saddle. "Cause all I've ever seen you do is work."

"That's because I'm here to work, not to have fun." The pitch of her voice was coming down and her death grip on his shirt loosened.

"It's a shame you think you can't do both, Buttercup." He reached around her to find the reins. "Cause around here we work hard." He shifted a little closer. "But we sure as hell play hard."

CHAPTER SEVEN

THIS WAS INSANE.

She'd presented in offices. In kitchens. Even in backyards.

Never on the back of a horse. This was probably a first in the world of interior design.

"Show me what you're thinking."

His voice was so close. So low. Almost like he was sharing a secret with her.

"Here?" Nora gripped the papers she'd spent all day and half the night working on as the wind whipped across the open land, threatening to steal them away and send them flying.

"You got a better option?"

Definitely. "How about inside? Some sort of normal place where I don't have to worry about falling to my death."

Brooks' arm tightened where it still wrapped around her waist. "You don't have to worry about falling, Buttercup. This isn't my first rodeo."

"Ha." He was full of jokes today. Dad jokes.

"The back of a horse is a normal place around here." Brooks took the stack of papers from her hand.

But he kept them right where they were, which meant both his arms were now wrapped around her.

On one hand it was the best thing that could have happened considering she was fairly certain her ass was going to hit the ground at some point.

On the other hand it was the worst thing that could happen. For obvious reasons.

Brooks flipped open the front of the folder holding the loose sheets, revealing the print out of one of the digital renderings she worked up. "That looks nice." He lifted the page, turning it sideways to orient it the correct way. "It looks like a little bitty farmhouse."

Nora huffed out a breath. He was serious about doing this here. "That is the least expensive and easiest to achieve of the options I came up with." She pointed at the color scheme running across the bottom of the page. "We could do it in a standard white or we could make it red to match what you have here at the ranch."

"Why would I do that?"

Nora lifted one shoulder. During her late night she'd come up with all sorts of ideas. Some of them good.

Some of them probably nothing like what Brooks' was envisioning. This was one of those ideas.

"I thought maybe you might end up deciding to hang onto it and rent it out as part of Red Cedar Ranch." It was actually one of the first things she thought of. She couldn't be the only person who hated the idea of being stuck at someone else's mercy. "Not everyone loves the idea of a bed and breakfast. It doesn't really offer much in the way of privacy."

Brooks was quiet for a minute. "That never occurred to me."

"I just thought it was worth putting out there." Nora snagged the top paper away, revealing her second option. "This one is the most expensive. If you wanted to sell this as a family home this is what you would need to do in order to make that happen."

"That looks quite a bit bigger."

It was bigger. She'd expanded the side of the house that included the bedrooms. Nora pointed to the addition. "Most families want at least three bedrooms. And most women want an en suite."

"Seems like you did a little research last night."

"This is all just common sense." She actually had done a little research, but wasn't going to tell him that. "It looks like most houses around here probably even have at least four bedrooms." Nora flipped to the next page, which showed the back elevation of the larger floor plan. "I actually added two more bedrooms and a bathroom off the largest."

"How much do you think a place like this would go for?"

Brooks seemed to genuinely want to know what she thought, which was a stark contrast with how she was used to being dealt with.

"I'm not sure. I would say getting the opinion of a realtor would make sense before you make any firm decisions." While she might be able to help him come up with different options, the final decision would have to be up to Brooks. She simply didn't know enough about Montana or the local housing market to make an educated decision.

And didn't have time to learn.

"I've got a buddy that sells houses. Maybe we can meet with him tomorrow."

"We?"

"I hired you for your opinions, Buttercup." Brooks leaned a little closer. "And I plan to get as many as I can before you hightail it back to the city."

"I don't normally offer those kinds of options. I'm a designer. Not a real estate guru."

"But you are something I'm not." Brooks paused. When he spoke again his voice was different.

A little deeper.

"A woman."

"Your mother is also a woman." And his mother had no shortage of opinions.

"I don't want her opinion. I want your opinion."

"Why?" Maryann had excellent taste. She'd done an amazing job with her own home and probably could have done The Inn on her own if time allowed.

"Because she tends to think her way is the best way." Brooks flipped the folder closed. "And you are open to other people's opinions."

Yet another unexpected compliment. "I try to be."

"You do a good job. That's why I hired you."

Nora chewed her lower lip. The folder was closed and their discussion about the house seemed to be over, which meant she was now stranded on the back of a horse in the middle of a pasture.

Tucked against Brooks Pace, his arms still wrapped around her.

It was one of the things she missed most about being in a relationship. Physical closeness. Not sex or even anything that led up to it.

Just the quiet moments curled up together.

Not that she'd had many of them.

Her time with Dean was dominated by his mother. She monopolized all his free time. All his attention.

Any Nora got seemed to irritate the hell out of her, and Dean was nothing if not a doting son.

But she was used to being on her own most of the time so it took her years to realize maybe her relationship with Dean wasn't great.

And that his closeness with his mother wasn't normal.

The rocking of Shadow's steps worked her closer to Brooks. Closer to the man she was supposed to be getting away from.

Nora risked a peek behind them, being careful not to lose her balance. Not that it would matter. The second she shifted Brooks' arms tightened.

"You okay, Buttercup?"

"I was just trying to figure out where we are." Specifically how far they were from the main house. Her car.

Her way out.

"We're headed to the northwest corner of the property."

"That doesn't help me." Nora looked to the right of them.

Field.

To the left.

More field.

"Behind The Inn."

"Oh." She relaxed a little. They were going to The Inn. A place where there would be other people. A place where she wouldn't be alone with the cowboy holding her a little too close.

Which was what she wanted. To not be alone with Brooks Pace.

In spite of the disappointment suggesting otherwise.

"I want—" The deep drawl of his voice was lost in the wind moving around them.

Nora leaned back, angling her ear his way. "What?"

Brooks closed what little space remained between them, his chest pressing against her back as his lips moved to her ear. "I said, I want to show you some of the ranch."

Nora tucked her head so he could hear her. "I've already seen The Inn."

He stayed close, his lips hovering distractingly near to hers. "We're not going to The Inn, Buttercup. We're going *past* The Inn."

"How far is that?" The question wasn't as loud as she meant for it to be. Mostly because she was struggling with thoughts of what Brooks' lips might feel like.

"You have other plans?"

She watched each word come out of his mouth. Watched the way his lips wrapped around them.

Her thoughts about his lips dropped to more indecent locations, making her stomach flip and her thighs clench.

"No." It was barely a squeak. She cleared her throat and tried again. "No other plans."

She should have other plans. Primarily getting the hell away from this man before she decided staying close to him was a brilliant idea.

The lips that were slowly torturing her to a sex-starved death curved in a smile that seemed like it was from something other than amusement. "Good." He tipped his head toward the mountains looming in the distance. "Now turn around and enjoy the ride."

He was talking about the horse. The horseback ride.

She stared at the mountains, willing her thoughts away from any other sort of ride Brooks Pace might take her on.

And tell her to enjoy.

Is this what being single was like? Constant suffering?

She hadn't had this problem in Seattle. She'd gone a full three months problem free after her break-up with Dean.

Maybe that was because she was still in shock over what had happened, and now the shock was wearing off.

Rubbed away by a cowboy with rough hands and dusty boots.

Now she was thinking of his hands. The way they would scrape against her skin—

She needed help.

Nora dropped her head back. A natural reaction to being overwhelmed.

Except this time it didn't offer her the respite she needed.

This time her head landed right against Brooks' well-muscled shoulder.

"Are you fallin' asleep on me, Buttercup?" His hold tightened a little more.

"Yup." She went along with his assessment. Hopefully he thought he was boring her to death.

Instead of what was actually happening.

She tried to straighten away, but Brooks held tight.

"Don't be sorry." His frame rocked with each shift of Shadow's body, the smooth back and forth not doing anything to help her cause. "I used to fall asleep on my horse when I was a kid." He smiled at the memory. "My dad used to have to come out and hunt me down because my horse would just walk me around like that."

The thought of a dark-haired little-boy-Brooks passed out across the back of a horse shifted her thoughts.

But not to anywhere less problematic.

"The farthest my parents had to go to find me was my room." While her memories weren't bad, they certainly didn't make her smile the way Brooks smiled at his.

"I would imagine it's different growing up in the city."

She nodded, her head rocking against the spot where it still rested against his shoulder. "There weren't any horseback naps, that's for sure."

His laugh was soft, but still vibrated through her. "That's a damn shame."

Was it?

She'd never considered her childhood lacking. Her parents both had good jobs that provided them with anything and everything they could ever want. Toys, televisions, trips.

But even on trips their lives were still very much the same. They might do some sightseeing, but once they were finished, each of them went their separate ways, spending most of their time apart.

"I'm not sure my father could have chased me down on a horse." She loved her dad. He was smart and focused and hard-working.

But a cowboy he would never be.

"Nothin' wrong with that. Everyone's good at something different."

Brooks' response sat warm and solid in her chest. "You're good at everything."

He could run a ranch. Change a car battery. Build houses.

Two-step.

"Not everything." His head tipped her way and he gave her another of those stomach-flipping smiles. "Just most things."

And now she was back to thinking about his lips.

"Are we close to where we're going?"

"You in a hurry?"

Yes. "I was just curious."

"We're close."

"I haven't seen The Inn yet." She'd been watching, both hoping to see The Inn and dreading it.

"We're not going to The Inn."

"But you said—"

"I said we were going *behind* The Inn." Brooks pointed to their left. "The Inn's way over that way."

Nora looked in the direction he pointed. If she squinted hard enough she could almost make out the line of the roof.

Or maybe it was a stick.

Or a cow.

She faced forward, staring ahead. This was turning out to be one hell of a bad decision, but all she could do now was try to keep the damage to a minimum.

So she faked falling asleep, keeping her eyes mostly closed as they continued on.

The sun was low in the sky when Brooks finally slowed Shadow to a stop. “We’re here, Buttercup.”

She pretended to stir awake, sucking in a breath as she straightened away from the heat of his body.

In front of them was a line of mature trees. Something sat in the branches of the thickest one. She tipped her head to one side, trying to get a better look.

“Come on.” Brooks easily swung off Shadow’s back, his boots gracefully hitting the ground. He reached his hands up to her. “I’ll catch you.”

Nora shook her head. “I’ve heard how this works. Brody fell on his ass trying to catch Clara and the same thing happened with Mae.”

“Mae was trying to kick Boone in the nuts.” He lifted his brows. “Should I be worried?”

She looked off to one side as she pretended to think. “You did force me onto the back of a horse.”

He grinned up at her, not looking the least bit sorry. “You got a nap out of it.”

She couldn’t tell him he was wrong. “If you don’t catch me I’m going back to Seattle and you can figure the house out on your own.”

“Deal.” He wiggled his fingers at her. “Come on, Buttercup.”

Nora immediately dropped off. The best thing that could happen was if she hit the ground. Then she could go back to Seattle and forget all of this.

Brooks Pace included.

Unfortunately, he caught her.

Unfortunately, he didn't let go once he had her.

Unfortunately, she didn't hate being wrapped in his arms, his clear blue eyes fixed to hers.

"I didn't kick you in the nuts."

His head barely shook. "I didn't drop you. Guess that means you're stayin'."

"Seems like." She struggled to even blink. Looking away was impossible.

Why did he have to be so handsome?

So coordinated?

So thoughtful?

So—

She fought the urge to look at his lips again. "Why are we here?"

Brooks' arms slowly eased away. "I want to show you the first thing I ever built."

"It's a little late for me to worry about your credentials."

He laughed and she felt a little proud that it was because of her. She wasn't usually what most people would call funny.

"Come on." He pressed one hand to the small of her back, urging her toward the towering trees.

Nora picked her way through the overgrowth, carefully scanning each spot before she stepped.

"The cows haven't been out here in a while." Brooks lifted a branch blooming with honeysuckle out of her way. "That means no cow patties."

"Good to know." She stepped in a rutted spot and tipped sideways, immediately grabbing onto Brooks for stability. “I’m definitely not wearing the right kind of footwear for this excursion.”

“I’ll give you a heads-up next time.” Brooks pushed another branch out of the way as they closed in on the wide base of the tree she’d noticed earlier. “Then you can be prepared for off-roading.”

“If you’re going to make a habit of this then I might rethink our partnership.” She stopped at the base of the tree as her eyes skimmed up, stalling out at the thing she hadn’t been able to identify before. “Oh wow.”

“I’m not sure it qualifies for a wow, but I’ll take it.” Brooks stood close, but he wasn’t looking up.

He was looking at her.

“You made this?” Nora reached out to rest one hand on the ladder leading to the most beautiful treehouse she’d ever seen.

“It’s an on-going project.” Brooks’ eyes lifted to the structure fifteen feet above their heads. “You want to go up?”

“I’ve never been in a treehouse.”

“That doesn’t surprise me.” Brooks gripped the ladder and shook. It didn’t budge. “These are new. Replaced the original rope ladder last year.”

Nora stepped to the base of the rungs and stared up. “The original?”

“I built this when I was a kid. Hauled everything out here myself.”

She turned to peek Brooks’ way. “You built this when you were a kid?” When she was a kid she spent her time watching television and eating Doritos.

While Brooks was riding horses and climbing trees.

And building houses in them.

“I’m going to be disappointed if you don’t go up there, Buttercup.”

For some reason it seemed like he really would be.

Nora lifted one foot to the bottom rung and climbed on. She'd been at the top of her fair share of ladders so she shouldn't be nervous.

But it wasn't the ladder that was the problem.

And the feeling in her belly might not be nerves.

Brooks started up behind her, keeping pace with her steps. The ladder led to a porch of sorts with handrails that made it easy to pull up the rest of the way.

Nora stepped onto the narrow space and turned.

From this spot you could see everything. The Inn. The main house. Acres of pasture dotted with the black bodies of cattle. The mountains in the distance.

All of it at once.

It was breathtaking.

"I thought you were coming up here to look at my handy work." Brooks stood at her side but like last time his eyes weren't on the view.

They were on her.

She patted the rail surrounding the small deck. "Seems sturdy."

The rails were painted the same white as the siding of the small structure. The decking under her feet was stained a rich brown that matched the shaker-style shutters flanking the windows.

The freaking thing had shutters on the windows.

Nora went to the door. It was stained the same color as the floor and shutters. She turned to Brooks and lifted a brow. "You built this as a kid?"

"It's been upgraded."

That was an understatement.

Nora twisted the knob and pushed open the door.

She sucked in a breath.

The place was flipping furnished. A leather sofa ran the length of the longest wall. An upholstered ottoman sat in front of it with a stack of books about everything from cabinetry to drywall finishing piled in the center. A tiny bank of cabinets took up the back corner. A single-cup coffee maker sat on the butcher block counter with a rack of pods lined up beside it. A cow hide covered the floor, finishing off the rustic décor.

She turned to face Brooks where he lingered in the open door.

He still watched her, but this time uncertainty lingered in his gaze.

Which made no sense. There was nothing to be uncertain about here.

"Brooks." She stalled out when something caught her eye.

Candles. There were scented candles stacked on the counter and the small end table.

On a tray on the ottoman.

That was when she realized what he'd really brought her to see.

The place where he hid from the world.

CHAPTER EIGHT

"THANKS FOR MEETING me here." Brooks shook the hand of his longtime friend, Tanner.

"No problem." Tanner took off his expensive sunglasses and squinted at the little house. "You already bought this place?"

"Yup."

"That's too bad." Tanner shook his head. "I probably would have advised you against it."

"I wouldn't have listened." He was going to do his part to help Camille out and paying her outright for this house did just that. Took it off her hands in a simple, stress-free interaction.

"You're planning to renovate and resell?" Tanner walked toward the porch, the shine of his leather shoes looking more than a little out of place next to the overgrown lawn and scattered gravel of the drive.

"That's the plan." Brooks glanced back as Nora's rental car pulled in and parked next to Tanner's BMW.

She climbed out of the car looking like she was walking into an office building.

Not an abandoned house.

Her long hair was shiny and sleek. Just like the rest of her. Fitted pants. A fancy shirt and shoes that would end up ruined in a week around here.

She gave Tanner's car a sideways look as she passed. "This is your interior designer?"

"Yup." Brooks didn't like the way Tanner was watching Nora. He cut in front of his friend and made his way down the stairs. "Mornin'."

She gave him a smile. "I thought you weren't a morning person."

"Work's still got to get done." He stood between Nora and Tanner. "You didn't have to get dressed up for this."

"I didn't want your realtor friend to think you'd hired someone unprofessional."

"I don't give a shit what he thinks."

Her dark brows came together. "Then why is he here?"

"I don't give a shit what he thinks about *you*." His second explanation didn't come out any better.

Unfortunately there wasn't time to dwell on it because Tanner was elbowing his way in at Brooks' side, a toothy smile on his clean-shaven face. "Hello."

Nora's smile was different when she turned it toward Tanner. Like she had to force it into place. "Hello." She adjusted the bag over her shoulder, holding it with one hand while she shoved the other Tanner's way. "Nora Levitt."

Tanner took her hand, keeping it in his a little too long. "Tanner Carmichael."

Nora's forced smile held as she pulled her hand free. "What do you think of the house?"

"What do *you* think of the house?"

Brooks slid Tanner a sideways glance.

This was a bad idea.

"How's your fiancée doing?" Brooks almost grinned as the question came out. Nothing like the reminder of your better half to make a man remember his manners.

"She left me for a woman she met at work."

Nora's eyes widened. "Oh my gosh." One hand went to her chest. "I'm so sorry."

Tanner shrugged it off. "She's a great girl. I'm glad she found what she was looking for."

Nora's smile turned genuine. "That's a really good way to look at it."

"It's the truth." Tanner turned toward the house. "Let's go check this place out." He held one hand in the direction of the door. "After you."

Nora glanced Brooks' way before slowly passing them and heading into the house. Tanner had a stupid grin on his face as he followed behind her. "I take it you've been here before?"

"I have." At least she gave Tanner the same short answers she gave him.

"I'm not sure our friend here made a good purchase." Tanner stopped in the living room and frowned at the fireplace. "It's rough."

Nora stood a little taller. "Anything's fixable."

"Not anything." Tanner walked to peek into the two bedrooms. "It's small. It's not been kept up. The lot is a mess." He crossed his arms across the sharp lines of his high-end suit. "Brooks isn't giving you much to work with here."

Nora's chin lifted the tiniest bit. "I disagree." She walked toward the kitchen, closer to where Brooks stood, stopping just a couple feet away. "The floor plan leaves plenty of options for expansion. The lot is large and flat." Her eyes came Brooks' way. "And as far as the condition of the house itself, I have no doubt Brooks will be able to bring it up to anyone's standards." She dug into her bag, fishing out the folder of ideas she'd shown him the night before.

But this time when she opened it the top sheet looked much different.

"Here's what I'm thinking." She passed the paper Tanner's way. "It takes it to a four bedroom, but makes the best use of the existing footprint, which will keep costs to a minimum." She moved closer to Tanner, leaning to point to the different parts as she explained. "It will also add another bath and adjust the living area to an open concept which will make it feel larger and more modern." Nora's dark eyes came to Brooks before sliding away. "But the esthetic will make it warm and inviting. Comfortable for family living."

Tanner studied the paper. "I can see why Brooks hired you." He passed the paper back, tucking one hand in his pocket as his gaze lingered on Nora. "I'd love to discuss more of your ideas over dinner."

Nora stared at him for a second. "Oh." Her eyes widened. "Oh." Her fake smile was back, stretched too tight across her face. "I'm actually headed back to Seattle." She backed away from Tanner. "I only stayed for this as a favor to Brooks."

Tanner appeared shocked that she turned him down.

He wasn't the only one.

Tanner screamed city boy. He'd moved away from Moss Creek right after graduation and never looked back. He lived the kind of life Nora did.

And she'd turned him down flat.

Tanner pulled out a business card and held it Nora's way. "In case you change your mind."

She pinched the card between two fingers and shoved it into her purse without looking at it. "Do you think we are on the right path here?"

Brooks had to smother a smirk. Not only had she shut Tanner down, she'd immediately gone right back to the business at hand.

"I do. I think you'll make money. How careful you are will determine how much." Tanner rocked back on his heels. "I'll be happy to list it when it's finished." He tipped his perfectly groomed head Brooks' way. "Friend discount of course."

"Appreciate it." Brooks reached out to shake his hand. "Thanks for coming all the way out here."

"Anything for you." He slapped Brooks on the shoulder but his attention stayed on Nora. "This guy saved my ass more than once."

"If you hadn't had a habit of picking fights you wouldn't have needed it saved." He and his brothers served as back up for Tanner more times than he could count.

"You know I don't deal well with bullshit." Tanner shook his head. "Still don't." He pointed Brooks' way. "Only now I fight with lawyers."

That was probably more his speed. Tanner might look like he could do some damage. He was in good shape. Clearly lifted a weight or two.

But that didn't mean shit when someone came at you ready to knock the hell out of you.

Tanner tipped his head Nora's way. "It was a pleasure to meet you, Miss Levitt."

Nora's smile was a little more genuine this time. "You too."

Brooks stood at the door and watched Tanner walk to his car, cell already pressed to his ear.

"You're friends with him?"

Nora's voice was closer than he expected.

She stood right at his side, watching as Tanner backed out, offering a little wave as the realtor pulled away.

"Tanner is a good guy." He still believed that. In spite of the fact that he'd blatantly hit on Nora right in front of him.

Not that his friend couldn't.

Nora wasn't his.

She was single. Smart. Talented. Funny. Interesting.

The kind of woman a man would be proud to have at his side.

His partner.

"I'll take your word for it."

Brooks studied the line of her profile. The clench of her jaw. "You didn't think so?"

"He reminded me a little of someone I used to know." Nora pulled her purse closer. "I shouldn't hold that against him I guess."

He waited. Hoping she'd give him a little more of the story.

A little more of herself.

But like always, she went quiet.

Brooks went to where the file she brought sat on the kitchen counter. He picked it up, flipped open the cover, and stopped.

He stared at the paper inside. He'd caught a glimpse of it earlier when she passed it to Tanner.

But now that he was seeing it full on, it was clear Nora had changed more than a little of her initial design.

He turned to face her. "What's this?"

She shrugged and turned away. "It's why I'm here. To help you fix this house up."

"This isn't the same plan you showed me yesterday."

"I showed you a few plans yesterday." Nora kept walking, putting more space between them.

"And this was none of them." Brooks started to walk after her. "This is new."

"Am I not allowed to update a design?" She walked a little faster, heading toward the other end of the small house.

She wasn't going to outrun him. There wasn't anywhere for her to go.

"You are allowed to do anything you want." He held up the paper. "But this isn't what you want."

She suddenly spun his way. "You don't know what I want."

"I don't think I'm the only one." Brooks pointed at her. "I don't think you know what you want either."

Nora stood a little taller. "I do."

"You gonna try to tell me you want to go back to Seattle?" He eased in a little closer. "Cause if you wanted to be there you'd be there right now." He stopped right in front of her. "Instead of here with me."

"You're paying me to be here." She thought it proved her point. Thought it explained away her presence.

"You could have turned me down." It was what dragged his ass out of bed in the mornings.

Thinking about how Nora decided to stay.

Wondering why.

"I was being nice."

"No you weren't." He edged closer, unable to keep his distance anymore. "You're here for the same reason I am."

He'd denied it.

Swore to himself it just all worked out this way.

That he rushed to buy Camille's house to help her out.

But that wasn't the only reason he did it.

Nora's eyes narrowed. "And what reason would that be?"

"To figure this out."

She stalled out, her mouth dropping open for a split second. "There's nothing to figure out."

There sure as hell was. He'd seen the way she looked at him last night.

Watched as she pretended to sleep, leaned back against him.

The change that happened when he showed her his hideaway.

The place no one else had ever been.

No one but her.

And now she'd changed her whole design to match that place. That place that mattered to him like little else did.

"There's nothing to figure out." Nora's shoulders straightened as she repeated her claim.

"Liar."

Her nostrils flared. "There's not."

He moved in closer, letting his body push into hers. "Say it again."

Her eyes widened and her breath caught. "There's nothing." It was a whisper.

A whisper of a lie.

A lie he wouldn't let her keep telling him.

Brooks' hands went to her face, fingers lacing into her hair as he leaned close, the sweet smell of her skin teasing him. Testing his commitment to the moment.

The act.

"Tell me this is nothing and we pretend none of this happened, Buttercup."

"Why do you keep calling me that?" Her lips nearly brushed his as they moved.

He smiled. "Because you always nut up."

"Not always." She didn't come closer, but she wasn't pulling away.

So he held steady. Waiting her out.

"You changed your battery. You learned the two-step. You rode a horse. You stand up to my mother." He took a deep breath, stealing a little more of the scent of vanilla and honeysuckle that always surrounded her.

Not the kind of perfume he imagined a city girl would wear.

Because deep down he didn't think Nora was really a city girl.

She was a city girl who didn't know any better.

And he was working hard to show her better.

But he wanted to work harder.

Show her more.

Prove Moss Creek was worth considering.

That he was worth considering.

"I love your mother. You all act like she's this wild woman and she's actually the sweetest thing."

"She never came at you with a switch."

Nora's lips twitched, almost moving into a smile. "I'm sure you deserved it."

"I for sure did." Brooks let his fingers dig deeper into the thickness of her hair. "What about it, Buttercup?"

"What about what?" She acted like she didn't know what he meant.

That was okay. He'd let her.

"You gonna prove me wrong or are you gonna nut up again?"

He knew what she'd pick. She couldn't stand not to.

Because while his mother was straightforwardly intent on proving what she was capable of, Nora was not.

She still fully planned to prove what she was capable of, she just didn't care who else knew.

It was to prove it to herself.

"This is a bad idea."

"That depends on how you look at things."

"We're working together."

"So?" He let his thumbs rub across her temples, pressing just a little as he went.

Nora's eyes rolled closed in a way he'd kill to make happen again. "You're distracting me."

"You distract me every second of the day."

Her eyes snapped open. "Really?"

"Is that hard for you to believe?" Brooks worked back across her temples, hoping to ease the tension forming between her brows.

"Yes." The word whispered free as her eyes dropped closed again.

"It shouldn't be. You're hell on a man's focus." He managed to get a little closer as her full lips barely parted. "Makes for a long day."

"I—"

"Nora."

Her lids slowly lifted. "Hmm?"

"I'm gonna kiss you unless you tell me not to."

Her eyes dipped to his lips like they had the night before. He'd been sure she was thinking about a moment like this.

Now he had confirmation.

"It's a bad idea."

"That's not a no."

"It should be."

"But it's not."

Her lips pressed together.

And for the first time he was happy Nora Levitt didn't have anything to say.

He waited a heartbeat longer, just to be sure.

Just to give her all the time she needed.

Because he wanted her to be sure.

The tips of her fingers barely brushed the front of his shirt as her eyes stayed on his.

Brooks leaned closer, stealing the last bit of distance between them.

"Hello?"

Boots banged up the front steps.

Nora tried to step away from him, but Brooks held her tight, pushing her body behind his as a large form came through the door.

"Brooks." Officer Grady Haynes gave him a grin. "I thought that was your truck out there."

"You thought right." Brooks liked Grady. He was a hell of a cop and a hell of a pool player.

But right now he deserved a full ass-kicking.

Probably wouldn't even fight it if he knew the circumstances.

Nora peeked out from behind him.

Grady's eyes widened as they bounced from Brooks to Nora. He immediately took a step backwards, moving toward the door. "I just wanted to check in. Make sure everything's good here. We've been keeping an eye on the place. Make sure no one bothered it." He tipped his head Nora's way as she stepped up to Brooks' side. "Ma'am."

She smiled. "Thank you for watching the house for Camille."

Grady nodded. "Sure thing."

"Camille gettin' ready to fix it up?" Grady wasn't moving as fast as Brooks hoped he would.

Nora shook her head. "Brooks bought it from her. He's going to fix it up."

Grady's brows lifted. "When'd you do that?"

Brooks hesitated. The full truth of what he'd done might make Nora feel a little—

Pressured.

"Recently."

"Good for you. It'll be a nice project." A call came through the radio strapped to the shoulder of the vest he wore. The muffled voice said something about a property dispute.

Grady shook his head. “Mrs. Patterson’s fighting with her neighbor about the rose bushes again.” He lifted a hand as he walked out the door. “See y’all later.”

His steps down the wood risers almost echoed through the silent house.

Brooks stood, fixed in place as Nora circled around him until they were face to face again.

Her chin lifted, angling her eyes toward his. “When did you buy this house?”

“Recently.” He repeated the same answer he gave Grady, hoping it would be enough.

Knowing it wouldn’t.

“How recently?” Her face was impossible to read. She might simply be curious.

She might also be considering running out the door.

“Very recently.” He’d had cash and no need for inspections. The deal was done in two days.

“The date. What day did you purchase this house?” She wasn’t backing down.

Not that he expected her to.

Brooks eyed the door, trying to figure out if he could block her escape.

“Please tell me.” There was a softness in her question. And something else.

Something that made him want to brawl with whoever made her need to hear this.

Made her need to know the length he went to to keep her here a little longer.

Brooks met her eyes, soaking in the first bit of insecurity he’d seen in her. Hoping he could take it and make it his. Rid her of it forever. “Friday.”

CHAPTER NINE

FRIDAY.

Brooks bought Camille's house Friday.

"But you'd planned to buy it for a while." That's what it was. What it had to be.

She was ridiculous to think it was anything else.

His head slowly moved from side to side. "No."

No.

He had not been planning to buy it for a while.

She swallowed, trying to keep her mind from running with this new information.

Making it something it wasn't.

"Why did you buy it Friday?" It was difficult to breathe around the anticipation clogging her throat.

It was like her whole body was waiting to hear his answer before it decided to keep functioning.

"I think you already know the answer to that, Buttercup." Brooks came close again.

The urge to flee was strong. She was ready to kiss him before.

As ready as she could ever be.

But now...

Now things were different.

"But if you want me to tell you I will."

Hearing it would be too much. It would make it impossible to deny.

And right now she needed to be able to deny it just a little.

Otherwise—

“What did you think of the new design for the house?” Panic made her try to change the conversation. Shift Brooks’ intense focus off her so she could breathe again.

But his focus went nowhere. It stayed right on her, his blue eyes steady as he continued to close in on her. “I think you changed it to what you thought would make me happy.” He shook his head. “But I don’t want to talk about that right now.”

“We should talk about it. It’s why I’m here.” The reminder wasn’t so much for him as it was for herself.

She was here to do a job. For the man prowling across the floor like an animal about to attack.

And he was about to attack her.

It would be something she might never recover from.

How did a woman go back to men like Tanner and Dean when she’d been ruined by a man with a slow drawl and skills that surely had no end?

How could she find suits and ties sexy after seeing the way dusty jeans and faded t-shirts wrapped around Brooks Pace’s body?

Hell.

He might have already ruined her.

“Damn it.” Nora pointed his direction. “You’re a pain in the ass, you know that?”

His brows lifted and his boots slowed to a stop.

She wiggled her finger around him, pointing to the face that was too handsome. The body that was too solid. The hands that were too—

Were too—

She was about to say something. Something important.

"You're not so problem-free yourself, Buttercup." Brooks was moving again. "I thought I had it all figured out, but you keep showing me how much I don't know."

She started to back away. Not really on purpose. It just seemed like the best option.

Before his cop friend showed up Brooks said he was going to kiss her. Gave her the chance to say no.

It didn't look like he was going to be so patient this time.

Not that it mattered. When it came down to it she didn't have the ability to say that single word.

Or the desire.

And now he knew it.

"We should think about this." Nora tried to force her brain to do exactly that.

It complied. Just not in the way she intended.

It happily traipsed off with visions of Brooks' hands and lips on her.

"I have thought about it." He continued coming for her. "Every night while I'm layin' in the bed that still smells like you."

Her stomach clenched at the thought of Brooks in bed.

How did cowboys sleep? Probably not in anything decent.

"You're the one that put me there."

His lips slowly curved in a smile that almost made her trip over her own feet. "I have a mind to do it again."

Her back bumped into the end of the short bedroom hall. "It's a long walk from here."

"It would be worth it."

She swallowed hard.

She'd gone from being undesirable to the man she'd been with since college to having a man willing to carry her miles to his bed. "You don't know that."

"I'm figurin' it out real quick." Brooks closed in on her.

She sucked in a breath as his body came to hers, hands pressing to the wall at each side of her head instead of going to her hair like they did before.

"We're back where we started, Buttercup." He leaned close, his warm breath whispering across her skin as he leaned close to her ear. "And I'll give you the same warning I gave you before."

She'd been wrong.

"If you keep giving me the chance to say no then I might do it."

"That's the whole point, Buttercup."

"Are you going to do this every time?"

"Are you already plannin' to let me kiss you more than once?"

Shit.

"I'm not planning anything. I'm just wondering."

Brooks pulled in a deep breath against the skin of her neck. "How about we just start with this one and worry about the next one later." His lips brushed against her as they moved, teasing her with a touch so soft it sent goosebumps racing across her skin.

"Now it sounds like you're expecting I'll let you kiss me more than once."

Brooks suddenly straightened, his gaze serious as it met hers. "I don't expect anything from you, Nora." He shook his head. "Not ever."

Ruined. She was definitely already ruined.

And he hadn't even kissed her yet.

"I'm not going to say no." She'd been delaying the inevitable and it was only making things worse.

Making it more difficult to find any distance from Brooks. Any barriers to put between them.

She braced, expecting him to kiss her right away. Take what she'd given.

He didn't.

Instead the hands pressed to the wall slowly came closer, sliding over her skin. She could almost count the calluses as they scuffed her cheeks, reminding her of how hard he worked each day. How hard he worked to help take care of his family.

The tips of his fingers worked into her hair as his palms cradled her face with a gentleness that nearly buckled her knees.

He'd barely touched her and she was already going to hit the floor.

It didn't bode well for her.

His thumbs came to slide over her lips, the slow scrape making her suck in a breath.

She knew this about him. Knew everything he did was slow and methodical. The way he walked. The way he talked.

Now she knew it carried over into other things.

Things that could definitely benefit from his attention to detail.

Brooks' nose slid along the side of hers. "You are not what I was expecting, Miss Nora."

She couldn't answer him even if she had something to say. All her focus was on where his lips hovered over hers.

Where his hands warmed her skin.

Where his body held hers upright.

His lips barely brushed hers in a slow pass that wasn't nearly enough. A noise that could best be described as a whimper created itself and fell from her lips.

Brooks pressed closer, his hands suddenly becoming firmer where they held her. A low sound rumbled through his chest as his mouth covered hers completely.

Another damn whimper fell out, but this one didn't drop free.

There was nowhere to go.

She grabbed onto him. Fisting both hands in his shirt as his tongue traced the seam of her lips before dipping between them.

Her head started to spin as she held on for dear life.

Brooks was the only constant. Holding steady as everything she tried to know fell away. Leaving only the truth.

A truth that wasn't easy to face.

She pushed at his chest, hating herself for it.

She wanted to stay here. Close to him. Wrapped up in the world he spun for her, weaving it into a web she could happily die on.

Brooks' lips immediately pulled from hers. "What's wrong, Buttercup?" There was no anger in his words. No frustration.

Just calm concern.

And it made everything worse.

He should be mad at her. Irritated at the situation.

She certainly was. And she was the one creating it.

"I have to go." Nora ducked to one side, rushing around him. "I'm sorry." She rushed for the door, turning before going out. "I'm sorry."

Then she raced away, across the porch and down the stairs, falling into her rental car before sending a spray of gravel dust flying as she backed down what almost qualified as a driveway.

What in the hell was wrong with her?

Lots of things. That was for sure.

Normal women didn't run from men like the one in her rearview mirror.

Nora cranked up the air as she drove down the unlined street, angling the vents at her sweating armpits.

She'd just kissed Brooks Pace.

Not only that. She'd made it clear she expected it to happen again.

And then she ran away.

Like a chicken. Definitely not like the Buttercup he called her. There was no nutting up done today.

Nora forced slow breaths in and out as she tried to figure out where in the hell to go from here.

Seattle should be a consideration.

But the thought of going home didn't sit as right as it used to.

"Damn it." She stopped at the sign at the end of the street and let her head fall to the wheel.

She had one job. One task.

Finish The Inn and go the hell home.

She should never have taken Brooks up on his offer. She should have turned him down and run away. Clearly she was good at it.

But now she knew he'd bought that house for her.

Sort of.

The honk of a horn sent her sitting straight up.

Left her disappointed when it belonged to a blue truck instead of the red one she'd been hoping to see.

Liza Cross pulled up beside her, window rolled down, a wide smile on her face.

Nora pressed the button to lower her own window.

"He makin' you crazy already?"

"Something like that." Nora didn't even try to smile back. There was nothing to smile about.

She accidentally decided to want Brooks Pace.

Then she accidentally let him know it.

And she'd seen what he was like. The man bought dedication and drive in bulk.

"You want to come hang out at my place?" Liza wiggled her brows. "Ben's smoking a brisket for lunch." She paused. "And I've got enough alcohol you'll be able to forget all about Brooks Pace for the day."

****

"THIS ISN'T WINE." Nora stared down into the glass Liza handed her.

"I didn't say it was." Liza clinked her glass against Nora's. "I just said I had enough of it that you could forget a certain Pace man who's making life difficult."

Nora took a drink of the cold beverage. It was sweet and fizzy and a little sour. "You have no idea."

"I can imagine." Liza drank down a few gulps before setting her drink down on the table next to her. "The men around here are good at being pains in the ass." She looked out over the yard just behind the farmhouse at Cross Creek Ranch. "But they're useful as hell."

Nora watched as a row of cowboys worked at a giant grill, cooking burgers and hot dogs. A thin trail of smoke eked from a black drum, scenting the air with the odor of burned wood. "Do they cook a lot?"

She was used to the way things worked at Red Cedar Ranch. Maryann did all the cooking and the men did all the eating. She assumed that was how it always worked.

But to be fair, her knowledge was limited.

"They do." Liza leaned back in the rocker set on the open back porch. "They started doing it after Ed died." Her expression changed, turning almost sad.

"Did he die a long time ago?"

"Five years." Liza picked up her drink and swallowed down a little more.

"It must be hard to run a ranch without him." As far as she knew Liza didn't have any kids to help her the way Maryann had her boys.

"It was harder to run a ranch with him." Liza's gaze hardened as she looked out over the fields around the small farmhouse. "He nearly ran this place into the ground." The icy edge of her tone was unmistakable. "Among other things."

"Is it doing better now?" She was hesitant to ask the question, but it also seemed wrong to try to change the subject.

Liza's expression softened, her eyes settling on where Ben, the head ranch hand, opened up the smoker and pulled out a large slab of meat. "It is."

Nora watched the men as they plated up the items from the grill, stacking everything into large foil trays before heading toward the large building at the back of the yard. Two of the men pulled the sliding doors open and they all started filing in.

Liza stood up and snagged her mostly-gone drink. "You ready to eat?"

Eating wasn't high on her list right now, but she'd found out firsthand what happened when she didn't eat.

She ended up in Brooks' bed.

Nora glanced down into her cup.

She had to think about this too hard.

"Come on Levitt. Stop thinking about him. You'll have plenty of time for that later." Liza skipped down the steps and headed to the building.

Nora followed behind her, leaning to get a better look at the interior of what appeared to be some sort of mess hall.

A kitchen sat at one side of the room. A large refrigerator sat at each end of the workspace with a line of cabinets between, broken up by two ranges and two sinks.

"The kitchen in the house is too small to cook for this many people so we built this four years ago." Liza pointed to the sliding doors. "When it's nice we pull those open. In the winter we keep them closed and build a fire."

Nora peered toward the large stone fireplace at the end opposite the kitchen.

"It's nothing fancy, but it gets the job done." Liza went to one of the refrigerators and pulled out a large tray of potato salad and passed it Nora's way. "Set that up on the island for me."

Nora took it and turned toward the island wrapped in the same stone as the fireplace.

Ben was at her side almost immediately. "I got that." He snagged the tray and set it on the counter before going to Liza's side and grabbing the next item she passed out.

Three trips to the island later there was coleslaw, fruit salad, and banana pudding lined up with the meat and potato salad.

"Ma'am." One of the ranch hands passed her a paper plate and a set of flatware. He tipped his head toward the spread. "Ladies first."

Nora glanced around. Everyone seemed to be waiting on her.

She stepped up to the island. The men immediately fell in behind her, moving along as she worked her way down the row of food.

After taking a little taste of each item she turned to find Liza.

She caught sight of her friend, standing close with Ben, their voices low in a hushed conversation.

After a few seconds Ben walked off, looking...

Frustrated.

Nora considered staying put.

But Ben didn't seem to be the only one upset by their interaction.

She made her way to where Liza stood in the corner, staring out across the open room. "Hey."

Liza gave her a smile that didn't look even a little real. "Hey. Your lunch good?"

Nora hadn't touched it. "It is. Thanks for making it." She leaned against the same wall Liza was backed up to. "Are you gonna eat?"

Liza let out a little breath. "I'm not really hungry."

"I get it." Nora poked at the pile of fruit.

"Why do things have to be so complicated, Levitt?"

Nora shook her head. "Hell if I know." She dropped her fork, giving up any attempt at eating.

"I thought things would get easier." Liza's eyes fell to the ground. "But they just keep getting harder and harder."

Nora nodded along with Liza. "These cowboys don't help."

Liza's head snapped her way. "They don't, do they?" She shook her head. "Pains in the ass. Every one of them."

Nora pursed her lips as she let the fact settle in. "It's not just the cowboys. They're all pains in the ass." She lifted one shoulder. "At least the cowboys are easy on the eyes."

Liza's head fell back on a laugh. "That makes it worse."

Nora started to laugh with her. "It does."

"Damn it, Levitt." Liza straightened. She pointed to the plate in Nora's hands. "Stop pretending to eat and let's go get shitfaced."

CHAPTER TEN

"DON'T YOU LOOK like a ray of fuckin' sunshine." Brett stood in the doorway of the cabin, giving Brooks a once-over. "What in the hell happened to you?"

"Nothin' happened." Brooks sat in his recliner with a can of peanuts, tossing them back one by one, cracking into them with his molars.

"You skipped dinner."

"I skip dinner all the time." It was something he'd caught no small amount of hell over in his lifetime.

"Yeah, but you're not usually sittin' here starin' at a blank television screen when I get home." Brett stepped inside and swung the door closed behind him. "This doesn't have anything to do with a certain interior decorator, does it?"

"Nope." He'd lie until he was blue in the face. It was no one's business.

"Good." Brett went to his own recliner and started working his boots off. "Cause Grady was feeling awful bad, thinkin' he interrupted somethin' today."

Damn Grady. You'd think he'd be better at keeping his mouth shut considering his line of work. "Where'd you see him?"

Now it was Brett's turn to clam up. "Nowhere."

They stared at each other for a minute.

Brooks reached for the remote and threw it Brett's way. "Pick something to watch."

He didn't bother paying attention to what his brother switched on. He wasn't going to see any of it.

He shouldn't be in a bad mood. Nora running away was probably a good thing. Meant she felt something.

But it also meant he couldn't go near her right now.

Meant he had to give her time to come to terms with things.

And that irritated the hell out of him.

He'd seen what could be and then had it ripped away before being sent to the back of the line to wait his turn.

Brett bounced a pillow off the side of his head. "You gonna pout all night?"

"Probably." Brooks stared at the television without seeing a lick of what was there.

Brett sighed and pushed up from his chair. "Want a beer?"

Brooks shook his head. "Nope." He wanted to be ready the second Nora decided to head his way.

Hopefully it wasn't three days from now. That would only leave him the weekend to convince her to stay.

And there were no more houses to buy.

Brooks' cell started to ring as Brett fished around the fridge.

The number was a familiar one.

He answered the call from the head ranch hand at Cross Creek. "Hey, Ben. Somethin' wrong?"

They'd helped out at Cross Creek more than a few times over the years. The ranch was still recovering from the mess its former owner landed it in and they ran on a small crew that couldn't handle much more than the daily workload. That meant when something came up, they needed help.

Help he and his brothers were happy to offer.

"You might want to get your boots back on."

It was a welcome distraction.

Brooks tucked the phone against his shoulder, dropping the peanuts to the side table as he shifted the recliner upright. "Put your beer back, Brett. Ben needs help."

"Just yours." The light sound of female laughter carried through the line. "I believe I have something you might want to come get."

Brooks stopped, one foot half shoved into a boot. "What in the hell happened?"

"Sloe gin."

"Who in the hell gave her sloe gin?" Brooks crammed his foot the rest of the way in and was up and grabbing his keys before Ben answered.

"You know damn well who gave her sloe gin." Ben's voice lowered. "You're not the only one's got a problem on their hands tonight."

"A problem?"

"You might want to brace yourself." Ben chuckled. "I don't remember her having this much to say before."

****

HE HEARD HER before he saw her.

Which was probably a good thing. Gave him a minute to prepare for the sight in front of him.

Because it was Nora Levitt barefoot, sitting next to Liza Cross in front of an open refrigerator, eating banana pudding straight from the tray.

With her hands.

Both women's eyes came his way as he walked into the small kitchen of the farmhouse at Cross Creek.

Then they immediately started to cackle, falling in opposite directions as the pudding slid to the floor between them.

"They've been like this for an hour." Ben stood at his side, hands on his hips.

Nora was the first to work her way back upright, using her palms on the floor to walk her upper body back into a sitting position, each move leaving a print of vanilla on the linoleum.

Liza rolled to her hands and knees before reaching to grab one of the chairs at the small table occupying the center of the small room. She unsuccessfully tried to pull herself up, instead sliding right back to her butt, laughing her ass off as she did.

"Hell." Ben edged around the mess on the floor, going to Liza's side and reaching for her.

"I'm fine." She tried to push him away, but ended up pushing herself backward.

"Time for bed." Ben hefted her up from the ground before scooping Liza up fireman style. He glanced Brooks' way as he passed. "Good luck."

"Same to you."

Brooks watched as Ben disappeared up the narrow stairs, taking the woman he'd been in love with for years to the bed she occupied alone.

When he turned back Nora's eyes were on him. They were a little glassy, but still focused. "Why are you here?"

"For you."

It was a simple answer to a simple question.

But his question for her was more complicated. "Why are *you* here?"

Nora blew out a breath, bits of her hair flying up from the gust. "Life." She reached for the pudding.

Brooks stepped in, stealing it from her reach. "You got something against spoons?"

"We decided it was better not to make more dishes to do."

Brooks surveyed the mess across the kitchen floor. A capless bottle of pressurized whipped cream sat on its side. A mostly-empty bag of shredded cheese was stuck half under the fridge with slivers of cheddar scattered around it.

Dishes were the least of their issues.

He set the pudding on the counter and reached for Nora. "How about we get you up so we can get this door closed?"

"Liza was hot." Nora let him pull her to her feet. Her body swayed, forcing him to pull her close.

"Well she's in bed now, so I think it's safe to close it." Brooks kicked the can of whipped cream out of the way so he could get the appliance shut tight.

"I shouldn't have let you kiss me."

"We can talk about that later." Right now his primary objective was getting Nora out of Ben's way.

"Okay." Nora leaned into him as he turned from side to side.

"Where are your shoes?"

She looked down at her feet and stared.

"We'll get them tomorrow." Brooks tried to get her walking but she stayed put, yawning long and loud.

Leaving him in the same boat Ben was in.

Brooks hooked one arm across her back and one behind her legs and lifted her up. Nora immediately wrapped her arms around his neck and dropped her head to his shoulder. "Are you going to carry me to your bed again?"

Ben wasn't kidding.

"Well I don't know where your bed is." Brooks made his way back to the front of the house, managing to pull open the door and let himself out into the night. The outside lights were all off, making it dark as hell as he worked his way down the gravel drive to where his truck was parked.

"It's so loud here at night." Nora yawned again. "It's all the bugs."

"There are bugs in the city, Buttercup."

"You can't call me that anymore." Her voice was sleepy but also surprisingly serious.

"If you don't like it I won't call you that."

"I *do* like it." She huffed out a long sigh. "But I didn't nut up today. I ran away."

"Don't worry about that right now." Brooks shifted his grip, getting one hand on the passenger's door and pulling it open. He propped her into the seat and reached down, grabbing her bare feet to tuck them inside.

"I'm a chicken."

"You're not a chicken." He lifted her feet, picking a blade of grass from between her toes before settling them into the floorboard.

"Yes, I am." Nora yawned again as she slumped down in the seat.

Brooks reached in to buckle her in. "Go to sleep, Buttercup."

"I'm not..." Another yawn. "Buttercup."

He wasn't going to argue with her.

Not ever.

Brooks closed the door.

"You got her?" Ben stood on the porch looking his way.

"She's asleep." Brooks walked to the front of his truck. "I can come back tomorrow and help clean up that mess."

Ben shook his head. "Don't worry about it." He pointed to where Nora was sitting, head back, mouth open. "You just get her home."

Brooks stopped.

Get her home.

This wasn't her home. She'd made that real clear more than a few times.

Thinking one kiss might have changed her mind would be foolish.

He gave Ben a wave. "Thanks for keepin' her safe."

"Anytime."

"I guess we'll find out." Brooks climbed into his seat and started the truck, the sound of the engine almost smothering out the snoring beside him.

Nora slept the whole ride to his cabin, one arm draped across the console, her hand brushing his knee with each turn.

The lights were off when he pulled up. Chances were good Brett put two and two together and figured out what was going on and made himself scarce.

Brooks got her out of the truck and into the house without waking her up, which probably said more about sloe gin than it did his carrying skills.

He kicked the door to his room open wide, making sure not to knock her head on the jam as he passed through. For the second time he laid Nora Levitt across his bed.

And for the second time he wasn't the reason she found her way there.

Nora's hair was a mess. Her skin was sticky from banana pudding and whipped cream. Bits of cheese clung to her shirt and her feet were filthy from whatever outdoor activities she and Liza partook in before settling down for their late night snack.

He snorted out a laugh.

It made sense sloe gin got her, because she sure as hell got him exactly the same way.

She was sweet as shit. Unassuming.

She snuck up on you and when she finally hit it was hard as hell.

Nora and sloe gin both packed a punch.

He reached to pull down the covers, working them under her body before pulling them up and over.

Brooks silently grabbed a pair of pajama pants and a t-shirt from his drawer and crept to the bathroom, showering off before brushing his teeth. He yanked open the door and jumped back.

Nora squinted in the bright light of the bathroom, one hand coming to cover her eyes. "I'm sticky."

"That's what happens when you eat banana pudding with your hands."

"I already told you." Nora stumbled past him to the sink and started scrubbing at her hands, one eye barely cracked open. "We were trying not to make more dishes for her to have to wash."

Her squinty eye went down to where cheese shreds were stuck to her arm. "Ew."

"You wanna take a shower?"

"Yes." Nora reached for the button of her pants.

Brooks snagged a clean towel from the rack and passed it her way. "I'll find you something to wear."

He shut the door and stared at it.

"Hell." He wiped one hand down his face and went to his room, digging through drawers for something that might fit her at least a little. The best he came up with was a worn t-shirt and a pair of Christmas boxers.

The shower shut off just as he made it back to the door. "I think I got something that will work for you."

Nora cracked the door open and snagged the items before closing the door again.

He backed against the opposite wall and waited. A minute later the door opened. The towel he'd given her was wrapped around her head and she was wearing the shirt and shorts.

Or they were wearing her.

He tried not to notice the way the soft fabric of the top did little to hide what was beneath it. "They're a little big."

"But they're not covered in pudding." She glanced down at the clothes wadded in her hands. "And dirt."

"Dirt?"

Nora's lips pursed. "We might have been running around the yard catching lightning bugs."

"You and Liza were chasing lightning bugs?"

"She found out I'd never done it before and made me do it." Nora's eyes dipped to the floor between them. "I'm sorry Ben called you."

"I'm not."

"You should be." She tucked the clothes tighter to her chest. "You should be in bed, not taking care of me."

"I've waited a long time to have someone to take care of, Buttercup." Hopefully she was still drunk enough to forget this conversation in the morning. "You should go back to bed." Brooks turned, intending to make his way to the recliner.

"Is that what you want? Someone to take care of?"

He stopped, taking a minute to think over her question. He tipped his head in a single nod. "It is."

"I don't like being taken care of."

He turned to face her.

"It makes me feel guilty."

"Guilty?"

Nora nodded. "I feel bad. Like I should be taking care of myself."

"I know you can take care of yourself." She would have been fine at Cross Creek. Maybe a little achy from sleeping on a linoleum floor. Maybe a little cold from laying in front of an open fridge.

But she would have been fine.

"Then why did you come get me?"

"I already told you." Brooks waited to see if she might remember. "Because I wanted to."

"Why?"

"I wanted to be the one to take care of you." He took a step in her direction. "I wanted to be the one to make sure you had what you needed." Another step. "I wanted to be the one to keep you safe."

Her lips rolled inward, sliding against each other as she stared at him. "Do you like to be taken care of?"

He never really thought about it.

But now that he was—

Brooks shook his head. "No."

Nora chewed her lower lip. "I take care of people too." She scrunched up her nose. "That's sort of how I ended up here."

"You ended up drunk on sloe gin because you were taking care of someone?"

"Liza and Ben had an argument." The towel on her head started to tip. "I was trying to make her feel better and didn't realize how strong that stuff was."

"No one realizes how strong that stuff is." Brooks glanced at Brett's closed door. As much as he hated it, now wasn't the time or place for them to be having this discussion. "You should go to sleep."

"I'm not tired."

"Then just rest."

Nora came his way, her bare feet moving across the worn wood floor. "I don't want to rest."

"You were just passed out an hour ago."

She continued coming his way. "So?"

"So I'm pretty sure you're still at least a little drunk, and that means you need to drink some water, take some Ibuprofen and go the hell to sleep." Brooks went to the kitchen, hoping to speed this process up. The sooner she was behind a door, the better.

"You're trying to take care of me again."

"I'm not planning on stopping." He snagged the bottle of pills off the counter and dumped two out into his palm. He held out a glass of water. "Here."

Nora shifted the clothes in her arms, tucking them under one elbow before taking the glass of water. "Do you just want me to feel guilty forever?"

"No. I want you to not feel like shit tomorrow." He snagged the wad of clothes and passed off the pills. "Because we have a lot to talk about."

And the list kept growing.

"Then let's talk." Nora shoved the pills in her mouth and washed them down before shoving the cup his way.

Brooks lowered his voice, stepping closer. "Tomorrow."

Nora crossed her arms. "Now."

She was serious.

Brooks raked one hand through his still-damp hair. This was not what he'd been expecting.

He thought Nora would sleep soundly like last time, giving him the night to think.

Another surprise from sloe gin.

"We can't talk now." He kept his voice just above a whisper as he glanced toward Brett's room.

Nora slowly turned to look down the hall, understanding dawned in her eyes.

Good. Now he would have a little time to think.

To figure out how to proceed.

"Let's go somewhere else."

"What?" Where did the woman who never wanted to talk go? The one he had to pry more than a few words out of?

Right now he wanted her back.

"Let's go somewhere we can talk." Nora lifted her chin. "Somewhere private."

She had somewhere in mind. He could see it on her face.

"You want to get on a horse in the middle of the night?"

"Will you talk to me if I do?"

He should have left her at Cross Creek. Should have let Ben deal with the both of them.

Hell, he and Ben both should have probably left them alone.

"Damn it." Brooks went to his room and grabbed the biggest sweatshirt he could find, coming back out into the hall to yank it over her head. "Making me drag your barefoot ass halfway across the ranch in the middle of the night."

He was talking to himself now. It was better than talking to her.

Because talking to her was going to make him lose his mind.

CHAPTER ELEVEN

"WHAT ARE WE doing?" Nora held tight to Brooks as he stomped across the yard toward his truck, carrying her on his back.

"Do you see any horses here?"

He sounded angry.

Which made sense.

She was being a pain in the ass.

But time was of the essence.

The more her liquid courage wore off, the more likely she was to clam up. Go back to her normal self.

And right now she was pretty sure her normal self sucked.

Brooks pulled open the passenger's door and turned, dropping her into the seat. The leather was chilly where it met her bare thighs. "I'm not trying to be a pain in the ass."

"Good to know this is how it is when you're not trying." He closed the door on her.

She pressed her lips together. The urge to keep things to herself was already starting to creep in.

But she'd poured her heart out to Liza. The least she could do was pour it all over Brooks too.

Especially since he was a big part of what was starting to fill it.

He slammed his door a little harder than normal and crammed his key into the ignition before backing out of the spot in front of the cabin and heading toward The Inn.

Nora fingered the worn hem of the sweatshirt he'd added to the shirt and shorts she was wearing.

"Thought you wanted to talk, Buttercup."

"I don't like to talk." She didn't talk to her parents growing up.

Didn't talk to Dean.

Didn't talk to any of the people she used to claim as friends.

Not about important things.

Like how she felt.

Brooks hit the brakes, the tires skidding to a stop on the gravel. "Then what in the hell are we doing?"

"I just said I don't like to talk, not that I wasn't going to." Nora wiped at the tiredness making her eyes burn.

She just wanted to go to sleep, but if she did that then she'd just be running from two things.

What waited for her in Seattle.

And Brooks.

She huffed out a breath, killing the last bit of time she could afford to spare. Hopefully this was like ripping off a Band-Aid.

"I came here to run away." Nora abandoned the hem of the shirt and went to work on a bit of fingernail polish that was already chipping away. "But just for a little bit."

Brooks didn't immediately respond, but he started driving again. He stared straight ahead, turning the truck onto an almost nonexistent lane that was little more than matted grass. "What did you run away from?"

She felt like a coward even admitting it. "Everything."

"That's not real specific."

"It is though." She'd lost everything in one fell swoop of a penis venturing into foreign lands. "My ex cheated on me and decided he liked her better."

Which meant everything Nora thought was hers went to someone new.

The apartment.

The dog.

The friends.

The job.

The man and his mother.

That last bit wasn't worth much though.

"I had to move out. Find a new job. A new place to stay." She glanced at Brooks. "Everything."

He didn't say anything.

She wanted to do the same.

Her feelings were always just that.

Hers.

Giving them to someone else felt like she was burdening them.

Dumping something that wasn't their problem on their doorstep.

The truck bounced along the ground as Brooks drove across the field. "I thought we had to ride a horse to get here."

She would have done it too. Barefoot and braless.

Because she was Buttercup.

And it was time to nut up.

Brooks finally looked her way. "You really want to ride a horse like that?"

"I woulda."

He stared at her for a minute before huffing out a single breath of amusement.

The headlights flashed against the line of trees that already seemed familiar. Her eyes easily found the wood structure hiding behind leafed-out branches.

He parked the truck and immediately got out.

Nora reached for the handle but stopped, dropping her hand and waiting for Brooks to open it instead.

It seemed like that might be important to him.

"Thank you." She gave him a little smile.

He was quiet for a minute. "You're welcome."

Her solitary childhood caused all sorts of problems she hadn't really noticed until recently.

She'd ended up emotionally stunted. Stifling down any sort of emotion she didn't necessarily want to acknowledge.

And her own feelings weren't all she'd ended up accidentally ignoring.

"I like when you open the door for me."

Brooks tipped his head. "Good." He turned his back to her. "Come on."

Tonight was full of firsts.

First time chasing fireflies.

First time hanging out with a friend and talking about real things.

First time eating banana pudding with her hands.

First piggy back.

"I've never done this before." Nora grabbed on and let Brooks swing her away from the truck.

"Gone across a ranch in the middle of the night barefoot and wearing someone else's underwear?"

"I meant the piggy back, but the other's true too." Nora held tighter as the headlights switched off.

Everything was suddenly very dark.

"Can you see where you're going?"

"We'll find out."

She tried not to laugh, but it came out anyway.

"Don't laugh. If I go down we both go down." Brooks pushed through the branches separating them from the ladder leading to his hideaway. "And I'm pretty sure if we hit the ground we'll both need a tick check."

Nora tucked her legs higher.

Brooks stopped. His hand came to one of hers, pulling it free of his neck and putting it on something solid. "There's the ladder."

Nora grabbed on as Brooks transferred her over to the wood rungs. "Thank you."

She started climbing. Her eyes were adjusting to the dark, but it was still hard to see anything. She ran out of rungs and felt around for the rails that would help her up onto the platform, but her hands kept meeting air. "Brooks?"

His body came up behind hers, pressing warm against her back. "I'm right here." He ran one hand down her arm, fingers circling her wrist and moving it to the rail she'd struggled to find.

"Thank you." Nora managed to somewhat gracefully make it up and onto the decking.

Brooks was at her side immediately, one arm around her. "Head toward the door."

She shuffled across, being careful not to topple over the side. Her hand hit the knob and she twisted, opening the door and immediately stepping inside.

In the dark it was easy to notice the whole place smelled like him.

Felt like him.

"Do you come here a lot?" Nora felt her way across the small space, looking for the couch.

A dim light suddenly switched on, illuminating the room in a soft glow. Nora turned to find Brooks standing next to a small lamp she hadn't noticed before. "I come here enough to have solar panels on the roof."

"Oh." She wiggled her toes against the smooth wood.

"You done talking already?"

She wanted to be done, but so far shutting her mouth had done nothing but make her look like something she wasn't.

Ungrateful.

Stuck up.

A bitch.

So it was time to start spitting it all out. Even if it sucked.

And it did.

"If I don't go back to Seattle then they win." Dean's mother never liked her. Never thought Nora was good enough for her sweet angel baby.

Dean's mother provided him with everything. His apartment. Everything inside it. Company car. Esmerelda Remington owned every bit of Dean's life, and by extension all of Nora's too.

The woman had taken no small amount of pleasure in watching everything Nora had being ripped away. She'd even showed up to watch the movers take away the few items Nora claimed as her own, a smug smile on her nipped and tucked face.

Brooks' expression hardened. "Who's they?"

"Everyone."

Like everything it sounded like an exaggeration.

But it wasn't.

"My ex. His mother. My—" She corrected herself. "*His* friends." Nora swallowed down the lump she'd tried to fight into nonexistence. "Everyone."

She couldn't let them prove she was nothing without them.

Even though it was probably true.

Brooks' gaze was steady as it fixed on her face. "Who cares if they think they win?"

"I do."

"Why?" Brooks came closer. "Do you respect them?"

She snorted. "No."

"Then why do you care what they think?"

It was sound thinking. The problem was, everyone included one more person.

"I care what I think though." Deep down she was worried they might all be right.

That without them she *was* nothing.

"If I can't do it on my own then everything I had was because of someone else. Not because of me." She'd worked her ass off to prove to Dean and his mother that she was just as capable as everyone at the company they allowed her to work for. That she deserved the job Esmerelda gave her.

Building success on her own would finally show them she was more than they thought.

"If you can't do what? Rebuild the exact life you just had?"

"Yes."

"Is that what you want?"

"It's not about what I want. It's about knowing I can." She swallowed as her throat got tighter. "Knowing they didn't break me."

"I think they did." Brooks shook his head. "If you think doin' something to spite them is worth more than being happy then you're definitely broken."

"But—"

"But what? You think they wouldn't love knowing you're making yourself miserable because of them?" He came a little closer. "I think the best way to spite them is to do what makes you happy." His voice lowered. "What makes you happy, Buttercup?"

"I don't know." She clamped her lips together, stopping anything else that wanted to come out.

It was harder than normal because right now she actually wanted to say more.

Wanted to tell Brooks how she felt.

He reached up to slide a bit of her still-damp hair between his thumb and finger. "I think you're startin' to figure it out."

"I don't want to be a chicken." It was what sat squarely in between them. "Not going back to Seattle feels like running away."

"From what? A bunch of assholes?" He edged closer. "I'd run away from them and not think twice."

"But they'll think—"

"Who cares what they think?"

She stared up at him. "What do you think?"

"I'm tellin' you what I think. I think you should do what makes you happy. Screw everyone else." He paused. "Including me."

She'd ended up spending her entire adult life trying to prove her value to people who only really valued themselves.

And now it suddenly felt like she'd wasted so many days. Hours. Minutes.

Never worrying about her own happiness.

Because she never really had any.

"This place scares me." It was almost impossible to admit.

"We didn't have to come here."

"Not this place." Nora glanced around the small space. "I love this place." Her eyes dipped to where her feet nearly touched his. "Moss Creek. It scares the shit out of me." She blinked a few times as her eyes got watery. "Everyone wants to make sure you're okay and feed you and know how you feel."

"People take care of each other here."

The edges of her eyes started to sting. "No one's ever taken care of me before."

As a kid she was largely on her own while her parents worked, leaving the house in the morning and coming home late at night. She got herself up and dressed and on the bus as early as elementary school.

Then she met Dean, going from one extreme to another. His mother took care of everything and she got to ride along, there but not really a part of the care and concern. Even the job his mother offered was called a favor. Something she was forever indebted to them for.

Brooks' hand eased up against the side of her face, sliding into her hair to curve around the back of her head as he pulled her close. He was warm and solid and offered something she craved in the deepest, darkest parts of her.

Comfort.

It was something she pretended not to want. Not to need.

There was no reason to acknowledge it. Comfort and support weren't anything that was available to her.

Not until she came here.

But letting it in meant she would know what it felt like.

And the loss of it would be unbearable.

"I think there's plenty of people that would like to take care of you if you'd give them the chance."

Nora wrapped her arms around his waist, holding tight to something she might not know how to do without already.

She closed her eyes, turning to press her face to the wall of his chest.

Brooks' hand moved down the back of her head, smoothing her hair with a soft touch. Each stroke was almost unbearable, tightening her throat to the point she could barely breathe.

She squeezed him tighter, holding on like he could keep her from shattering. Keep her together.

Whole.

She sucked in a breath, digging deep for the last of the false bravery spurring her on as she tipped her head to look his way. "Is one of them you?"

She'd never asked anyone for anything. Never felt like she could count on them to follow through.

Letting herself believe Brooks wanted to take care of her was dangerous. It carried the possibility of a disappointment that would do more damage than Dean and his mother could ever consider inflicting.

But she still wanted to think it might be possible.

His fingers traced along her skin, raking down her cheek as his eyes held hers. "Does it seem like I waited for the chance?"

Her chest squeezed and her lungs stalled.

She'd been so willfully blind. Out of self-preservation and fear.

Brooks was already taking care of her. The battery in her car. The wine episode.

Most recently the sloe gin episode.

Even now, he was out in the middle of the night halfway across the ranch because she wanted to talk, just to make sure anything she said would stay between only them.

He made her a liar in the best possible way.

Nora pushed up on her toes and pressed her lips to his.

As a thank you. As a show of appreciation.

As a connection. One that was so much more than any before it.

Brooks held very still as she looped both arms around his neck, pulling in an attempt to get closer to him.

To this man.

To this cowboy she swore never to want.

Never to need.

His hand tangled in her hair as his mouth slanted across hers, deepening the kiss she started.

Nora tiptoed higher, fighting more of her body against the hard line of his.

Brooks was so solid. So strong.

So sure of everything.

It made her feel stronger. Surer.

Mostly about him.

"Brooks." His name felt at home on her lips. Like it belonged there.

"You can't say my name like that, Buttercup." There was a ragged edge to his voice.

To the air running from his lungs.

"But I like your name," she dug her fingers into his hair, keeping her mouth on his, "Brooks."

A deep sound rumbled through his chest. It was something she'd never heard before.

And it was impossible not to react.

The gravely noise shot straight through her, pulling her nipples tight before settling to an ache that pulsed between her legs and dragged out a whimper of need.

"Christ." Brooks pulled her body tight to his, palm gripping her ass as the hard like of his dick pressed against her belly. "You're killing me."

She didn't want him to die, but the fact that this man wanted her that much filled the parts of her that always felt hollow.

Empty.

"I don't like that you're smiling about that, Buttercup." Brooks pushed against her, moving her across the floor toward the couch that dominated the space.

"I like that you want me." The admission came easily.

"Want is an understatement." Brooks wrapped one arm around her waist, tipping her down toward the cushions.

Nora held onto him, making sure he came with her. The second his body hit hers she went for the waistband of his pajama pants.

Brooks pulled back. "None of that."

She froze.

Didn't he just say he wanted her?

That it was an understatement?

Brooks chuckled, low and deep as he leaned against her, snagging her hands from between them and lifting them over her head. "This isn't a fully-equipped cabin. Understand?"

"No." Her eyes fell closed as his free hand slid up her side, skin to skin under the layers he'd put on her.

"There's no condoms here, Buttercup." His fingers found a nipple, rolling it with the perfect amount of pressure.

She used to love this place. Think she could live here forever.

Now it might as well be a prison. "Why not?"

"I don't bring women here, Nora." His head lifted, eyes meeting hers as his fingers continued their slow torture. "Just you."

Under normal circumstances the relevance of that would have made her happy.

Right now it just added to the frustration twisting her body under his.

"You seem frustrated." His lips moved across her jaw as the hand on her body shoved up the layers between them, baring her skin to the air and his mouth.

Both found her at the same time, the lock of his lips on her breast bowing her back. The hand pinning hers in place released, and she immediately grabbed for him, holding on as he pulled at her flesh, stroking against it with tongue and teeth.

Driving her to the brink of something she might not be able to survive.

One wide palm slid up her thigh, pulling it open, making room for his body to settle between her legs.

Which would be fantastic.

If the damn cabin was *equipped.*

"Let's go back to the cabin." Nora pulled at him. She would run there barefoot at this point.

Whatever it took.

"I'm not fucking you tonight, Buttercup." Brooks' nose slid along her neck. "So get that idea out of your head." The hand on her leg slid higher, fingers spreading wide across the front of her thigh. The pad of his thumb traced across the hem of the shorts that were now hiked up and twisted.

"Why not?" He wanted her. She wanted him.

Wasn't that the best reason for it?

"Because I'm not rushing with you."

She wanted to rush.

Sprint right toward penetration.

The skim of his thumb shifted a little to the left, dragging closer to the part of her that ached for contact.

For touch.

For him.

Nora gasped when it slid closer, dragging along her labia. Every bit of focus she had went to where he touched her in slow, sweeping strokes.

The next pass went right across her clit, making her whole body jerk. His pressure lightened immediately, and the next drag of Brooks' thumb rolled her eyes closed.

He gripped her other thigh, tucking it higher and holding it while his thumb continued its perfect torture, each pass bringing her closer and closer to the edge.

When his mouth went back to her breast it was too much, the pull as he sucked it deep sending her over, clawing and clenching as everything spun around her.

Then suddenly the darkness seemed darker.

The quiet, quieter.

But she was nowhere near alone in the silence.

Brooks was there. Holding her tight. Keeping her close as he sat up, pulling her body across his.

"What about you?" Nora tried to straighten.

"What about me?" One wide hand tucked her head into the crook of his neck, palm staying on her cheek as he scooted down and kicked his feet up on the ottoman.

"You didn't—"

"Don't need to." He pulled her a little closer. "Go to sleep."

She yawned. "We're sleeping here?"

"Unless you want to go all the way back to the cabin."

"I like it here." It was a more general statement than he probably realized.

Which was good.

"I'm glad." Brooks' words were softer and his breathing was slower. Deeper.

The rise and fall of his chest under her cheek made her body heavy. Her head cloudy.

Cloudy enough to block out all the things she'd been letting run it, leaving just enough space for a single seed to spread. One thought to grow into a question she'd never been brave enough to ask herself.

What would it be like if she stayed here?

****

THE SMELL OF coffee hit her before the pounding in her head.

Again.

Nora pressed one hand to her head and groaned. Quietly.

"Morning." Brooks stood at the small bank of cabinets in the corner.

"What time is it?"

He turned toward her, a paper cup in one hand. "Early."

"I thought you weren't a morning person?"

"We've got lots to do today, Buttercup." He held out the cup of coffee. "We need to get movin' if we're gonna get it all done."

Nora shifted on the sofa, working her way up to a sit. She took the cup and peered in. "This is the fanciest treehouse ever."

"Not quite." Brooks went back to the single-serve maker. "It'll be better once I get electric run out here."

"You're going to run electric to it?" He was really committed to having the ultimate man-cave.

"I'm runnin' electric to my house. This'll end up with it by default." He dropped a plastic pod into the hopper and clicked the lid into place before pressing the brew button.

Nora glanced out the front window. "There's a house out here?" She'd only come here once in the daytime, but she was fairly confident there was no house.

"Not yet." He turned to face her, leaning back against the counter as his coffee started to pour. "I'm in line after Boone and Mae."

"Oh." She sipped at her coffee. Black wasn't normally how she took it, but right now she was willing to drink anything that might help dilate the blood vessels pulsing in her brain.

Brody and Clara's house was already under way. The foundation and the framing was complete. From what Clara said they had about two more months before it would be finished.

She'd helped here and there when Clara got stuck between options on the large, traditionally-styled home.

"What kind of house are you going to build?" Mae and Boone were building something that looked like it could be the Wooden Spoon's half-sister. It was different in shape, but had the same dark blue color palate and large, floor to ceiling windows.

Brooks turned to the coffee pot and slid his cup free, capping it with a lid before facing back her way. His gaze leveled on her.

"That's going to depend, Buttercup."

CHAPTER TWELVE

"WHERE ARE WE going?" Nora sat in the passenger's seat, still wearing his clothes.

And still barefoot.

"First we're going to your hotel." It was going to be a more involved trip than she realized.

Because it was time for Nora to be where she should have been from the beginning.

"Then?"

"Then we're going to make some firm decisions on the house."

"Did you decide what you want to do?"

"I said we, Buttercup. *We're* making decisions." He turned her way at the single stoplight in downtown Moss Creek. "We're a team on this. I can't do it without you and you can't do it without me."

Nora went quiet, going back to the silent woman he was used to.

But this time he didn't mind.

Because he wasn't quite ready to tell her all he was thinking either.

She was staying about thirty minutes away, and by the time they reached the limits of the larger city, his stomach was growling and he was ready for another dose of caffeine. “You hungry?”

Nora shifted in her seat, pulling her bare legs up under the oversized sweatshirt swallowing her up. “A little.”

“Good.” He pulled into the line of a chain coffee shop and ordered his drink and two scones before turning to her and lifting one brow in question.

“Are both those scones for you?”

He shook his head. “One’s yours.”

“Can I have a caramel macchiato?”

“You can have anything you want, Buttercup.” Brooks added Nora’s drink choice to his order before pulling around.

“I don’t have any money.”

“You don’t have any shoes either.” He passed his credit card to the woman at the window, tipping his head in thanks as she passed their items through.

Nora peeked into the bag as he pulled away. “Liza and I had fun I think.” She pulled out one of the scones, passing it his way. “I’ve never done anything like that before.”

“I’m sure she’d love to do it again.” He glanced Nora’s way. “Ben might hide the sloe gin though.”

“That’s probably a good thing.” Nora sighed. “We were both just upset.”

“What were you upset about?” He took a bite of the cinnamon pastry as he pulled onto the main road leading to the extended-stay hotel Nora had been calling home for the past month.

“Mostly you.” She rubbed her lips together, eyes on him.

“It won’t be the last time.” Brooks turned into the lot of the hotel. “I’m sure you’ll be upset with me before the day’s over.”

“Why?”

Brooks parked in front of the main entrance, shutting off the engine before turning toward her. "Cause we're packin' all your shit up and taking it back to Moss Creek."

Nora blinked at him, scone hovering in front of her mouth. "Where in Moss Creek?"

"Anywhere you want to go." He had a few ideas in mind, but the final choice was hers.

But she was coming to Moss Creek come hell or high water.

"You can stay at The Inn. You can stay with Liza. Anywhere you want."

He wanted to say she could stay with him. It's what he wanted. To be close to her.

To give her what she'd clearly never had.

Which explained why she struggled to accept it.

Nora turned to look at the large building, she slowly chewed through the bite of scone in her mouth. Finally she looked back his way. "Okay."

"Good." Brooks was out of the truck before she could rethink, heading around to her side, still wearing the pants and shirt he slept in along with the slippers he usually wore around the house.

Nora smiled out at him as he opened her door. "We look homeless."

"We look like we had an interesting night." Brooks held one hand out to her and she immediately grabbed on, holding tight.

"Maybe we did." Nora walked barefoot down the sidewalk, looking comfortable and relaxed for the first time. "I've never slept in a treehouse before."

"That was the most interesting part of your night?" The automatic doors opened and they passed through the lobby, headed for the front desk. "Not sitting in a pile of cheese eating pudding with your hands?"

"I've done that before."

"Does that count as grazing?"

"I've been thinking about that." She stopped at the counter and gave the woman behind it a nose-wrinkling smile. "Hey, Lisa. I might have lost my key card."

The older woman glanced his way before looking back at Nora. She leaned in closer, giving her a wink. "Looks like it was worth it." She pulled out a new card, swiped it through the coding machine, and passed it across the counter, wiggling her painted-on brows. "Have fun."

Nora's smile was the most genuine he'd ever seen it. "Thanks."

She snagged the card and turned toward the elevators, pressing the button to bring it their direction. Her lingering smile was almost hidden by the curtain of her dark hair.

Brooks reached out and pushed it behind her ear. "What was it you were thinking about?"

"Why I graze." The elevator doors slid open and she stepped inside, her hand still tucked into his. "When I was a kid I just ate what was around. Snacking on what was easy since I was on my own so much."

A family with three little girls came in right behind them and Nora tucked close to his side, her soft body fitting right against his.

Brooks tipped his head at the man, who was eyeing them with a wary gaze. "Mornin'."

The man nodded back. "Morning."

"Mommy, why can she be barefoot but I can't?" One of the little girls pointed at Nora's feet before stomping her own.

"She's not supposed to be barefoot either." Brooks leaned down. "She's just not a good listener like you are."

Nora scoffed.

He grinned at her as he straightened. “Don’t act like it’s not true. I’m sure Ben told you not to take your shoes off last night.”

The doors to the elevator opened and Nora shot the mother an apologetic look as she passed out into the hall. “Ben didn’t tell me anything last night. He was hiding.”

“Ben Chamberlain was hiding?” He didn’t believe it for a second.

“That’s what Liza said.” Nora reached the door to her room and inserted her new card into the reader.

“Hiding. Ben was hiding.” It was still just as impossible to believe as it was the first time. The head ranch hand at Cross Creek wasn’t known for backing down from much.

Former bosses included.

“Maybe she said *avoiding*.” The lock clicked open and Nora twisted the levered handle, opening the door to her room.

“That sounds more right.” He could absolutely understand Ben staying away from Liza. She and Nora had a lot in common.

Including their commitment to doing what they thought they should do instead of what they actually wanted to do.

Nora went straight to where two large suitcases sat open on the bed. She fished out a set of socks and stuffed her feet into them before wiggling on a pair of sneakers.

“Didn’t expect you to own sneakers.”

She turned his way, eyes moving down his body. “Didn’t expect you to own pajamas.”

“I don’t.”

Her cheeks barely pinked up.

“Brett doesn’t appreciate it when I wear my real pajamas in the kitchen.”

Nora slowly turned away from him, her eyes widening a little more as she went. She flipped the lids of her bags closed and zipped them up before pulling them to their wheels.

"You are already packed?"

Nora's eyes held his for a quiet minute. "Unpacking was one step closer to staying."

She'd done everything she could to prove she really was leaving.

Always to herself.

Because to her staying meant she lost. Meant she was weak.

Meant she couldn't take care of herself.

"Come on." It was time for her to get the hell out of here. He reached for both bags and she let him take them. Following behind to grab another, smaller bag from the bathroom as they passed.

He loaded the bigger bags into the bed of his truck while Nora held the smaller one in her lap. She dug out a brush as they pulled away from the hotel and started working it down the length of her dark hair.

"You seemed friendly with the woman that worked there." He struggled not to watch her beside him as she went about a task she'd done countless times before.

But this time he was there to see it. A mundane thing that should be completely irrelevant.

Like brushing your teeth.

Except the mundane was what he'd been chasing. What he'd been craving.

"Sometimes I would sit with Lisa on her dinner breaks." Nora worked her hair into a braid as they drove back to Moss Creek.

Back to his home.

Maybe back to hers.

"She would show me pictures of her daughters and grandkids and tell me all about them." Nora's smile was sad. "Her husband died a few years ago and I think she's lonely."

"Are you lonely?"

Nora wound a band around the tail of her braid, eyes fixed on her fingers as they worked. "It's different for me."

"Why's that?"

Her dark eyes lifted to his. "I've always been lonely."

Brooks reached across the console, catching her hand in his and holding it tight.

It was impossible not to imagine a dark-haired little girl in a silent house, eating cheese and crackers.

Alone.

Learning she was the only person she could depend on. Going without someone to count on.

Living without support. Protection.

The kind of love he'd always had.

"What are your parents up to?" He shouldn't ask. It wasn't his business.

Yet.

But he needed to know if they'd gotten better. If they realized what their absence forced on her.

"Um." Nora smoothed down a little hair as it slipped free of her braid. "They travel a lot. I check in with them every few months."

Every few months?

It was difficult to keep his expression from showing how he felt. "That's nice for them."

Nora's face dipped toward her lap. "They aren't bad people."

He was going to have to disagree with her on that one. "Do they know you're here?"

"I left them a message."

His mother practically knew when he took a shit. If he flew states away she'd call him every day to make sure he was eating and sleeping.

Hell, she'd probably show up to make sure he wasn't lying.

"I'd hold back on telling my mother any of that."

Nora laughed. "No shit." She let out a long breath, her expression turning serious. "I don't know how to act here."

"Act however you want to act. No one here wants you to be anything other than who you are, Buttercup."

She went quiet, but her hand stayed in his the whole ride, even as her eyes were far away.

Working through something only she really understood right now.

He should take her straight to The Inn. Let her get set up in a room. Get changed into whatever she wanted to wear.

But he'd just finally started to get to the parts she hid away, and he wasn't quite ready to give that up yet.

As they moved through town Nora rolled down her window, the warm summer air catching in the strands curling against her skin. Her hand stretched out the opening, fingers spreading wide in the wind.

Her eyes closed as the angle of the sun stretched across her face.

He turned away from Red Cedar Ranch, heading toward the little house that might be the beginning of what he'd been looking for.

The truck bumped across the rutted driveway. Nora's eyes opened, immediately going to the house.

She smiled.

This time she didn't wait for him to open her door. She barreled out of the truck, sneakers hitting the dirt as she jumped free.

She reached the front of the truck and turned toward him.

Like she was waiting for something.

Waiting for him.

She reached up to slide a bit of loose hair behind one ear. The wind almost immediately pulled it free, sending it curving back against the smooth slope of her jaw.

He'd looked at her a hundred times, but for the first time he got to really see her.

Not the woman she tried to be. The one who hid behind clipped words and short conversations.

The one who thought she had to prove she was strong. Unbroken.

Right now Nora looked anything but broken.

"You ready to make some decisions, Buttercup?"

Her eyes held his for a few seconds. She slowly nodded. "I am."

"Good." Brooks walked to her side, taking her hand in his as they made their way to the porch.

"I want this place to look like your cabin."

"I want you to—"

"Do what I want. I know."

Brooks pushed open the door and she went inside.

"I want it to look like your cabin." Her eyes roamed the room like she was seeing something he didn't. "I want people to feel the same way walking in here that I felt walking in there." Nora dropped his hand and walked to the fireplace she always touched each time she came. One hand slid across the mantle, smoothing over the scarred wood.

"How did you feel walking in there?"

"Like I was someplace special." Her fingers traced the bricks. "Like I never wanted to leave."

She left the fireplace, making her way down the short hall to the larger of the two bedrooms. She turned in place. "Is the water on here?"

"And electric." He'd made sure they were both hooked up first thing. "Bathroom's stocked if you need to use it."

Nora reached out to run one hand down the faded wallpaper peeling away from the plaster. "Can I stay here?"

"No." He shook his head, rejecting the idea immediately. "The place has been vacant for long enough that someone might try to break in. I'm not risking—"

"You could stay here with me."

That stopped his argument cold.

"I mean," she looked out toward the hall, "there's two rooms."

That right there was the main problem with this scenario.

"Buttercup, I'm not sure how to tell you this." He walked toward her. Toward the woman wearing his clothes.

Standing in his house.

Taking over his life.

"But I'm not so interested in separate rooms if you're in one of them."

Her eyes barely widened as he continued moving closer.

The idea was growing on him. Quickly. But that didn't mean it was what would be best for Nora. "If you want to be alone then you should go to The Inn."

Her lips pressed together, rolling inward as she barely shook her head. "I've been alone my whole life, Brooks." Her eyes rested on his. "I'm tired of being alone."

He caught her face in his hands. He didn't want to try to convince her to stay in Moss Creek.

He wanted her to decide that on her own.

But he wouldn't hold back on certain truths. Truths that might help her decision along.

"You'll have to work hard to be alone here, Buttercup."

CHAPTER THIRTEEN

FOR A SECOND there she thought he was going to kiss her again.

It didn't happen.

And it was disappointing as hell.

"Where are we going now?" Brooks hadn't even unloaded her bags. He'd just packed her back up in the truck and now they were back on the road.

"We're goin' to my place." He glanced her way. "You need to put on some real clothes and I need to make a few arrangements."

"Aren't you supposed to be helping at the ranch?"

"My schedule is flexible now."

Nora pursed her lips at the short answer. Under normal circumstances she'd be glad for the quiet.

Glad?

No. She was just used to it. It was normal for her.

But maybe she needed a new normal. "Why is your schedule flexible now?"

"We've got more hands on deck." Brooks passed through town and made the turn toward Red Cedar Ranch. "And Boone's back, taking on his share of the work."

"So now you can do what you want to do instead of what you have to do."

Brooks' eyes came her way again. "Guess that makes two of us doin' what we want."

It was easier to focus on what Brooks wanted than what she wanted.

Her own wants were still a little wobbly.

"What else do you want to do?" Nora peeked into the bag where half of Brooks' scone still sat.

"Eat it." Brooks nudged the bag with his elbow. "Turns out scones aren't my favorite."

"You're sure?" He had to be hungry. The man usually ate at Maryann's in the morning and she'd seen the fallout from a ranch breakfast.

"I'm sure."

Nora faced him as she bit into the crumbly biscuit, trying to catch the mess with the bag. "You didn't tell me what else you want to do."

Brooks shrugged. "Get married. Have kids." He didn't look her way. "What everyone wants to do."

"Not everyone." She'd been lucky enough to put two and two together pretty early on, even before she overheard her parents one night, discussing how they couldn't wait to have their lives back once she was out of the house.

"What about you?"

It was a complicated question and brought on yet one more difficult emotion she worked hard to avoid feeling. "I don't know."

It was easier to claim indecision than the truth.

Being a bad parent was worse than being no parent at all. If she couldn't be what kids needed then it was better she didn't even try.

Better she be the one to do without than an innocent child.

Her desire to continue talking was suddenly gone. Doused like water on a flame. Pulling her back into herself.

And maybe that's where she belonged.

"My mom didn't know if she wanted kids." Brooks hand slid to hers, his fingers locking with hers and holding tight.

Nora's head snapped his way. "Your mom?"

He tipped his head in a nod.

"But..." Her mind wouldn't wrap around the thought of Maryann Pace as anything but a mother of a pack of boys.

As a woman who continued to collect anyone she thought needed more mothering. More nurturing.

More love.

"She was in college when she met my dad. She was on a date at a rodeo." Brooks' eyes finally came her way. "She left the rodeo without her original date."

"Bill Pace the woman stealer." It was easy to imagine. Even in his late fifties Bill turned as many heads as his wife did.

"They've been together ever since." Brooks' thumb stroked over her skin in a slow glide.

While it was easy to picture Bill as the handsome cowboy who stole Maryann's attention away, it was more difficult to place Maryann in the scenario. "I can't imagine your mom not being what she is."

"There's pictures." He lifted his brows. "I'm sure she'll show you. She loves to tell the story."

She could see why.

Maryann was on the other end of a decision that changed the entire trajectory of her life.

Without making that decision her whole world would look different.

The ranch was quiet as they pulled past the main house and headed toward the cabin Brooks shared with Brett. He parked the truck in front before coming around to let her out.

Nora balanced her toiletry bag as she slid free of the cab.

"Which bag do you want?" He reached into the bed of the truck and pulled both cases closer.

"The smaller one." She followed him up the steps and inside.

Brooks set her bag on his bed before backing out of the room. "Take your time. I'll be outside."

Then he closed the door, leaving her alone in his room yet again.

She walked to the bed, lifting the covers and peeking at the bits of grass and shredded cheese scattered across the pristine white fabric.

She was done drinking. It might make certain things easier to face, and it might land her in Brooks' bed, but she always ended up there alone.

Always alone.

Nora unzipped her bag and flipped open the lid, grabbing out a pair of blue jeans and a t-shirt. She fought the urge to look around too much. It felt invasive, especially after holding back on so much of her own life.

A few minutes later she was dressed, deodoranted, and her braid was reworked into a ponytail that was more likely to survive the day.

Nora zipped her bag back up and dragged it to the door. When she pulled it open there was no sign of Brooks.

She rolled her bag down the hall toward the front door, expecting to see him on the other side.

But the porch was empty.

So she tugged her bag along, down the steps, and back to the side of the truck before hoisting it up the side.

Suddenly all the weight of the luggage was gone.

"I'm gonna need you to get a little more patient, Buttercup." Brooks was close at her side, easily lifting the bag into the truck bed.

"You wanted me to just stand here and make you do all the hard work?"

"Putting a bag in a truck isn't hard work." He turned to face her. "And yes."

She tried to stay on topic, but it was impossible. "You changed your clothes."

"Did you want me walking around like I was?"

She didn't mind how he looked before, but pretending she didn't really prefer how he looked now was even more impossible. "How many cowboy hats do you have?"

"Enough." He looked down at the jeans she'd owned forever, his eyes lingering longer than she expected. "How many pairs of those you got?"

"Here?"

"It's only helpful to me if they're here."

"A few pair." She'd brought them, not knowing exactly what all she'd have to get into while working on The Inn. Frequently she ended up pitching in on a job. Helping with cleaning, painting, and anything else that needed done.

But that might have been because she was always given the clients with the smallest budgets and worked hard to get them the most she could, even if that meant she had to do more work. "These are my work clothes."

Brooks lifted a brow. "I like your work clothes."

She tried not to smile.

Tried not to let his compliment go to her head.

But it was one more impossible thing to add to her list.

"Thanks." Nora stayed put, hoping maybe he'd finally move in closer.

Offer a little more of the touch she craved.

"Let's get movin'." Brooks opened the passenger's door. "If we don't get everything done you're stuck at The Inn tonight."

She didn't want to be stuck at The Inn. She wanted to be stuck alone—

Alone with Brooks Pace.

It was motivation enough to do as he said and she climbed into the truck and buckled up.

The second he turned over the engine she rolled down the window, letting in the warm air that carried a hint of cut grass and chlorine from the pool at The Inn.

The drive was quiet.

But not the kind of quiet she was used to. It wasn't empty. Void and bare.

This was as full as silence could be.

Their first stop was a home improvement store. Brooks caught her hand in the lot and held it as they perused appliances, picking out the ones that would eventually convey with the sale of the house.

Unfortunately, they had to be ordered, which meant there would be no oven or dishwasher anytime soon.

Not that it was a big deal. She'd been living in a hotel for a month. At least at the little house she wouldn't be alone.

Because she'd been alone enough to last a lifetime.

"I've got an idea." Brooks tugged her down another aisle, grabbing an abandoned cart as they went. He pulled a mini fridge off the shelf and stacked it inside before adding on a microwave and a toaster.

"It'll be better than camping."

His brows shot up. "You've been camping?"

Nora shook her head. "But I've seen it on TV, does that count?"

"No." Brooks snagged the cart and headed for the checkouts.

Ten minutes later they were loaded up and back on the road.

Nora turned to peek out the back window. "It's probably a good thing nothing was in stock. I don't think we could have fit it back there."

Brooks shot her a grin as he reached for her hand once again. "You'd be surprised what I'm capable of."

She definitely would not.

They passed the automotive store where they picked out a battery a little more than a week ago.

Back when she was sure she had to leave Moss Creek.

Back when she worked harder than she'd ever worked in her life to convince herself it was the only option, but with each passing day her need to prove what she was capable of to people who didn't matter dimmed.

Brooks pulled into the lot of the grocery store they'd also visited together. "You bringing me here so I can pick out some snacks?" She was teasing.

But the sharp line of Brooks' jaw made it clear he was not amused. "We're getting you some real damn food." His voice carried something surprising.

Anger.

Nora stared at him as he climbed out of the truck and walked around the front end, looking like he was ready to murder someone.

He pulled open her door and held out his hand. "Come on, Buttercup. It's time to start righting some wrongs."

****

NORA STARED UP at the little house.

"Somethin' wrong?"

She pointed to where her rental car sat. "My car's here." She'd left it at Liza's. Abandoned after their sloe gin-fueled evening of commiseration. "And there's flowers on the porch."

A large planter filled with trailing petunias spilling over the edges sat in the corner of the planked-wood porch. Next to the container of white and yellow blooms were two rockers that seemed identical to the ones at Red Cedar Ranch.

"I tried to tell you." Brooks got out of the truck without any further explanation, making her wait until he opened her door for clarification.

Nora turned toward him. "You tried to tell me what?"

"People around here will take care of you if you let them." He held his hand out, wiggling his fingers. "Come on."

She glanced toward the house, swallowing down the squeeze in her throat.

Things were about to get as complicated as she wanted to make them.

Nora took his hand and let him pull her toward the perfect pile of sunshine-colored bells. She reached out to run the tip of one finger along the edge of a white petal while Brooks unlocked the door. He pushed it open wide, revealing the second change to the little house.

The horrible smell from her first visit here with Clara, Mae, and Liza was gone by the time Brooks bought it, replaced with the stuffy, slightly-musty odor of a vacant home.

Not anymore.

Now the place smelled like vanilla and the lingering aroma of Pine Sol.

Maybe a hint of bleach.

Nora stepped inside and gasped.

The smell of the place and the flowers were the least of the changes that had happened while they were gone shopping.

A sofa sat on an area rug in the cleared-out living room, across from a television on a low stand. A soft-looking blanket was draped over the back of the overstuffed cushions and a few throw pillows were stacked in the corners.

Nora turned to face Brooks. "What happened?"

"You wanted to stay here."

"But I was fine staying here the way it was." She would have been happy on an air mattress on the dusty floor.

Maybe even more than happy.

Brooks leaned against the casing of the open door, crossing his arms over his chest. "No one else was fine with it."

She peered down the short hall, knowing more was waiting to push her closer to something she'd only seen in other people's lives.

And never thought about having in hers.

It was too painful to think about. Wish for.

Because it made it impossible to keep ignoring how much she was missing.

How much she'd learned to do without.

"Go look." Brooks' voice was soft. Like he knew this was harder than it should be.

She didn't move.

"Come on." He came to her side, resting one hand on the small of her back. "We'll go look together."

"I can just look at it later." Nora tried to plant her feet. "We need to bring the groceries in."

"Gotta rip it off like a band aid, Buttercup." The pressure of Brooks' touch increased. "Time to nut up."

"I don't want to nut up anymore." Nutting up was overrated. "I want to be a chicken."

"No you don't." He pushed harder. "I'll pick you up and haul your ass in there if I have to."

Any other time the thought of being carried to a bedroom by Brooks Pace would have killed all the other thoughts wandering around her brain, but even that wasn't enough to push away the panic gnawing deeper with each passing second.

She did not want to go in that room.

Just like she hadn't wanted to stay in Moss Creek, Montana.

"I can't do this." She tried to keep the waver out of her voice. Tried to hide the emotions already twisting her vocal cords.

"You can do anything." Brooks stepped behind her and started pushing her with the full width of his body. "You can design houses and change batteries and two step. I know you can look at a little room." He pressed her along the hall. "Just take a deep breath and do it."

"Then what?"

"We deal with that later." One arm came around her waist as they pushed past the opening of the room.

A large bed stood in the center of the longest wall, positioned between the two windows that looked out over the front yard. White curtains draped across blinds that were a little too wide. A worn braided rug covered most of the small room's scarred wood floor, which had clearly been mopped within an inch of its life. Two small tables sat on each side of the antique headboard, a vase of pale yellow flowers that perfectly matched the quilt covering the bed topping each one.

She held on, keeping a death-grip on her composure.

Then she looked at the wall above the bed and saw something familiar, hanging on the plaster like this was where it was meant to be all along.

Both hands came to cover the lower half of her face, fingers digging into her skin as she fought to keep her reaction in check.

Brooks' hands stroked up and down her arms. "Just breathe, Buttercup. You'll get used to it. It's just gonna take a minute."

She shook her head, managing to fight out two words. "Your mom."

Maryann Pace was going to kill her. Death by doting.

"Not just her." Brooks' hands continued their slow path over her skin. "Liza brought your car here and the blinds and the flowers." He pointed to the rug. "That's from Mae's parents." He continued on, tearing through what she'd worked so hard to build. Ripping away the walls of denial she hid behind. "The bed was mine when I was a kid." He paused. "Hopefully the mattress is new."

A horrible-sounding snort-laugh nearly made her choke on her spit.

"See? I told you you'd get used to it." His arms came around her waist, pulling her body back against his. "This is how it is here, Buttercup. Everyone's wanted to take care of you since the second you showed up. They were just waiting until you were ready."

She wasn't ready. Not by a long shot.

There was no way to be ready for something like this.

Someone like this.

Because at the end of the day all of this was because of one person.

The person who saw through all her bluster. All the lies she hid behind out of self-preservation and fear.

Fear of learning what it was like to be taken care of.

What it was like to no longer be the only person on your team.

What it was like to no longer be alone.

She'd wasted a month fighting it. Fighting the people here.

Fighting him.

But she didn't want to fight him anymore.

Didn't want to fight herself.

Going back to being alone would be impossible.

Unthinkable.

Which meant she had to figure out how to not be alone.

CHAPTER FOURTEEN

HIS MOM HAD gone overboard.

He was expecting a bed with some sheets and blankets. Maybe a chair or two.

Instead, she'd scrubbed and completely furnished the place in under four hours.

But that was what happened when Maryann Pace was finally able to drag another person into her web.

Even if they came kicking and screaming. Like Nora.

And it clearly wasn't getting any easier for her. After a lifetime of counting only on yourself it would be tough to trust someone else to not let you down.

"Why don't you take a minute and I'll go get the groceries?" He started to back away, intending to give her the minute she needed.

Instead Nora sucked in a deep breath and spun to face him, her face frozen in an uncomfortable-looking smile. "I'm fine." She pushed past him. "I can help."

And then she was gone, running from the house again.

At least it wasn't because of him this time.

Brooks went to the front window to watch as she attacked the bags of groceries with a frown so deep her brows almost touched.

But Nora didn't look angry. She looked focused.

Completely intent on what she was doing.

But he was pretty sure that focus wasn't for the groceries she looped over her arms like it was an Olympic sport. "Damn it." He went out the front door she'd left open and down the steps. "You don't have to carry them all at once, Buttercup."

"I just thought it would make things easier." She fished the last bag from behind the seats then worked one butt cheek against the edge of the open door, bumping back into it hard enough to almost get it closed. She scowled at the unlatched door.

He crossed his arms. "And did it?"

"Maybe." Nora gave the door a gentle tap with one hip, pushing it fully closed. She smiled that same, awkward smile from before. "See? Fine?"

"I didn't ask if it was fine." Brooks watched as she hustled past him. "I said, did it make things easier?"

"And I said *maybe*." Nora huffed her way up the steps and into the house, successfully avoiding the point he was trying to make.

That might not be all she was working to avoid.

"*Damn it*."

Her wail had him running, taking the steps in a single stride in his rush to get to her side.

He found her standing in the center of the little kitchen, bags strangling her wrists, face scrunched up in an awful way, tears streaking down her skin.

"*Fucking cobbler*." She grabbed at the bags, trying to fight the tangled loops off her arms. When they wouldn't come easily she started yanking, sucking in short, loud breaths through her nose in between sobs.

He was done. Done letting her find her own way through this.

"Stop." Brooks dropped to one knee at her side and went to work on the bags.

Nora's crying immediately ceased, her cheeks puffing out as she held it in.

"Not the cryin'. You can cry as much as you need to. Let that shit out." He freed the first of the sacks and set it on the floor at her feet.

Her head dropped back and she stared at the ceiling. "I – don't – want – to – cry." Each word was stopped by a jerky breath. "I – don't – like – it."

Another bag came off.

"Just because you don't like it doesn't mean it doesn't need to happen." The woman was clearly backed up, which made everything leading up to this moment make a hell of a lot more sense.

She was scared to break the seal. Afraid of what might happen once she stopped smothering out how she felt.

Instead pretending she didn't feel at all.

Her head violently shook from side to side. "I – can't."

"We've talked about this, Buttercup. You can do anything you want to do." Two more bags went on the floor, freeing up her first arm.

Her hand immediately went to her face, covering it.

"Stop doin' that too." He went to work on the other arm, frustration making his words sharper. "Don't hide what you're feeling from me, Nora."

Her eyes suddenly dropped to where he knelt. They were wide and wet. Red-rimmed and bloodshot. "I'm sorry." The apology was muffled behind the cover of the hand still pressed to her face.

The last of the bags came off in one twisted section. They were barely on the ground before he was back on his feet. Brooks caught her second hand as it attempted to join the first. "No." He shook his head as he pulled her other hand away. "No more hiding from me."

He'd had enough. Enough of her thinking no one else cared how she felt. Enough of her holding back.

Her lips pressed together so tight they turned white. Her skin was blotchy and mottled and her nose was red.

She looked miserable.

And he still wasn't letting her go. Because misery loved company, and it was time Nora had all the company she could stand. "Fucking cobbler?"

She stared at him for a second before her face crumpled up and she nodded. "Fucking cobbler."

Two words that broke the well wide open.

She started to sob again.

He pulled her close, holding her tight as she cried into his chest, tears soaking into his shirt, into his skin.

Into his soul.

He stroked down her hair. Rubbed her back.

As she started to calm he rested his chin on her head, closing his eyes at the sag of her body against his.

Nora wanted to go back to Seattle to prove the bastards there hadn't broken her.

But she was broken long ago. There was nothing left to break.

That was the real reason she didn't want to stay in Moss Creek.

She was afraid they could put her back together again.

She went quiet except for the soft sound of hiccupping.

"You ready to take a break now?"

She nodded against his chest, face pressed where he couldn't see it.

Brooks caught her face with his hands, forcing it up until her eyes met his.

He'd worked hard his whole life and being with Nora wasn't going to be any different. Making her his wasn't turning out to be easy.

But that was okay. Maybe better than okay. Anything worth having was worth working for, and Nora Levitt was sure as hell worth having.

Worth earning.

He'd seen it with his brothers. Seen what they went through to find the women they loved.

To prove they were worth loving back.

That's what he wanted.

What he ached for.

A woman worth working for.

Brooks leaned down to brush his lips over hers. He'd wanted to kiss her all day, but there was no time for anything that kissing might have wanted to lead to.

And he wanted to take his time with her.

Because this was it. This was what he'd been hunting.

Who he'd been hunting.

He straightened. Nora's eyes stayed closed for a second before fluttering open.

One little kiss and her whole expression was different. Softer.

More relaxed.

It pulled him in for another.

Her arms came around his neck as she pulled closer, her body pressing into his as she pushed up on her toes. One hand knocked the brim on his hat as she worked her grip tighter.

He'd intended another sweet press of his lips to hers. Planned to kiss her one more time and send her to the couch while he put the groceries away. Instead he went with her, dragging her body across the room before taking her down to the cushions.

He'd wanted someone to feel close to.

The connection he knew was possible.

It sounded perfect. Ideal.

But staring it down was a whole lot different than he expected.

Nora's legs wrapped around his waist as they fell, locking tight as her back hit the couch, making it impossible to keep his weight from landing full-force.

But she didn't seem to care. Her arms held him as tight as her legs, keeping him closer than he should be.

Because getting close to her was supposed to go slow. It was supposed to be like a well-planned attack. One she would remember.

Instead he was struggling to breathe. Fighting the barriers of clothing keeping his hands from her skin.

He wanted to touch her.

No. This was something else.

Need.

He needed to touch her.

Needed her to touch him.

Nora grabbed the hat barely hanging onto his head and yanked it free, tossing it over the back of the couch. The second it was set free her hands went straight to the hem of his shirt, yanking it up between them with a pull hard enough to do damage.

The sound of popping seams only spurred him on more.

Knowing she was fighting to get to him.

That she wanted the closeness as much as he did.

He'd been looking for his match, not realizing the full extent of what that would mean.

Matched attraction.

Matched need.

Matched desire.

It was unimaginable.

Uncontrollable.

Unstoppable.

Her lips pulled from his only long enough to get the shirt she'd torn over his head and off his arms. Then she had him again, fingers digging into his face as she pulled it back in.

Her hands moved over his chest and across his stomach before grabbing tight to the waistband of his jeans.

He should stop her. Stop this.

Rein it in before it got out of hand.

But instead of working the button free her hands shoved inside, bypassing what he thought was a barrier in less than a heartbeat.

Her grip had him almost immediately, pulling out a groan as she fisted him tight. The only thing saving him was the constraints of the denim limiting her movements.

Not that it was helping much.

Just the feel of her skin on his had his hips pushing into her, looking for more friction. She gasped when he pulled back before shoving close again, managing a couple inches of glide along her palm.

Her hand suddenly pulled free, stealing the sensation driving all his thoughts.

Unfortunately now she was hard at work on the fly of his jeans.

He hadn't been prepared for a race, and he sure as hell hadn't been prepared for Nora to run as fast as she did.

Or as hot.

But maybe it wasn't just Nora running fast and hot.

It was them.

Together.

Because he was doing exactly what she was doing. Fighting clothes, not caring what happened to them as long as she was closer to him.

Nothing mattered as long as he could touch her.

Feel her.

Taste her.

The shirt that made her look like she belonged in Moss Creek hit the floor a second before whatever bra she was wearing joined it.

He should have taken the time to look. To appreciate every second of this. Her body. The way she moved.

The way she sounded.

But right now all of that was killing him. Torturing him with a need that accelerated at a pace he'd never experienced.

The soft fullness of her breast in his hand wasn't enough. He needed it in his mouth.

Under his tongue.

The arch of her back as her nipple tightened to a point didn't satisfy him in the slightest.

Neither did the lock of her fingers in his hair. The writhe of her hips under his.

The sound of his name on her lips.

They all just made it worse.

He fought her jeans. The ones he'd loved seeing so much. The way they curved against her body like they were made for it.

But right now it wasn't her body.

It was his.

And he needed to prove he was man enough to own it.

The black panties barely caught his eye as he ripped them away, sending them wherever everything else that was in his way went. Even the sight of her fully naked body didn't slow him down. Didn't calm the fight he was feeling.

Brooks gripped her thighs, fingers digging into the soft flesh as he shoved them open wide, his mouth on her the instant there was space.

Waiting for any part of her was unbearable. He wanted it all.

Needed it all.

And he needed it now.

Nora cried out immediately, her voice filling the house as he filled his need and satisfied hers.

She bucked under him, like he'd loosened some wild part of her and it wanted free.

He wanted to set it free.

And then he wanted to do it again.

Her thighs locked around his neck, pinning him in place as her whole body went tight, almost convulsing around him as she came under his tongue.

And it wasn't enough.

There might not ever be enough.

She clawed at his skin, grabbing at any part of him she could reach, using her legs to force his body back up hers, holding tight as she pushed against him.

Sending them over the edge of the couch to the rug covering the scarred wood floor.

The impact stunned him long enough she managed to gain the upper hand, the straddle of her thighs pinning his legs together as she finished undoing his pants and started yanking them down his hips.

He grabbed her and pulled her against him, shoving at the coffee table one of the many people who wanted to take care of Nora brought over and put right in his way. Instead of scooting it tipped over, sending the perfectly positioned tray on top of it and the items it contained scattering across the floor.

The lid came off a small wood box emblazoned with the logo for Cross Creek Ranch and a whole row of condoms fell out.

Fucking Liza Cross for the win.

He was going to send her flowers.

And someone to clean her kitchen.

Maybe ship Ben Chamberlain his own wood box.

Brooks rolled toward the mess, sending Nora's body under his once again as he grabbed for the strip of protection that was saving his life right now.

Saving his sanity.

Because for the first time in his life he had to have a woman.

Had to own her.

Had to make her see she should be his.

That he could take care of her in every fucking way there was.

Brooks managed to get one hand on the condoms but lost his balance, forcing him to drop them to keep from banging his head on the edge of the coffee table.

He wasn't fast enough to grab them a second time. Nora beat him to it, tearing one free and throwing the rest over her head before ripping one edge of the single loose. Her eyes held his as her hands dipped between them.

Her touch was torture. Too slow. Too methodical. Too purpose-driven.

He wanted her wild again. He wanted her as desperate as he was.

Brooks grabbed the hands slowly killing him, pulling them from his dick and pinning them above her head, holding them in place with one hand while he finished the job she started.

Her lids drooped when he slid the head of his sheathed cock along her slick slit, dragging it in the slowest sweeps he could manage, fighting the need to sink into her.

To fuck her until all she knew was his name.

Until she forgot what it was like to be alone.

Until the only life she could imagine was with him.

It was the only option she had. The only one he was willing to live with.

He notched his dick into place, barely pressing his hips forward as his thumb found her clit.

She tried to push up against him. Tried to gain what he held back.

He held firm, refusing to give in. He hated to do it, but it was a necessary evil.

Second ticked by as he fought the tightness already pulling at his balls, threatening to stop this before it could really get started.

"Brooks." Nora grabbed at him. "Please."

He let her pull him closer, hoping it would distract him, refocus the mind intent on ruining his plans.

It didn't work. He was lost at the press of her breasts against him as she arched closer. His hips pushed forward, sinking his body into hers.

Time wasn't on his side.

Not even a little.

But he'd die before he left her wanting.

Left her thinking she was ever second on his list.

Especially second to him.

"I need you to help me out here, Buttercup." Brooks kept his hand between them. "We're working on a tight schedule." He dropped his head, catching a nipple with his mouth and pulling it deep, rolling his tongue across the pebbled tip as his hips and thumb worked in time.

Then he started to count.

Anything to steal a little focus from the tingle at the base of his spine. The pull so tight it ached.

She made it to one hundred. One hundred of the longest seconds of his damn life.

Barely a minute in a half. He should be ashamed.

But when Nora wailed his name into the air all he felt was relief.

Relief and pure fucking pleasure.

Pleasure that wasn't just physical. Wasn't just the release he'd been chasing.

Because this wasn't setting anything free.

Nothing was going anywhere.

Including Nora Levitt.

CHAPTER FIFTEEN

NORA PRESSED HER lips together, trying to stifle the laugh threatening to come out.

Who laughed after something like that?

A woman who was walking the line of losing her mind, that's who.

Which is what she was right now.

One step away from crazy.

And it felt fricking amazing.

A snort broke free. She pressed one hand to her face, trying to smother out anything else that might try to escape.

Brooks' hand had hers in an instant, ripping it away.

Revealing the smile she'd been covering.

His brows jumped up as she started to cackle.

Maybe two orgasms put her in a better mood.

Maybe a man not even getting his pants all the way off bolstered her confidence.

Or maybe she was just flipping happy for the first time in...

In...

Ever.

"I'm not gonna lie to you, Buttercup. This is sort of hurting my feelings."

That just made her laugh harder.

Mostly because the man that might have her walking wrong for the rest of the day and had the audacity to look embarrassed by it.

She grabbed him by the neck and pulled him down, meeting his lips to hers. The kiss lingered, going from a smashing of lips to something that might make her consider not walking for the rest of the day at all.

The flex of his dick made her gasp.

"You're going to end up with ice cream melted all over the floor if you're not careful." His fingers skimmed up the side of her ribs, pausing to pluck at her nipple.

Her eyes rolled closed. "I don't care."

She should care. She should be more than fine with what he'd given her already.

But it didn't feel like enough.

His lips trailed along her jawline and down her neck. "I do."

"Why?"

"Because we need it." His body slowly eased out of hers in a drag that made it obvious he was just as interested in staying here as she was.

"What do we need it for?" She wasn't big into food in general, but she'd lick a line of cookies and cream off anywhere he wanted her to.

"Holy hell, Buttercup." Brooks' head hit the center of her belly and stayed there for a few long breaths before his eyes lifted to hers. He stared at her for a minute. "Shit."

She sat up as he stood. "What?"

"You." He pulled his pants most of the way up as he turned toward the hall, looking over his shoulder to point a finger her way as he walked. "You're going to be a problem."

She scoffed as he disappeared, coming back a few seconds later to stare at her a little more, his blue eyes turning midnight. "And for the love of God, put your damn clothes on."

She grabbed the closest thing and pulled it over her head, tugging it down into place. "There. Happy?" She smiled at him, because she sure as hell was.

His nostrils barely flared. "No."

Nora glanced down, head bouncing up before going back down again to the t-shirt she'd grabbed.

It wasn't hers.

It was his.

She smiled again.

"Christ." Brooks wiped one hand down his face as he turned from her and stomped to the kitchen.

She crawled up onto the couch, kneeling to lean against the back, watching as he started digging through the groceries, wearing nothing but low-slung jeans and cowboy boots. He came up with the carton of vanilla he'd picked from the freezer section during their shopping trip.

"Why do we need ice cream?"

He did a slow spin in the empty kitchen. "Damn it."

She stayed put as his stomping went to the front door, yanking it open before the pounding of his boots went down the porch and hit the bare gravel of the drive.

A minute later he was back, carrying the box containing the mini-fridge. He set it on the worn linoleum, next to the bags she'd carried all at once, wanting to pay him back in some small way for what he'd done.

Because habits were hard to break. Even when you might want to.

Nora stood from the couch and went to his side. "Thank you for doing this for me."

"Not sure who I'm doin' this for anymore." Brooks grabbed the cardboard flaps at the top of the box and pulled, tearing them loose from the staples holding them in place.

She held the box in place as he reached in to pull the appliance free. "Who else would you be doing it for?"

Brooks set the fridge on the floor before working it back against the wall where a full-sized unit would soon be. "You're not the only one here, Buttercup."

She smiled at his back.

She wasn't the only one here. For once.

She'd always been alone, even when she physically wasn't. Her parents. Dean. The friends that were never really hers.

She was still alone, even when she was with them.

Which was the worst kind of alone.

As Brooks plugged in the fridge she bent to dig around for the items that needed to go inside, lining them down the counter as she found them. Brooks packed them in, managing to get everything into the tiny space.

Nora moved on to the pantry items. She grabbed a box of cereal and pulled open one of the cabinets.

It was full. Stocked with coffee and filters and sugar and pancake mix and syrup. "Your mother knows we don't have a stove to cook on, right?"

Brooks leaned in to peek over her shoulder. He started opening the cabinets, revealing all sorts of things, including a crock pot and both an electric griddle and an electric skillet.

How in the hell had Maryann managed to come up with all this stuff in such a short period of time? "Does she just have extras of these lying around?"

"She likes to be prepared." Brooks scooted the boxes and containers his mother brought to one side and started adding in what they'd bought. "And I can guarantee she called in every favor she had if she needed to."

"Why?" It was difficult to wrap her mind around the extent Maryann had gone to.

"Because you wanted to stay here and like it or not, you were hers the minute you stepped foot into town." Brooks put up the last of the food and turned to face her, leaning back against the counter, his eyes moved over her for a second. "You ready for dinner?"

Time had gotten away from her today, flown by faster than ever before. Normally she would have fished out something simple to fill her belly while she spent time working on her next job. Maybe caught up on some of her favorite shows.

But this was a different sort of situation and she couldn't imagine Brooks eating a container of yogurt and a handful of almonds on the couch. "What are we having for dinner?"

He pointed to where her bags were stacked in the entry. "How 'bout you pull out all your house ideas and we decide what we're doing here while I heat us up something to eat?"

Maybe dinner with Brooks wouldn't be so different from what she was used to after all.

Except for the alone part.

By the time she retrieved the folder containing her plans for the little house, Brooks had the microwave in and unpacked with a tray of shredded barbeque beef heating inside.

She opened the file on the counter next to where he was lining up buns, pickles, and chips, and went to work spreading out the stack of ideas, starting with the first one and ending with the last. All in all she'd come up with four separate plans for the new life this house was about to embark on.

And one was her clear favorite.

She pointed to it, not giving him the chance to ask, because she already knew he would. "I like this one best."

He lifted a brow at her. "You're serious?"

Nora nodded. "Completely." It was the middle of the road as far as cost was concerned. It used the existing hardwood floors, but also included the additional bedrooms this area probably required.

It opened up the kitchen, but simplified her plans for the design.

That was what this was all about. Simple. Cozy. Comfort.

Just like the place that inspired it.

"You want to make it look like the treehouse?" Brooks was clearly skeptical.

"Definitely." There wasn't a doubt in her mind that was how this house was supposed to look. How it was supposed to be.

"Because you like it, or because you think I like it?" Brooks untwisted the tie holding the bag of buns closed.

"Both." It was an easy answer. One she didn't have to think about for a second.

Brooks picked up the pickle jar, gripping it tight as he popped the seal on the lid. "I'm not sure we can live here through a renovation like that, Buttercup."

"Why not?" It's not like they were doing much to the existing bedroom, and the footprint of the kitchen would remain largely unchanged with the addition of a peninsula where a wall currently was being the most major change.

"Construction is messy. The place will be filthy all the time."

"It wouldn't be that bad." She tried to sound nonchalant. Like the thought of going to The Inn alone didn't bother her.

"I'm not letting you live in a construction zone, Buttercup." Brooks grabbed the beef from the microwave and slid it onto the counter. "It's not happening."

Her chest was tight. Tight and uncomfortable in a way she'd worked hard to avoid.

Brooks lifted two paper plates from the stack and dropped a bun onto each one before using a plastic fork to pile a mound of beef into the center of each one. He added pickles and the top buns before passing one plate her way. "We can't stay at my place. Brett will lose his shit."

She took the plate as a little of the squeeze released. "He doesn't like you having company?"

Brooks paused, something unspoken passing across his eyes. "Somethin' like that." He took his own plate and grabbed a pack of potato chips from the counter before going to the couch. He stood looking down at the upturned table. "Shit."

"I forgot about that." She started to smile again, a bubble of laughter coming right behind it.

Brooks' eyes came to hers and for a second she thought he was going to go on about hurt feelings again.

Like he had anything to be hurt about.

He started to crack a smile. "Remind me to send Liza flowers."

"*Nice* flowers."

Brooks set the items in his hands on the sofa and went to work pulling the table back upright. Once it was back in place he moved the chips to the top before sitting down with his plate and lifting one arm her way. "Come on. Time to eat."

She dropped down beside him, leaning into his side as his arm wrapped around her shoulders, pulling her as close as he could manage with two plates of food involved.

Nora lifted her feet to the edge of the table as she picked up her sandwich and took a bite. It was nothing more than ready-made beef, but it was the best thing she'd eaten in a long damn time.

Definitely better than cheese and crackers.

"What do you want to do with the fireplace?" Brooks propped his feet up next to hers, relaxing back against the cushions as he ate with his free hand.

"I think we should paint the brick and put a wood mantle on it." She could see it like it was already there. "And we should finish the floors the same way." She pointed toward the front door. "And the door too."

"Kitchen floor?" He polished off his sandwich and reached for the chips.

"Tile." She closed her eyes, imagining what the house would look like. "Maybe slate."

"We can go pick it all out next week." He was quiet for a second as she continued to envision the space around them. "Unless you have somewhere else you're plannin' to go."

Her eyes snapped open at the uncertainty in his voice. "Are you asking if I'm planning to go back to Seattle?"

"I'm just askin' what your plans are for next week."

"Well." Knowing she wasn't going back and voicing it were two different things. "I was thinking of extending my stay in Moss Creek." Her next breath wasn't easy to take. "Indefinitely."

Brooks' head barely tipped. "Good."

"Then I think we've got somethin' else to shop for." He stood from the couch, glancing back her way. "But you'll need pants for it."

****

THIS WAS NOT what she expected when Brooks said they had something to shop for.

"What's wrong, Buttercup?" He stood at her side, waiting for her to take the steps in front of them.

"This is huge." She looked down the side of the fifth-wheel camper he wanted her to go through.

"It's not just for us." Brooks nudged her with one hand, urging her toward the entrance. "Brody has three kids he wants to take camping at some point."

She eyed the outdoor entertainment center that included a television and a mini fridge. "This isn't what I think of when I think of camping."

"You sayin' you'd rather have a tent?"

"No." She was definitely starting to warm up to country life, but that still sounded awful.

"Then get your ass up those steps so we can make some decisions."

"Why do I have to decide?" She felt bad enough thinking she was the one deciding how Brooks would spend whatever the amount of money one of these cost, but now she was the one making that decision for Brody and Clara too.

"Because someone has to decide, and you're a good decider." He pushed harder against her back. "So go start deciding."

She huffed out a breath and started up the steps into a camper that was probably nicer than a lot of apartments.

But wouldn't be good for a family.

The living room area had recliners in place of a sofa, and the kitchen was oddly laid out. Plus the only beds besides the main one had to be created from the dinette and the loveseat.

The next option was a little better. It had two couches and a half bath off the back entrance.

But it still wasn't quite right.

Finally they came to a unit that had everything she thought a family would want while they spent weekends hiking and making smores. A functional kitchen with lots of room for snacks. A bunkhouse with its own television. Plenty of seating room for everyone to be together.

Nora dropped down onto one of the couches.

Brooks eased down beside her, wrapping one arm across her shoulders and pulling her close.

She leaned into him, resting her head against his shoulder. "I think Brody and Clara and the kids will really like this one." Her throat was a little tight, but in a happy way.

"I think we'll all get plenty of use out of it." Brooks leaned in to rest his chin against her head. "So this is the one?"

She nodded. "This is it."

It sounded like an insurmountable task at first. She had no clue what a family needed in a camper.

At least she thought she didn't. "There's probably even enough room if they decide to have more kids."

"I'm positive Brody is gunning for that." Brooks stretched his legs out in front of him. "I'd say Mae is dealing with the same problem."

Nora leaned to look his way. "Already?" Mae and Boone hadn't been back together for very long.

"Life's short, Buttercup. No reason to waste time."

She was a little stunned at his words.

At the ones he didn't say, but she could hear all the same.

Brooks wasn't wanting to waste time.

The salesman who'd been following them around with bated breath came into the camper, eyes bright with the hope that she'd finally made up her mind. "Did we find what we were looking for?"

Brooks' eyes stayed on her. "I believe we did."

CHAPTER SIXTEEN

BROOKS STARED UP at the ceiling, listening to the sound of Nora snoring softly beside him.

He'd woken up easily at a time he would normally be struggling to drag his ass out of bed.

Maybe it was because they went to bed early after he barely managed to get Nora inside before she crashed and burned.

Not that he could blame her. They'd had a big day.

But right now sleeping was the last thing he wanted to do. It felt like a waste of time.

Time that suddenly felt more important than it used to.

Brooks eased his arm from under her, carefully working free of where she curled around him, legs and arms draped haphazardly across his body. Nora sucked in a deep breath, rolling to her back as his feet hit the floor.

Then she started to snore again.

He slowly backed out of the dark room, making his way down the hall to the coffee pot in the kitchen. After dumping in some grounds and switching it on he fished through the fridge, digging out the makings for a decent breakfast. He switched on the griddle and turned up the heat, the line Nora's papers still spread along the counter catching his eye as he did. He flipped through them as the griddle warmed up, looking at all the designs Nora came up with.

Her talent was as obvious as her attention to detail. She'd worked up cost estimates and timelines for each one.

He lingered over the most recent plan. The one that looked like the treehouse he'd worked on for years, improving it past the point of reasonability.

She'd taken the best parts of it and worked them into this house, somehow managing to give it the same sort of feel he'd worked so hard to come up with. It'd taken him years.

And she did it in an evening.

Brooks flipped another page, expecting to see the cost analysis.

Instead a printout of an email stared back at him.

The text was short but nothing anyone would call sweet.

Miss Levitt,

Since your contract with Red Cedar Ranch was signed during the time that you were still an employee of Remington Designery, half of the agreed-upon fee is ours. Submit this payment to accounting immediately. If funds are not received within five business days legal action will be taken to recoup the monies due.

Esmerelda Remington

Owner and CEO, Remington Designery

45 Hightower Place, Seattle, WA 98161

His fingers itched to crush the paper between them. Turn the email into the same trash as the woman who sent it.

Instead he sorted the pages, putting them back exactly how they were, making sure the email was completely hidden.

Because if he looked at it again, chances were good he'd send an email of his own, and that's not where he and Nora were yet.

Yet.

The smell of hot metal pulled his attention back to what he was supposed to be doing. By the time he had the griddle loaded with bacon the coffee was finished brewing. He poured out a cup and made his way through the house toward the bedroom, still fighting down the anger threatening to make him bring up something that was none of his business.

Yet.

Nora stirred as he walked in, one arm flailing to his vacated spot.

She jerked upright, head snapping to the side he'd slept on.

"Coffee?" He held the cup out to her.

She covered her mouth as she started to yawn. "Why are you up?"

"I've got to work." He passed over the coffee.

She took the cup. "Oh." Nora looked toward the windows. "What time is it?"

"Four-thirty."

She smoothed one hand down the side of her head, working the hair away from her face as she took a drink of coffee. "Is this when you always get up?"

"This is when I'm supposed to always get up." He usually struggled to drag his ass from the bed, frequently skipping breakfast so he could spend a little more time under the covers.

"Okay." Nora dragged the blankets off her body, revealing the same shorts and shirt he'd given her two evenings ago after her night of fun with Liza Cross. She turned to let her feet dangle off the side of the bed, toes barely grazing the rug. "That might take some getting used to."

"I've been waiting almost thirty years to get used to it." The smell of bacon forced him to back away. "So you might not want to get your hopes up."

Nora stood as he reached the hall. "Is that bacon?" She followed him, bare feet padding across the floors as she carried her coffee, sipping it every few steps.

He'd never had a morning like this.

Mornings after a fun night, sure.

But that's not what this was.

This was something completely different.

"And pancakes." Brooks snagged the bowl of batter he'd mixed up and poured a few pools into the vacant spots on the griddle.

"You're actually making a 4:30 wake up seem pretty appealing." Nora came close to his side, watching as he worked.

"It's nothing fancy."

Her eyes came to his. "Maybe I wasn't talking about the breakfast."

Brooks leaned down, catching her lips with his.

It should feel strange. Like they were playing house.

But it didn't.

It felt almost normal. A level of comfortable he'd never experienced.

None of the awkwardness that frequently permeated these types of situations.

Maybe because this morning had little in common with previous situations.

Nora leaned into him, breathing deep, staying close even after he had to end the kiss to flip bacon.

"What are you going to do today?" Brooks turned the pancakes, working everything around to make enough space to add another pool of batter.

Nora grabbed a paper plate and lined it up next to the griddle just as the first set of pancakes needed to come off. "I should probably go thank your mom."

"You will make her day." He knew damn well his mother was holding her breath until she got to see Nora, hoping to finally suck her into the Pace family pool.

Nora gave him a little smile. "Good." She was quiet while he finished cooking. Silent as she helped plate up their breakfasts.

It wasn't until they were on the couch, feet on the coffee table that she finally spoke.

"What would you think if we went to dinner at the ranch tonight?"

He knew she was chewing on more than bacon, and he'd been around Nora enough to know he'd eventually find out what it was that was working through her mind. "I think it would be fine. As long as you like chicken tacos."

Her brows lifted up. "Chicken tacos?"

She seemed surprised by the dinner his mother had planned for the evening.

She was going to end up real surprised if she followed through with going.

"And rice and beans." He sipped at his coffee, washing down a mouthful of syrup and pancake.

"Huh." Nora shoved in the last bite of her two-cake stack. "I thought she mostly made meat and potatoes."

She did. His mom had a solid rotation of exactly that. It made shopping and cooking easy. Everyone knew what was for dinner on any given night.

But tonight she was making something different.

"A real dinner two nights in a row." Nora smiled at him. "I'm a lucky woman." Her eyes dropped to his plate.

He picked up the single slice of bacon there and held it out to her.

Her smile widened as she took it. "Thank you." Nora snagged his empty plate and stacked it on hers before standing up and heading to the kitchen. "Is there anything I can do while you're gone?" She tossed their plates into the trash and went to the sink, switching on the hot water and adding in soap before grabbing the cooled griddle and wiping the extra bacon grease into the trash can with a paper towel.

"We should probably firm up some paint colors." Brooks poured the rest of the coffee out, splitting it between their two cups. "You could pick out counters and countertops too if you have time."

"When do you think you'll start demo?" Nora dipped the non-electric end of the griddle into the water and started scrubbing.

"Camper's supposed to be delivered late next week. Once that's set up we can clear this place out and start working." He'd gotten to know some of the guys who worked on The Inn and a few of them were looking for side work, which meant he had extra hands available for the tasks he couldn't do completely on his own.

Nora's lips pressed into a frown. "I feel bad that everyone worked so hard on getting this place habitable and we're only going to use it for a week."

"Buttercup, those people would have done anything to get you to stay." He wanted her to know how important she was to everyone around here.

Not just him. Not just his mother.

Nora was quiet as she continued to clean the griddle within an inch of its life.

It was hard not to push her. To keep from pointing out everything she'd been working so hard not to see.

But even though this felt comfortable and normal, it was still new.

Very new for her.

She finally rinsed the griddle off and went to work drying it before sliding it back into place in the cabinet. "I don't want people to feel like they have to do things to get me to stay." Nora stared down into her coffee cup, the line between her brows growing deeper by the second. "That wasn't fair of me to make them feel like that."

"You're important to them." Brooks leaned against the counter beside her. "Wouldn't you want someone important to you to stay close?"

Her eyes eased his way and the line of her lips softened, the edges barely curving. "I guess so."

He leaned to press another kiss to her lips before straightening. "I need to get my ass in gear."

Nora stayed in the kitchen while he went to shower off and dress for the day. When he came out of the room she was still standing at the counter, this time with her laptop set up in front of her, scrolling through lines of paint colors.

"Working already?"

Nora's eyes rolled his way, stopping to slowly work their way down his frame. "Uh-huh."

Brooks snagged his hat off the coffee table and settled it on his head as he walked toward her. He tipped one finger under her chin, lifting it up for a goodbye kiss. "Have a good day, Buttercup."

She gave him a little smile. "I think I will."

He turned and she snagged him by the hand, halting his exit. When he faced her she was chewing her lower lip, dark eyes holding his. "Be careful."

"I will." He took another kiss before forcing his boots out the front door, making sure the deadbolt was in place before heading to his truck. Usually the hardest part of going to work was the getting out of bed part.

Today it was something else he struggled with.

As he drove to the ranch Brooks called Grady. He didn't like the idea of Nora being at that house alone all day. While it was clear someone was living there from her car in the driveway and the flowers on the porch, it still didn't sit well.

Knowing Grady was still making his passes of the place settled the irritation threatening to make him turn the truck around.

"Brooks Pace." Grady sounded bright-eyed and bushy-tailed when he answered. "What can I do for you?"

"I was wondering if you were still driving past Camille's place? Keepin' an eye on it."

"I try to. Why? You got something there you're worried about?"

"I do."

"I'll try to look a little more then. You getting started on the renovations?"

"I plan to start demo in the next couple of weeks." It'd seemed like a great idea at the time. The house was a way to keep Nora here longer. Keep her close.

Now that she was close, he hated the thought of spending all his time working instead of with her.

"I'll be interested to see what you do with it."

"Come by anytime."

"Thanks. I might do that." Grady said his goodbye and Brooks was hanging up the call just as he pulled up in front of the main house. His brothers were already out in the yard, saddling up horses as the sun started to lighten the horizon.

Brett was set apart from the rest of the men, frowning hard as he worked. Brooks rounded up Shadow and led him to where Brett was saddling up his own horse. "Mornin'."

Brett didn't glance his way. "Yup."

Brooks looked to where Brody and Boone stood with their dad and the hands working with them this morning. They all seemed oblivious to Brett's bad mood. "Somethin' wrong?"

"There's a lot wrong." Brett mounted up.

Brooks pulled up onto Shadow's back and settled into the saddle. "Want to talk about it?"

Brett jerked his head to one side. "Nope." He turned his horse toward the back pasture, heading out at a decent pace.

Brooks nudged Shadow in the direction of his dad and brothers. "Any of you know what's wrong with Brett?"

Brody glanced out at where Brett rode. "It's probably got to do with The Inn."

"The Inn?" Brooks turned to peer back at the house before facing his brother again. "Or someone who works there?"

Bill Pace hooked one boot into a stirrup. "Leave your brother alone." He swung into place, the height of his horse setting him taller than anyone else in the group. "A man's gotta be miserable before can appreciate bein' happy." He squinted in Brett's direction. "And that one's gonna be miserable as hell."

"If that's true then I should be happier than any of you assholes." Brody's eyes went to the porch as Clara stepped out with one of his twin daughters on her hip. She smiled his direction, his face lighting up at her attention. "So I'm gonna say it's probably true." He was already headed her way. "I'll catch up."

Boone shook his head. "He keeps lookin' at her like that she's not gonna fit in her wedding dress."

"The wedding's two weeks away." Brooks watched as Brody dropped off his horse and climbed the stairs. "He can't do much harm in two weeks."

Boone snorted. "I bet he'd try like hell though." He fell in line beside Brooks as they followed their dad out. "You talk Nora into stayin'?

"Seems like." He didn't want to get ahead of himself. "I guess we'll see."

"We'll see? You haven't asked her to stay?" Boone seemed almost appalled.

"I don't want her to feel like she has to decide right away."

"Why the hell not?" Boone pushed the brim of his hat back, revealing more of his shocked expression.

"It has to be her decision." He'd lined everything up for her to stay. She had a job. A place to live.

But the final choice had to be hers. He couldn't make her stay.

"Shit." Boone shook his head. "You're scared she's going to leave."

It was something that always hung in the back of his mind.

Nora had been adamant that she didn't like Moss Creek. That she would be going back to Seattle.

That she was leaving.

Ignoring the fact that it might still happen seemed foolish.

"You can't go into something like that scared, man. It'll make you hold back." Boone shook his head. "You gotta go full on or you'll always wonder if you coulda done more."

"If it's right then it won't matter what I do."

"Don't be a dumbass. You can't just sit on your ass and expect a woman to know what you're thinkin'. Especially one like Nora." Boone shook his head. "The kind of shit you want would never occur to her. Not after what she's been through."

Brooks let out a long breath. It was the downside to all the love and support his family had to dish out.

If one person knew something, they all knew it and apparently they all knew about Nora's past. "I was hopin' Mom would keep what I told her to herself."

Boone leaned his way as they passed a couple of hands. "I haven't talked to Mom."

There was only one other connection and it didn't involve him at all. "Mae." She and Liza were best friends and Nora spent a whole night with Liza and sloe gin.

Boone tipped his head. "She's ready to roll heads."

In all honesty, so was he. Especially after the email he saw this morning. "The woman she used to work for is claiming Nora owes them half the money she earned on The Inn. Says she's obligated to split it because she was still under contract with them."

Boone let out a low whistle. "Was she?"

Brooks shook his head. "I don't know."

"She didn't say?"

"A copy of the email they sent was in a pile of the papers for the house." He sucked in a lungful of the early morning air, hoping it would relax the anger still lingering. "She doesn't know I saw it."

"You gonna ask her?"

"Not my place?"

"Isn't it? Don't you want to be the one she talks to about shit like this?" Boone clicked his tongue. "Women don't just give you a place in their life. You've gotta tell 'em you want it, and then you've gotta prove you deserve it."

"That's what I've been doing. Whatever she wants is what I make happen." It's what he'd watched his father do for years. What he'd been waiting to do for the right woman.

"Maybe it's not always what she wants that's important to her." Boone shot him a wink before turning and taking off, catching up with their dad at the head of the pack, leaving Brooks behind, giving him too much space to think about what exactly he meant.

And how in the hell that was supposed to help him.

CHAPTER SEVENTEEN

"THEY'RE PERFECT." NORA smiled at the vase of flowers.

The older balding man who passed them across smiled back at her. "I'm glad you like them."

She'd spent most of the day trolling around Moss Creek, checking out everything it had to offer. From the little jewelry shop to the boutique filled with scented soaps and candles, to the florist who was taking a matching set of the flowers on the counter in front of her out to Cross Creek Ranch.

"I love them." Nora grinned at him. "I might have to come back and get some for myself."

"You come back anytime you want, Miss Nora."

She carefully slid the boxed-up arrangement off the counter. "In that case I might be back tomorrow." She used her backside to push open the door. "Thanks again."

The street outside was quiet but not empty. Across the street the Wooden Spoon was in the final stages of construction after being set on fire by Camille's horrible ex.

It was a reminder that things could technically be worse. Dean and his mother hadn't tried to burn anything down.

Esmerelda was just trying to bully her into handing over money that didn't belong to them. Not by a long shot.

She'd been terminated the day she discovered Dean boning another woman in their bed. Anything she had at the office was packed up into a box and set on the sidewalk outside within hours.

Like his mother knew it was coming.

Her first conversation with Maryann didn't happen until eight weeks after that, making it easy to separate the two halves of her life.

One was dominated by a viper in Calvin Klein.

The other was filled with women who supported and appreciated each other, giving her a taste of what it might be like to be a part of something like that. And while it was terrifying, there was nothing else she'd ever wanted more.

Except maybe Brooks Pace.

Nora made her way to where her rental was parked along the street, managing to get the arrangement inside without pouring water anywhere important.

She fell into the driver's seat, closing her eyes and taking a minute to breathe.

She'd gotten very good at only seeing what she wanted to see, how she wanted to see it. It was a form of self-preservation. A way to keep from having to acknowledge things she didn't want to face.

But the blinders always slipped at some point, leaving her with glimpses of what lurked around the edges.

And right now there was a lot lurking.

Storage units. Bank accounts.

Threats of litigation.

She'd spent the whole day ignoring it, a complete turn of the tables she'd been sitting at.

Now Moss Creek was her focus. The thing she used to pretend nothing else existed.

But it was still there.

Waiting.

Nora started the engine, turning up the music, trying to drown out the thoughts creeping in.

The trip to the ranch was shorter now that she wasn't two towns away. She did the full drive with the windows down, enjoying the warm air tangling her hair into an unconquerable mess she'd have to fight with later.

It was worth it to stay in the moment. To keep her mind where it had to be.

Just for a little bit. Long enough for her to wrap it around the possibilities she faced.

Maybe faced.

Brooks hadn't expressly asked her to stay. Not outside of the scope of their project.

He'd done many things to make her think he might be leaning that way, but if she'd learned nothing else about herself it was that she was good at seeing only what she wanted to see.

And right now what she saw was a full driveway.

The space in front of the main house at Red Cedar Ranch was lined with trucks, which meant everyone was still out in the fields. Nora parked next to Brooks' truck and wrestled the flowers back out of the front seat, balancing them on one hip as she grabbed for her purse, blindly pulling it free and hooking it over her shoulder as she walked toward the house. The gravel was much easier to maneuver in sneakers than it had been in the flats she normally wore, one pair of which was still somewhere on Liza Cross's property.

The door to the house opened as she climbed the stairs.

"Flowers!" The little voice could only belong to one of two people.

Nora leaned to peek around the side of the arrangement, finding one of Brody's daughters staring up at the yellow and orange blooms. Her smile was wide and dimpled like her daddy's. "You brought me flowers."

Clara rushed down the hall to scoop Michaela out of the way. "If you love the flowers then you have to give her room to get into the house, Little Monster." She backed to one side, giving Nora an apologetic smile. "We have manners, I swear we do."

"She was perfectly polite." Nora gave Michaela a wink as she passed.

"Who's here?" Maryann's voice carried in from the kitchen. The sound of it made Nora's stomach clench and her throat tight.

This was uncharted territory for her.

A step that went way out of her comfort zone.

Maryann appeared in the doorway, wiping her hands on the apron tied around her middle. Her expression immediately went soft.

And a little hesitant.

"Aren't those beautiful." Her eyes stayed on the flowers as Nora walked into the kitchen, using the vase as a buffer she didn't need as much as she expected to.

"Roger says hello." She set the vase on the counter, away from the area Maryann used to lay out the meals she dished out in giant portions.

"I knew these were from him the second I saw them." She pointed to the green buds that perfectly complemented the warmth of the blooms around them. "Aren't these going in the flowers for the wedding?"

"I don't even remember anymore." Clara set Michaela on the ground. "I just told him he could do whatever he wanted."

"I don't think you'll be disappointed." Maryann leaned in to breathe the air against a rose. "Roger does beautiful work."

Nora stood at the counter, uncertainty keeping her from participating in the conversation.

What did families talk about? Did they offer to help or just jump right in?

She'd never thought of herself as stunted before coming here, but in this moment there was no denying it.

She'd led a life that left her poorly prepared for the Pace family.

"You want something to drink?" Maryann was already at the fridge. "I've got sweet tea if you'd like it."

"I would love some." Nora took a half-step Maryann's way. "I can get it if you're busy."

She'd never crossed the line here. Never moved from employee to more, thinking her relationship with Maryann had to be all business.

Maryann turned her way. "That would be lovely." She pointed at a cabinet to the left of the industrial-sized fridge. "The glasses are up there."

Nora pulled one out.

Then she took a deep breath before turning to Clara and Maryann. "Would you like some too?"

Maryann gave her a little smile. "I'd love some."

Clara lifted a half-full glass. "I'm already set."

Nora filled two glasses with ice and tea before taking one to where Maryann was working at the counter, shredding a head of cabbage. Nora set it off to one side so it wouldn't be in the way. "Is there anything else I can do?"

Maryann tipped her head toward a few limes. "Those need to be squeezed into this bowl here."

Limes she could handle.

Nora rolled them across the counter, making sure they were good and loose before cutting each one in half and working the juice into the bowl. By the time she was finished a line of men on horseback appeared at the edge of the yard, just beyond the chicken coop.

Brooks was easy to pick out of the crowd and not just because she knew what he put on this morning. The way he held himself was distinct. The set of his jaw. The angle of his head.

It was something she'd only allowed herself to notice for fleeting seconds, but the images of him stuck in her brain, perfectly preserved. For a while they were torture. Impossible to handle outside of complete denial.

If she didn't like cowboys then she didn't like Brooks.

If she didn't like animals then she didn't like Red Cedar Ranch.

If she liked the city then she didn't like Moss Creek.

But there was no way to keep going like that.

She did like cowboys. Specifically Brooks.

Animals were fine. Mostly the ones at Red Cedar Ranch.

The city wasn't anything special.

Not like Moss Creek was.

Maryann piled the cabbage on top of the lime juice then dropped in a handful of cilantro and salt and pepper, stirring it all together before pushing it aside.

"The boys are going to be here any minute." Maryann looked Nora's way. "You feel like pulling the sour cream out of the fridge?"

"Sure." She went back to the refrigerator, digging around as she looked for the sour cream. It wasn't on the top shelf or any of the ones under it. It was nowhere and she was starting to get frustrated with herself. She had to be missing it.

Nora took a breath and started from the top again.

Once again she came up empty.

It was a simple task and she was struggling with it.

She'd wanted to go back to Seattle to prove she was better than some people thought and now she couldn't even find freaking sour cream.

Once again she was coming up short.

"What are you lookin' for, Buttercup?" Brooks' deep voice sent her spine snapping straight, bumping her back into where he was leaned in close.

Disappointment flared, tightening her gut and forcing her to blink more than normal. "Your mom asked me to get the sour cream and I can't find it."

"I'd say that's because Clara's already got it on the table." He came in closer, wrapping one arm around her, keeping her close as he pulled her away from the fridge and out of the bustling kitchen. Not a single person seemed to notice their exit as he moved her out of the house and onto the enclosed back porch.

He pulled her in, wrapping both arms around her in a way that blocked out everything around them. "Just relax. Take a deep breath."

"I'm okay." She sucked in air, forcing down the upset threatening to embarrass her. "We should go back in."

"We don't go back in until you're ready."

"They will think—"

"They'll think I wanted you to myself for a minute." His head dropped down close to hers. "And they might judge you for gettin' so close to me after I've been out working all day."

She snorted out a laugh.

"How was your day?" His tone was soft and smooth. Like they had all the time in the world.

Nora closed her eyes and breathed deep, letting his calm soak into her. "I went to town."

"How was that?"

"It looks like they're almost done with Mae's place." Another deep breath, this one a little easier to manage. "I met the florist."

"Roger? My mom loves him."

"He loves her back." She smoothed one hand down the shirt covering Brooks' chest, breathing deep for too many minutes, trying to regain control over what used to be so easy to tame. "Why is this so hard?"

"Sometimes the best things are the hardest." He didn't seem to be bothered by the fact that his whole family was probably wondering where they were.

Wondering what was wrong with her.

"But this should be easy." These were the nicest, most thoughtful people she'd ever met.

Anyone in their right mind would love to be in her position.

"Says who? It's okay if you aren't ready." Brooks stroked down her back. "You want to go home?"

"No." She did want to go home, but not as much as she wanted to do this.

To nut up.

Nora sucked in a breath and stood straight. "Let's go eat."

Brooks smiled down at her. "I think you're going to be happy you made that decision." He took her hand and pulled her inside, leading her to the counter where Brody and Brett were still working their way through the buffet-style line, filling their plates with the tacos and rice and beans Brooks promised.

But that wasn't all there was.

Four bowls of salsa sat at the end of the line, along with five brand new bottles of assorted hot sauces.

Nora glanced Brooks' way as she edged along the counter.

Maryann never made spicy food. Definitely not five kinds of spicy food.

Nora assembled two tacos, topping each with shredded pepper jack and the salsa that looked the spiciest, before taking her plate to sit beside Brooks at the table.

She stared down at the meal that was most definitely made for her. There was only one way Maryann could know that she liked spicy food.

Brooks might not have said that he wanted her to stay out loud, but maybe that was okay.

Maybe this was good enough.

Hell, it should be better than good enough. The man told his mother about her for the love of God.

What did she want from him?

Nora picked up a taco and took a tentative bite, just in case Maryann brought her A-game to the spice show.

"How is it?" Maryann asked the question to no one in particular.

Or maybe only to Nora.

Nora nodded as she chewed through the perfectly spicy bite. "Really good."

Maryann gave her a quick smile before turning to her own food. "Good."

Once dinner was done Maryann pulled out three sheets covered in foil and lined them down the counter. Boone fished a giant container of ice cream from the freezer as his brothers came in beside him and started filling bowls. Each one got a scoop from every tray and a plop of vanilla on top.

"Now you see why I'm worried about my wedding dress fitting." Clara dropped into Brooks' vacated chair as Mae's butt hit the one on Nora's other side.

"You learn to pace yourself or else you end up only fitting into your shoes." Mae leaned one elbow on the table. "So." She wiggled her brows. "What's happenin'?"

"I don't even know where to start." Nora blew out a breath. "I got wasted with Liza and ate shredded cheese and banana pudding." She pursed her lips. "I'm staying in Camille's old house. I might have seen Brooks naked, and there's a chance I could end up living in a camper."

It sounded ridiculous strung together like that.

Clara nodded. "Makes sense."

"Does it?" Nora turned to her. "Because it sounds insane."

"Not when you're familiar with the Pace men." Mae eyed Boone as he added a second scoop of ice cream to one of the bowls. "And we're pretty familiar with them."

"I'm not sure I'm there yet." She still struggled to wrap her head around what was happening.

If it was really real.

"They're a different breed." Clara took a bowl from one of the twins as they helped their daddy and uncles dish out dessert. "Thank you."

"Welcome."

"They decide what they want and they just go get it." Mae shook her head. "Resisting is futile."

"I don't think that's what's happening."

Boone brought over the bowl with double the ice cream, hand delivering it to Mae with a wink. "Ma'am."

Mae's smile was only for him. "Thank you."

He shot her a grin and a look that promised ice cream was only one of the things he planned to give her before the day was over.

Nora turned toward Mae as Boone walked back into the kitchen to finish his chore. "I think you just got pregnant."

"No freaking way." Mae sucked a bite of vanilla off her spoon. "He knows if I end up pregnant before I'm ready he's dead."

"Is he ready?" She'd been with Dean for years and never once did they discuss marriage or kids.

Probably because he was still a child, letting his mother run his life.

And hers.

Not anymore though.

She'd been considering fighting Esmerelda over the money from her job with Maryann.

It was most of the reason she planned to go back to Seattle. To hire an attorney and finally stand up to them both. Prove she wasn't going to let them walk on her anymore.

Now that seemed less important.

"He was ready even before I took him back." Mae scooped up a bite of what appeared to be peach cobbler. "I think it's in their blood to want every kid they can talk us into."

Nora turned to Clara. She and Brody already had three between them, his twin girls and her son Wyatt. "Brody too?"

"He wanted our house to have six bedrooms." She shook her head as she ate her own cobbler. "But how do you say no to something that looks like that?" Her eyes landed on where her fiancé passed bowls out, sending each girl to a specific location, praising them every time they returned.

It was one more thing she wasn't sure how to handle. One more thing making her worry that even though she might think Moss Creek was meant for her, she might not be meant for Moss Creek.

CHAPTER EIGHTEEN

"CLARA'S PROBABLY ASKING her what she's wearing to the wedding." Brody stood beside Brooks, watching his fiancée as she chatted with Nora and Mae.

"Maybe." Brooks shifted around the ice cream as it melted across the layer of warm cobbler. He hadn't managed to take the first bite.

"You found a date yet?" Boone knocked Brett's boot with the toe of his own.

"Not bringin' one." Brett polished off the contents of his bowl before rinsing it off, loading it into the dishwasher and walking out.

"Been there." Boone shoved in a bite of blueberry and crust. "Glad I'm not there anymore."

"Where's that?" Brooks tried to force his attention away from where Nora sat with Mae and Clara, looking happier than he'd seen her.

Which was good.

One more reason for her to forget about Seattle.

One more reason for her to stay in Moss Creek.

"Misery." Boone lifted his brows as he scooped up more with his spoon. "I was there for a hell of a long time."

"You weren't the only one." Brody shook his head. "But you've got to go through it. The misery makes what comes after so much sweeter."

This was his second time dealing with this conversation and honestly it was two times too many.

"I'm sure not everyone goes through it." He'd been patient. Careful.

And it was paying off now.

Everything was falling into place.

Nora had friends. A job. A place to stay. People who cared about her.

They shared a bed. Shared a home.

No misery involved.

Boone snorted. "Dumbass."

"You're the dumbass." Brooks finally managed to pull his attention from Nora. "Your misery was your own damn fault."

"It's usually our own damn fault." Brody crossed one ankle over the other and relaxed back against the counter. "I got to be miserable twice."

Brody lost his first wife to a blood clot almost immediately after the birth of their twins, making him a father and a widower on the same day.

His eyes fixed on the woman who would soon be his wife. "But it was worth it."

Clara's head turned, eyes coming their way.

Mae was next, followed by Nora.

Mae huffed out a breath as she stood up, coming Boone's way with her empty bowl. She shoved it against his middle, leaning close. "You know it's rude to stare."

He grinned at her. "You're gonna have to get over it because I like lookin' at you." He leaned down, catching a kiss before she backed away.

Mae's eyes came Brooks' way. "We're going outside."

"Have fun."

Clara brought Michaela to Brody. He caught her as she tried to pass his daughter off, pulling her close to whisper something against her ear before letting her go.

Nora stood at the doorway, watching. Her gaze came to Brooks as Clara and Mae joined her. She gave him a little smile before being pushed into the hall and toward the front porch.

Boone shook his head as he turned toward the sink. "You're screwed."

"Why?" Brooks watched until there was no sight of Nora. He waited for the click of the front door as it closed, just in case she came back in.

Just in case she might need him again.

"The misery is coming." Brody stepped in beside Boone, sorting bowls and plates.

"It's not coming." Brooks couldn't even make himself irritated at his brothers. They might have fucked things up, but he'd been careful as hell. Waiting for the right time with the right woman.

Patience was a man's best friend when it came to finding a wife.

Wife.

The word settled in his chest.

It fell right into place just like everything else had with her. It might not have all been easy or simple, but not a single bit of it made him even close to miserable.

Anything worth having was worth working for. He put in the work and now it was paying off.

"Sure." Boone's brows almost reached the brim of his hat as he rinsed plates, passing them to Brooks to be loaded into the dishwasher.

Their dad joined them as their mother disappeared through the front hall, probably going to join Mae, Clara, and Nora on the front porch. He ran one hand down the front of his chest. "How was the spicy salsa?"

"I feel bad telling you how good it was." Brody handed off the last of the plates.

"I thought I might be able to sneak a little, but she watched me like a hawk." Their dad snagged one of the twins, scooping her up.

"She doesn't want to listen to you complain about heartburn." Boone reached out to tap one finger to the end of Leah's nose.

"Ew." She immediately swiped at it with both hands. "Your hands are wet, Uncle Boone."

"Come on." Bill moved through the kitchen, collecting his grandkids on his way to the living room. "Let's go watch our shows."

"What's he going to do when you guys move into your house?" Brody and Clara's house was coming along. They'd probably be able to move in shortly after the wedding, leaving the main house quiet for the first time ever.

"Probably come to our house every night." Brody grabbed a rag from the sink and started wiping down counters while Boone and Brooks finished loading the dishes. "Until one of you has kids for him to play with."

"I wouldn't hold your breath on that happening anytime soon." Boone glanced Brooks' way. "At least not on my end."

Brody's gaze joined Boone's, both fixing on Brooks.

"What?"

"You and Nora talked about kids yet?"

"No."

"But she knows you want a lot of 'em, right?" Boone added a pack of detergent to the washer before closing it up.

Brooks pulled the full trash bag from the can, tying the top off before heading to the back door.

"Holy shit. She doesn't know he wants a million kids." Boone followed after him. "That's a big thing. You can't just assume she knows it."

"Everyone here has big families." Brooks kept walking, hoping Boone would take the hint and drop the subject.

It didn't happen.

"She's not from here." Boone lifted the lid on the large outdoor can, holding it open while Brooks tossed the bag in. "You've got to make what you want clear so she can decide if it's what she wants too."

"Worry about your own relationship." He wasn't taking advice from Boone. His brother might be happily paired off now, but he'd fucked up just about as bad as a man could, almost losing the woman he loved forever.

Successfully losing her for a decade.

"I would if you were worried about yours."

"I don't need to worry." They'd given him shit for years about being picky. Now it was paying off.

Brooks went through the kitchen, past Brody as he headed for the front of the house. "I'll see you tomorrow."

He didn't want to hear any more of their bullshit. He knew what this was.

What it could be.

The chatter on the porch died the second he stepped outside. Four sets of eyes sat squarely on him.

But his eyes were only on one of them. "You ready?"

Nora blinked a few times, like he'd surprised her. "Yeah. Sure." She got up from the rocker where she sat, right next to his mother. "Thank you for dinner."

"We have it every night." His mother stood, looking more cautious than she usually did. "You're welcome anytime."

Nora leaned in for a quick hug. "Thank you."

She looked his way, thumbing over her shoulder. "I need to get my bag."

"I'll wait." He'd wanted her to come here tonight. Wanted her to see what a life in Moss Creek would hold for her.

What a life with him would offer.

But he was done hearing his brothers' bull and just wanted to go.

Wanted to be with her.

Nora came out in under a minute, bag on her shoulder. She gave the women on the porch a wave and an easy smile. "Bye."

Mae and Clara waved back, but his mother's eyes were on him, her lips tilting in what was almost a smile.

Probably because he'd finally managed to bring Nora around.

Like he intended.

A son who finally did it right from the start.

Both Brody and Boone got themselves banished to the cabins because of their mistakes.

Not him.

Brooks took Nora to her rental car, waiting while she unlocked it before opening the door.

She needed a real car. One that didn't cost an arm and a leg to rent.

Tomorrow he would take her to find one.

It would be one more item falling into place.

"I'll follow you." Once she was in he closed the door and went to his truck, backing out behind her, keeping pace as she drove toward the little house that would always be a physical reminder of their beginning.

Brooks relaxed more with each mile put between him and his brother's assumptions.

They were wrong. Eventually they'd figure it out.

Nora parked in the side of the driveway closest to the front door and Brooks lined his truck right beside hers. Another physical representation of what they were.

Side by side.

A team.

A partnership in the making.

Nora was quiet as she followed him up the steps, waiting while he unlocked the door.

But she was quiet a lot. It just meant she was thinking, and after today she had a lot to think about.

She'd spent the day in town. A town that she might soon call her own.

His mother made a dinner specifically for her, including three different types of cobbler.

She had friends, family, and a job all in one place. A happy life ready to be started and lived.

Nora was probably trying to figure out how to get her storage unit emptied without actually having to go back to Seattle.

Brooks closed the door, locking it tight as Nora set her purse on the coffee table. She sat down on the couch and stared at the fireplace.

"Did you have a nice night?" He was struggling with the patience he worked so hard to have.

But he needed to hear she was getting what she needed.

What it took to make her want to stay.

"It was fine." Her tone was flat and distant.

Not at all what he was expecting.

"I thought you'd be happy to see your friends."

"I was happy to see them." Nora ran her palms down the fronts of her jeans.

"Good." He took a step closer. "Did you like dinner?"

She nodded, her eyes still not coming his way. "It was nice of your mom to make that."

"She made it for you."

"I know. She told me." The last bit sounded off. Shorter.

Sharper.

"I think Clara and Mae were glad you came." He'd stand here all night and keep pointing out the reasons she should want to stay if that's what it took for her to see it.

"They said they were."

"Then why are you upset?"

Her head finally turned his way. "Why are you telling me how happy everyone else is that I'm here?"

"Because I want you to know that everyone cares about you."

Nora stood up. "Maybe I'm not worried about everyone else."

"What does that mean?"

Nora's shoulders shifted, squaring as they pushed back just a little. "It means you're the only one who hasn't told me they want me to stay in Moss Creek."

"It's not my place to tell you that."

She stood very still. "Why?"

"I can't be the reason you decide to stay here." It wasn't fair to ask her to uproot her whole life just for him.

It's why he worked so hard to show her what else Moss Creek had to offer.

"Can't be or don't want to be?" It didn't sound like an accusation but it felt like one.

But what he wanted didn't matter. Not when it came to something like this. "Both." The lie was for her. So Nora could make a decision she'd never regret.

"So you just want to play house with me until you decide if you like me enough to keep me?" Her voice cracked as the last words came out.

The wrongness of her assumption shocked him. Left him speechless.

Which was definitely the wrong thing to be right now.

Nora tipped her head in a little nod.

Then she grabbed her purse and was gone, rushing from the little house once again.

Leaving him staring after her as she pulled away.

CHAPTER NINETEEN

THIS WAS A bad decision.

But there was no going back. Not since Maryann Pace was sitting on the porch in a rocker.

Like she was expecting someone.

Nora parked her car and sat for a minute.

She should have gone to Liza's. Then she could be running barefoot through the grass without a care in the world.

But that wasn't what she needed right now.

Right now she needed wisdom.

Someone who understood where she was at.

And there was only one person she knew like that. Unfortunately, it was also the woman who brought most of her problem into the world.

Nora took a deep breath and forced herself out of the car. She gave Maryann a little wave as she walked to the porch.

No doubt Maryann was wondering what in the hell she was doing back here. She'd been gone less than an hour.

That was apparently all it took to realize you might have no clue what you're doing with your life.

What you're doing in general.

"Hey." Nora forced on a smile as she reached the porch.

Maryann rocked slowly, a sweater wrapped around her shoulders. She pointed to the chair next to her. "I saved you a seat."

"Thanks." Nora crossed to the rocker. She picked up a folded item from the seat and started to move it to the next chair over.

"That's in case you get chilly." Maryann looked out over the yard and fields. "Rain's coming in. It's going to cool off real fast."

Nora shivered, almost as if Maryann spoke the temperature drop into existence.

It wouldn't surprise her if she did.

"Thank you." Nora shook out the sweatshirt before pulling it over her head.

"I brought you out some tea too." Maryann nudged the glass closer.

"You brought it for me?" Nora pulled the length of the sleeves over her hands and looked down at the front.

It was emblazoned with a faded lion's head and the words Moss Creek Varsity Football.

"I figured you'd be coming back." Maryann rested her head back against the chair.

"How did you know that?"

Maryann's face tipped her way. "I've seen the look on your face before." She smiled a little. "In the mirror, many years ago." She turned back toward the yard. "I don't know if you know this, but I'm not from around here."

"Brooks told me. He said you met Bill at a rodeo and that you've been together ever since."

She snorted out a little laugh. "That's the version a woman tells her children." She glanced Nora's way. "Would you like to know what really happened?"

Nora nodded.

"I went to that rodeo with a man I'd been seeing." She lifted one shoulder. "I wasn't particularly taken with him, but he was studying to be an attorney and I thought that was a glamorous sounding job." She shook her head. "Then I saw Billy Pace. He was anything but glamorous, but there was something about him."

That's something she understood completely. "It was probably the hat."

Maryann smiled her way. "Probably." She sighed. "I spent the whole weekend with him, doing the kinds of things we only admit to our friends."

Nora leaned back in her chair, settling in for the rest of the happy story, glad it would take her mind off her own story that might not end up being nearly as happy.

"And then he left."

Nora blinked. Surely she hadn't heard that right. "What?"

Maryann nodded. "He packed up and came back here."

"Alone?"

"Alone."

"I thought—"

"You and me both." Maryann took a sip of her tea. "I thought he would ask me to go back with him. I thought he was feeling the same way I was, but when the time came he just left."

"Why?"

"Because he thought I would just know he wanted me to leave with him, and when I didn't he thought I didn't want to leave California. The man assumes everyone knows what he's thinking." She shook her head, but her lips held a smile. "He still struggles with it. Thinks I'm a damn mind reader."

Nora picked up her tea. "I think I'm with him on that one."

Maryann's smile widened. "I had to learn to pay close attention, especially when I ended up with four boys just like him."

"Brody and Boone don't seem like that."

"Only because they learned the hard way." She shook her head. "In hindsight I should have made it more difficult on Bill. It might have made my life easier over the years."

"What happened after he left?"

"I went back to my life." She tipped her head Nora's way. "Not the lawyer though."

"Then how did you end up with Bill?"

"He showed up at my apartment one day." Maryann's smile was soft and her eyes were far away. "With a moving truck."

"Did he tell you he was sorry?"

Maryann shook her head. "No."

"Did he tell you he loved you?"

Another shake. "No."

"What did he say?"

"He told me he was taking me where I belonged." She rolled her eyes Nora's way. "It seemed very romantic at the time."

"It's not unromantic."

"But it took him years to finally start telling me what he felt, and even then it was only because I threatened to leave him."

The revelation was stunning. "You threatened to leave him?"

"It was a knee-jerk reaction fueled by lack of sleep and too many mimosas."

She could see how that could happen. "That makes sense."

"As much sense as anything I suppose." Maryann pulled her sweater tighter as the wind started to pick up. "My point is, I was at fault too." Her rocking stopped. "I expected something from him that I was too scared to give."

Nora's heart skipped a beat. "Why were you scared?"

Maryann lifted a shoulder. "I suppose because it all happened so fast. I wasn't confident enough to tell him how I felt not knowing how he felt."

"Did you know how you felt?"

"Of course." She chuckled a little. "There was no denying that man made me feel things."

Nora chewed her lip as she mulled over all Maryann just shared.

How it fit into where she was right now.

Maryann turned to face her as the rain started, big drops hitting the grass. "My best advice is to start as you intend to go." She reached out and took Nora's hand in hers. "These boys are as good as men can be on their own, but they still need a little help." She squeezed. "And that includes the one I left a life behind for."

Nora held Maryann tight, clinging to the first bit of motherly advice she'd ever had in her life. "Did you ever feel like you didn't fit in here?"

Maryann's smile took on an understanding edge. "Every damn day." She held Nora's gaze. "But that's where you're one step ahead of me. You know who you are. What you bring to the table." She shook her head. "I was just a young silly girl in love with a cowboy."

Maryann gave her hand a final pat before standing up. "Don't ever wait for a man to tell you what he wants, Nora." She grabbed her tea as the rain picked up its pace, falling harder and faster. "You deserve to hear anything you want to hear, when you want to hear it." Maryann pulled the door open, shooting her a wink. "Give him a little hell just for fun."

Then she was gone. Dropping a bomb of advice and honesty and leaving Nora to process it on her own.

Alone.

Again.

"You left me."

She didn't mean to stand up. Didn't mean to suck in a breath at the sound of his voice. The sight of him standing there.

In the rain.

Already soaked.

She stood a little straighter.

Start as you intend to go.

It would be easy as hell to do exactly as Maryann did all those years ago. Run to him for simply coming after her.

But it wasn't enough. No matter what she wanted to pretend.

A lifetime of not enough didn't mean she should be grateful for anything.

"You should want me to stay for you." The next breath was shaky but she managed to pull it in. "You should ask me to stay if it's what you want."

"It's not about what I want." Brooks came a little closer, near enough she could see how wet he was. The way the fabric of his shirt fitted to his body like a second skin.

She could definitely see why Maryann did what she did.

But she wasn't going to ignore the first advice someone cared enough to offer her.

"It is for me." Nora edged toward the railing. "If you want me here I deserve to hear it." She swallowed down the nerves trying to stop her. "I deserve to know how you feel."

"My feelings don't matter."

The statement stopped her short.

Made her rethink what she believed.

What Maryann believed.

Maybe it wasn't that these men didn't want to share how they felt.

Maybe they thought their feelings always came second.

Until they were told they didn't.

She stood a little taller. "Then neither do mine."

"That's bullshit."

"You're the one that said we could be a team." She crept along the edge of the porch. "That's not how teams work."

"It is where I come from."

Nora stopped at the top of the stairs. "You're wrong."

That was the real reason Brody and Boone were the way they were. The met women who gave as much as they took.

Like Maryann.

Brooks just didn't see it.

"If we're a team then your feelings matter as much as mine do." Nora started down the steps.

"Get your ass back on that porch."

"No." She wasn't going to let him stand out in the rain alone.

She knew what it was like to be alone. To bear the burden of everything while everyone else got what they wanted.

And she sure as shit wasn't going to let Brooks do it.

"Goddammit, Nora." He pointed one finger at the house. "Go back on the porch."

"No." He didn't really want her on the porch anyway. If he did he'd run away. Take away the option she was choosing.

Him.

Nora went straight for him, blinking as rain collected on her lashes and soaked into her hair, matting it to her head. "If you want me to stay in Moss Creek you better say so, Brooks Pace. Otherwise I'm getting in my car and leaving."

His jaw flexed, the muscle twitching as he stared at her from under the brim of his hat. "I want you to do what you want to do."

For the love of—

"Fine." Nora fished the keys out of her pocket and started toward her rental car, ready to take this as far as she had to.

Because she was starting as she intended to go, and the way she intended to go was with a man who told her what he thought.

What he wanted.

A man who knew his feelings mattered to her.

She made it two steps.

Two steps before he caught her by the hand.

Two steps before he pulled her close.

Two steps before his body was against hers, the brim of his hat shielding her face from the rain as it continued to fall.

His eyes held hers for a few long seconds.

She didn't expect this to be easy for him. Nothing worth having was.

But he had to do it.

She lifted a brow. "You gonna nut up, Buttercup?"

Brooks snorted out a breath that almost sounded like a laugh. His blue eyes roamed her face, dipping to her mouth before coming back to hold her gaze. "Stay."

It wasn't a declaration of love.

She didn't need one.

It wasn't grand. It wasn't fancy.

But she would remember that single word forever.

"Okay."

His arms banded tight around her, pulling her close enough she could barely breathe as his mouth came to hers, warm and firm. She held on tight, arms gripping as the first clap of thunder shook the ground.

"Come on." He grabbed her like he always did, pulling her along where they needed to go, making sure she was in the truck first before jumping in and starting the engine.

Her teeth chattered as the cold and wet started to sink into her skin.

"I told you to stay on the porch." Brooks reached out to switch on the heat, angling the blowers in her direction.

"You were in the rain first." She fought the words out between shivers.

The wipers flipped at high speed as he drove. "That didn't mean you had to stand in the rain too."

"Yes it did." Nora tucked her arms close, trying to conserve heat.

"Is that how this is going to be? I do something stupid and then you do it too?"

"Pr-ob-ably." The tensing of her body broke the word up as she said it.

Brooks pulled up in front of the little house, parking before coming to get her, rushing her through the rain and up onto the porch. He shoved the door open and dragged her in.

She didn't even wait for him to get the door closed. "What else do you want?"

Brooks flipped the deadbolt on the door before slowly turning her way. “That’s a pretty broad question, Buttercup.”

“Then give me broad answers.”

“I’m not sure you want to hear my answers just yet.”

“If I didn’t want to hear them then I wouldn’t have asked.” Clara and Mae knew what Brody and Brooks wanted for their lives.

For their futures.

She wanted to know what Brooks wanted.

“I want what everyone wants.”

She shook her head. “That’s not an answer.” He’d given it to her before. A generic plan that most people had.

Brooks came closer. “Seemed like an answer to me.”

He was dripping wet, jeans and shirt glued to his body in a way that hid nothing.

She’d never seen him naked before. Not completely.

“It wasn’t.” She backed away as he continued to advance on her. “I want answers. Real ones.”

Brooks paused. “What do *you* want?”

“I’ll tell you if you tell me.”

He started moving again. “You start.” He closed in on her. “What do you want, Nora?”

That list was short and most of it was populated by items that included Brooks Pace.

Some of them proper.

Some of them not.

“I want to be happy. I want to be loved.”

“Everyone wants those things, Buttercup. You’re going to have to do better than that.”

Did he just use her words against her?

He did.

Nora kept backing up, trying to keep a safe distance between them. It was the only way to make sure she didn't cave in.

Didn't let him make her forget what she wanted.

What she needed.

Suddenly he was on her, fast enough she didn't have a chance, his wet clothes pressed tight to hers. "You're not sayin' much."

"You're distracting me."

"That sounds like a you problem." He pushed against her, shoving her through the house.

His eyes dipped to the shirt she wore. "Where did you get that?"

"Your mom gave it to me."

"Remind me to give her hell next time I see her." He grabbed the bottom of the sweatshirt and whipped it up her body, pulling it over her head and dropping it to the floor.

She fought to keep her line of thought as he found the bottom of the t-shirt she put on this morning. "Your mom said I have to make you tell me things or I'll regret it."

Brooks worked the damp shirt up. The second the air of the room hit her skin she started to shiver again.

"What do you want to know, Buttercup?" He worked faster, peeling off her jeans, taking her panties down at the same time.

"Everything."

"That'll take a while." He unhooked her bra and skimmed it down her arms.

Her whole body braced for the feel of his hands. The perfect way they scraped against her.

But they didn't come.

Instead he pulled back the covers on the bed and bumped her toward it with his body, pushing her until she dropped to the mattress. Then he tossed them across her, covering her to her chin with sheets and blankets.

He leaned to one side, working off a boot. "I want you to stay in Moss Creek." One boot hit the floor. "I want you to stay wherever I am."

The second boot thunked against the hardwood.

"I want to finish this house and then I want to buy another one." His hat went to the table beside the bed. "And I want you to keep makin' them look however you want."

His shirt was next.

She couldn't stop herself from staring as he shucked it over his head.

"I want you to tell that bitch you used to work for to kiss your ass." He unbuttoned his pants, dragging her eyes to where his fingers worked. "I want you to go with me to Brody and Clara's wedding."

He was all over the place now, but she barely noticed. All her attention was focused on where he raked down the zipper of his jeans.

"Then I want you to go with me to Boone and Mae's wedding." His hands went to his hips, shoving down the denim. "I want you to be at my side for everything." His dick bobbed free, long and thick, straining as he kicked his pants away. "I want you in my bed every night." Brooks grabbed the blankets and yanked them away, the heat of his body replacing them almost immediately. "I want to be the one who takes care of you." His lips brushed over hers. "I want to be the one who gives you what you need." His hands caught hers, fingers lacing together as he held them beside her head. "I want to be the one who makes sure you're never alone again."

His mouth was on hers, hot and hard, still telling her what she wanted to know.

That he wanted her.

Wanted her here.

Wanted her with him.

Just wanted her.

His mouth was on her neck. On her shoulders. "Stay with me, Buttercup." His lips wrapped around a nipple, tongue flicking it before pulling free and moving to the next. "Don't leave." He sucked at her, the pull of his mouth shooting straight between her legs, feeding the ache already there.

"I want to stay." She fisted his hair. Held him in place as he continued to build her need. "I want to stay with you."

A low rumble vibrated where his mouth pressed against her.

His lips came back to hers as his fingers worked the puckered flesh it abandoned, rolling each tight tip with a pressure that sent her hips rocking into him, seeking out that same friction and pressure. "Brooks."

She needed more.

Wanted more.

His hand pressed between her thighs, cupping tight against her. "What else do you need from me, Buttercup?"

Her eyes snapped open to find him watching her.

His lips curved in a slow smile that was almost a smirk. "You didn't think I'd be the only one making confessions tonight, did you?" The hand against her shifted to grip her thigh, pushing it out to one side as his weight left her. Brooks lifted up to his knees. "You know what I want." His free hand trailed down her center, tracing a line between her ribs and across her belly button before dipping lower to follow the seam of her pussy. "Now I want to know what you want."

Was it not obvious what she wanted?

"I can help you narrow it down." His hand on her thigh flexed, fingers sinking into her flesh as his other hand parted her, opening her most private spot to the heat of his gaze. "Touch or lick?"

Just the words made her heart race and her thighs clench. "Both."

His thumb slid against her clit, rolling over it in a steady rhythm as he leaned closer. "Turnabout's fair play, Buttercup. If you want answers from me then I'm going to expect answers from you." His fingers eased into her, rocking in time with the stroke of his thumb. He nosed along her neck. "I want to hear what you want from me, when you want it."

She clenched around him, wishing it wasn't his fingers.

Nora forced her eyes to his. "I want you to fuck me."

Brooks' nostrils flared. "You might be more than I bargained for, Buttercup." He grabbed her around the waist, pulling her to the center of the bed. "Might even be more than I can handle." His mouth was on hers again, tongue sliding past her lips as he fisted a condom down the length of his dick.

She hooked her legs around his, fighting closer. "Please, Brooks."

His head dropped to her shoulder. "I can't handle when you say please like that."

She leaned into his ear. "Please."

It was nothing she would have ever done. Not with anyone else.

But this wasn't anyone else. This was Brooks.

He wanted her. He appreciated her.

He took care of her.

And it made her different.

It made her what she never could be before.

The breathy word was barely out of her mouth before he was in her, sinking deep with a single thrust that pulled a groan from his chest.

She held on, rocking with him, riding every rake of his body into hers.

"Harder." She wanted more of him. More of this.

He gripped the headboard above her, fingers wrapping tight around the rails as his body flexed, muscles straining as he pushed into her, filling her completely before stealing it away.

With each thrust he ground into her, his pelvis rubbing her clit with a sort of friction she didn't know was possible.

It was too much.

The sight of his body as he worked. The feel of it as he moved.

There was no denying what he was capable of. No denying what she'd agree to because of it.

She'd give him anything he wanted.

Anytime he wanted it.

Babies. Marriage. All the houses he could find for her to decorate.

She'd do it all.

"Brooks." It was the only name she could remember. The only name that mattered.

She grabbed him, fingers digging into the thick muscles of his ass as he fucked her exactly how she'd asked him to.

Taking her down in the process.

But he went down with her.

Together.

Even in this moment, she wasn't alone, holding him as he held her, bodies taking as much as they gave.

Until there was no more to be had.

But still so much to be found.

CHAPTER TWENTY

BROOKS REACHED ACROSS the mattress, looking for the warm body that should be tucked close to his. His hand hit nothing but warm sheet.

He sat up, blinking away the sleep he usually fought this early in the day.

Light filtered in from the main part of the house, pulling him from the blankets. Easily luring him away from a few more minutes of rest.

Nora stood in the kitchen wearing the same pair of boxers he'd given her the night he brought her back from Cross Creek Ranch, and the sweatshirt his mother put her in the night before.

She leaned over the griddle, twisting the dial around, frowning at it as she moved it back and forth.

"Morning."

Nora jumped a little, swinging around to face him. "Don't sneak up on me like that."

"Wasn't sneaking." He went to the coffee pot she'd already managed to get running. "You were just distracted."

"I don't know how to use this thing." Nora went back to the knob as he poured out a couple cups from the freshly-brewed pot.

"What are you making?"

She sucked in a breath. "Well, I was thinking I could manage sausage and eggs." She picked up the English muffins from the counter. "To make sandwiches."

"I'm sure you can manage it." He leaned in close, stealing his first kiss of the day. "How'd you sleep?"

He knew how she slept. Like a rock.

A rock that snored.

"Good, I think." She tucked a chunk of dark hair behind one ear as she went back to the griddle.

"Then why are you up so early?" He relaxed against the counter, sticking close.

"I wanted to make breakfast for you." She peeled back the plastic on the tray of preformed sausage patties and wiggled a spatula under one, dropping it on the griddle. She smiled at the immediate sizzle. "I think I got it hot enough."

She looked so damn proud he couldn't help but smile. "Told you."

Nora grinned his way as she added two more patties. "Maybe tomorrow I'll try French toast."

"I'll eat anything you make me, Buttercup." Brooks drank down some of his coffee as she pulled out the eggs and cheese from the little fridge. "You'll have a whole kitchen to work in soon."

"I'm not sure that will improve the outcome any." Her eyes focused as she tapped an egg against the counter. "Pretty sure it has nothing to do with location or equipment."

"It just takes practice."

The tip of her tongue poked out the corner of her mouth as she carefully split the egg over the griddle. "Was your mom always a good cook?"

"To hear my dad tell it, she left a lot to be desired at first." From what he knew, his mother made the most random things at the beginning, combining foods that had no business being together.

And his dad ate all of it, probably even with a smile on his face.

Nora frowned, all her focus on the eggs as they tried to spread across the griddle. "I'll ask your mom."

Brooks pulled out one of the muffins and split it in half before dropping it into the toaster. "What are you doing today?"

Nora scooted one egg around. "I'm not entirely sure."

"You could always go into town. Check in with Mae."

"Maybe." She flipped an egg, smiling wide when it made it through the process intact. "I think I'm going to be good at this."

Brooks leaned in, pressing a kiss to her head. "I think you are good at everything you want to do." He set down his empty cup. "I'm going to go hit the shower."

He left her watching the food with a sharp eye. By the time he was finished with a quick clean up and dressed for the day Nora was stacking the sausage and eggs on toasted muffins. She shoved a paper plate with two sandwiches his way. "I did it."

"I knew you could." He took the plate and another kiss.

He didn't expect her to do this for him. Didn't necessarily need a woman who ran the kitchen and the house.

But he appreciated her effort. Especially since it was for him.

Nora plopped down on the couch beside him with her own breakfast.

Brooks snagged her legs and draped them across his lap. "You comin' to the house for dinner or am I coming home?"

Nora watched him for a minute, dark eyes making it clear she had something she wanted to say.

"I was thinking maybe we could go out for dinner."

"You got a place in mind?"

She set her sandwich down and rubbed her lips together. "Mae told me about a place in Billings."

"I'll take you anywhere you want to go." Whatever made her happy that's what he'd do. Not because he thought it was what would make her stay.

He just liked seeing her happy.

"Maybe we could find a dress for me to wear to Brody and Clara's wedding while we're out?"

It was a short jump for his mind to go from a dress for Brody's wedding to Nora finding a dress for another wedding.

One he was much more invested in.

"Buttercup," Brooks snagged her plate away, dropping it on the coffee table as he took her down to the cushions, "we can find as many dresses as you want." He nosed along her neck. "You might want to grab one for Boone and Mae's wedding while you're there. I've got a feeling it's coming sooner rather than later."

Her eyes went wide. "You think?"

He was positive. His brother wasn't risking losing Mae twice. Boone would have her locked down as soon as possible.

He understood the feeling.

Nora smiled a little. "So dinner and dresses?"

Brooks nodded. "Dinner and dresses."

****

HE WASN'T EXPECTING so many damn dresses.

Or expecting to be part of the selection process.

Nora stood in front of him, wearing the tenth dress that he would spend an entire night imagining on the floor. "What do you think?"

"I think you're too good lookin' for this to be a simple process."

Her smile was small but her whole face lit up.

He was learning Nora liked hearing all the things he thought about her.

Liked hearing his appreciation for what she did.

What she was.

And he was more than happy to appreciate what she was.

"This one looks better up top." The neckline was a little lower than the last few and it would torture him in a way he couldn't wait to bear. "And you look good in blue."

She looked good in everything, but he wasn't going to mention that right now.

Nora smoothed her hands down the pale blue fabric hugging the soft swell of her hips. "It's not too much?"

"I mean," his eyes moved down the body that would soon be under his, "it's plenty."

She huffed out a breath. "I wasn't expecting you to be so unhelpfully helpful."

"I do my best." He'd liked almost every dress she put on with the exception of one that looked like someone just cut a hole in a purple bag.

Nora even looked decent in that one.

But she didn't smile the same when she came out in it.

The woman helping them wandered over with two more dresses for Nora to add to her stack. "I found these and I thought they would look perfect on you." She passed them Nora's way. "Yellow will look so good with your skin tone."

Nora took the dresses and disappeared back into the dressing room. The woman who worked at the store turned to him. "You are the most helpful husband I've ever seen in here."

He didn't correct her assumption. "I try."

"You do a good job." She gave him a quick smile before rushing off to help another customer.

"Ready for the next one?" Nora's voice carried out from behind the door.

"I'm always ready, Buttercup." He leaned back in the chair he'd occupied for the better part of forty minutes.

Nora peeked out. "I might need a little help."

Brooks pushed up from the upholstered seat, going straight for where the door was barely open.

Nora turned her back to him, sweeping her hair to one side, revealing a partially zipped zipper. "I can't reach to get it the rest of the way up."

Brooks moved in close, blocking the gap in the door with his body as he slowly raked the zipper up. "Does this mean you'll need my help to get it off too?"

"Probably."

He leaned down close to her ear. "Then this one is my favorite."

But it wasn't just the fact that he would be the one lucky enough to get to help her out of it that made this one his favorite. The clerk was right.

Yellow was Nora's color.

It was bright and warm and vibrant.

Just like she was.

"Stop distracting me." Nora wiggled away from him. "We still have to eat dinner, cowboy."

"We might have to take it to go after seeing you in this dress."

Nora poked one finger into the center of his chest as he tried to come into the dressing room with her. "You keep your ass out there." She peeked around him. "That poor woman will think we're doing something terrible."

"It would be anything but terrible, Buttercup." His eyes drifted down the front of the dress the exact color of the flowers that would forever be hers. "And she thinks I'm your husband so it wouldn't even be a sin."

"You're a sin." She shoved at his chest. "Go sit down while I get dressed."

Brooks let her back him out of the room, grinning as she slammed the door shut in his face.

"Does she like the yellow one?" The clerk was back at his side.

"Loves it." Brooks glanced out the front opening leading to the indoor mall. He passed his credit card to the store employee. "Put whatever she wants on this." He walked toward the exit, snagging a sweater the same shade as the dress Nora tried on. "And this too." He wandered out into the open area, pretending he didn't know exactly where he was planning to go.

Pretending he was just killing time.

But right now killing time was the last thing he wanted to do.

Time suddenly felt limiting.

Confining.

He crossed his arms, walking past the display window of the store across from the dress shop.

Front and center was what he was looking for.

Exactly.

Brooks glanced back into the clothing shop, catching sight of Nora as she chatted with the clerk as she continued to browse.

He turned back toward the window.

He'd always taken his time. Put his faith in patience.

Been content to wait.

Not so much anymore.

He took another look at where Nora stood, sweet and smart and everything he never knew he wanted.

She was it. Every bit.

And it was time to quit being patient.

****

"THANK YOU FOR letting me pay for dinner." Nora walked into the house, setting her purse and the bag holding the sweater he picked on the coffee table as he followed behind with two yellow dresses covered in protective plastic.

He'd wanted to argue with her, but had plans that would make it a pointless waste of time.

Brooks carried the dresses to the bedroom closet and hung them on the rail. Nora followed him into the room, yawning.

He turned to face her. "I want you to marry me."

She froze.

Didn't move.

Didn't blink.

Didn't even breathe.

Just stared at him.

He knew this would be a surprise.

Knew she wouldn't see it coming.

But that didn't make the time less right.

He waited for her to respond.

Blink.

Breathe.

Something.

"Buttercup?"

Her mouth dropped open, hanging for a second. "I—" She shook her head. "I'm sorry. I think I just had some sort of episode."

Brooks took a step toward her, reaching into his pocket to fish out the velvet bag he'd taken in place of a box. He pulled the tiny drawstrings open and tipped what was inside out into his palm.

Her eyes widened as they landed on the ring.

He pinched the yellow diamond between his finger and thumb and held it up between them. "This is yours, Buttercup. Whenever you're ready for it."

Her eyes stayed glued to the ring as he moved closer. "You don't have to take it now, but you said you deserved to know what I want." He stopped. "So I'm tellin' you."

Her brown eyes lifted to his, holding a second before dropping back to the ring. "I don't know what to say."

"You don't have to say anything until you're ready to." Brooks dropped the ring back in the bag, pulling it closed before tucking it back into his pocket. "But I'll be askin' every day until then."

CHAPTER TWENTY-ONE

"HE'S ASKED YOU every night?" Liza shook her head from across the table. "I'm not sure I'd still have an empty finger."

"Do you want to marry him?" Mae sat next to Liza, eating French fries from her best friend's plate.

Nora sighed. "I don't know." It was the easiest answer. It sounded way better than the truth.

Which was that she hadn't thought about it.

She'd successfully avoided actually considering Brooks' proposal for over a week.

Managed to shut her brain down each time it tried to creep anywhere near that possibility.

Who married a man they'd been with for less than two weeks?

Crazy people.

"Be careful." Clara picked through the plate of nachos they were sharing at the pizza place that served as one of the handful of eateries in Moss Creek. "Next he'll be trying to sweet talk you into babies."

"They don't always go in that order." Mae sipped at her drink. "Boone doesn't care what order it happens in.

He just keeps throwing it at me hoping something will stick."

"Pretty soon you're going to have a house built and ready to move into." Clara shook her head. "Then he's really going to be ready."

"Has he actually proposed?" Nora couldn't help but feel hopeful that she wasn't the only one facing this situation.

"Not with a ring." Mae's eyes moved to hers. "Does Brooks actually have a ring?"

Nora pursed her lips, not wanting to admit the truth.

Mae's eyes went wide. "Holy shit."

Liza snapped forward, leaning closer. "What does it look like?"

It was perfect. "I haven't looked at it closely."

She had. Every damn time.

Liza fell back, hands covering her face. "You are killing me, Levitt."

"I just..." Nora blew out a breath, closing her eyes. "I can't think about it right now."

A wadded-up paper straw wrapper bounced off the center of her forehead.

She opened her eyes right as Liza stole Mae's discarded wrapper and launched it her way. "Stop ignoring."

Nora pressed her lips together.

Liza pointed one finger her way. "I remember what you told me, Levitt."

Damn sloe gin.

Clara and Mae's eyes came her way.

"I just can't deal with it right now." Nora dropped her head to her hands. There was too much going on. She was overwhelmed and doing her best to pretend certain things didn't exist.

Primarily ex boyfriends and their wench mothers.

"You missed out on a whole month of boning Brooks Pace because you refused to acknowledge that you didn't hate this place." Liza crossed her arms. "And I bet you're regretting that now."

Making her own friends seemed like a good idea.

Not so much now that they were staring her down.

Clara's eyes barely narrowed. "What's going on?"

Her next sigh was more of a groan.

Mae cringed. "That bad?"

"I used to work for my ex's mother." She'd never opened up to other women like this.

Never felt safe enough.

"When I caught her son in bed with another woman she fired me."

Every woman at the table gasped at the same time.

Liza was the first to speak. "That bitch."

"She's the reason I wanted to go back to Seattle. I wanted to prove that I was fine without her and her crappy son." Nora picked up one of the paper strips Liza tossed her way, and started smoothing it out. "I wanted to prove what I had wasn't just because of her."

She'd worked so hard. Busted her ass. Done things no one else would do. Taken jobs no one else would take.

Thinking at some point Esmerelda would see her as more than just someone standing between her and her son's grossly close relationship.

Liza's lip curled, lifting one side of her nose. "Who cares what that heifer thinks?"

"She's not a heifer. She's actually very glamorous." Esmerelda was attractive in the coldest way possible. "Like Cruella DeVille but without the puppies."

Mae snorted. "Sounds like she's got at least one puppy that follows her around."

Clara leaned into Nora's side, wrapping one arm around her shoulders. "I'm so sorry."

She could end the story there. Wrap up the intro into her recent past.

But it wasn't the part of the story that was keeping her from taking the ring that stared her down every night and putting it on her finger. "That's not even the worst part."

Mae's brows went up. "It gets worse than being cheated on and fired at the same time?"

Actually it did.

Because honestly the worst part of the cheating was the doctor's appointment afterwards.

And being fired from a job that was killing her? Not really awful in hindsight.

"She wants half my earnings from The Inn. She's trying to say I was technically still an employee of her company when I took the job."

That was the real slap in the face. That Esmerelda had taken everything and still wanted more.

Just to prove she could get it.

Mae's mouth dropped open. "You're not going to give it to her, are you?"

She didn't want to.

She also didn't want to deal with *not* doing it. "Maybe it would just be easier to do it and be done with her."

The pull to put it behind her and never look back was strong. Just as strong as her commitment to going back to Seattle used to be, but now that she'd finally given in to Moss Creek it was all she wanted.

Liza shook her head. "No way. Don't give in."

Clara was the only one not reacting to the information. She sat quietly at Nora's side, head tipped as she looked Nora's way. "I say give it to her."

"What? Why?" Mae was clearly flabbergasted by the suggestion.

"Because some things aren't worth fighting for." Clara lifted one shoulder and let it drop. "But some things are."

Her eyes came back to Nora. "Give her the money back and then take the damn ring like you want to."

Something inside settled.

The squeeze in her chest relaxed.

Nora turned to Clara. "It's not crazy?"

Clara smiled. "Who cares if it is?"

"The answer is none of us." Mae stood up. "We're all just as crazy as you are."

The waitress brought a bag containing four foam containers that held one lunch and two desserts, passing them off to Mae.

"You think we'll ever convince Camille to start having lunch with us?" Clara packed their leftovers into another box before snapping the lid into place.

"I hope so." Mae scooted her chair in. "Eventually she'll figure out we're just going to keep showing up with food and that it will be easier to just go with us."

Nora lifted her purse off the back of her chair, looping it over her shoulders as they walked through the restaurant. She understood Camille's hesitancy. "It's hard to adjust to a new life."

Clara nodded. "For sure."

They were all parked in the side lot. Everyone piled into their respective cars and headed to the ranch, taking Camille the lunch she'd refused to leave work for.

It was something Nora was familiar with. The need to prove you earned what you had.

To prove you were deserving.

But Camille needed to know she wasn't alone.

Hopefully it would help. Based on personal experience Nora was pretty confident it would.

She parked at The Inn, lining up next to Liza's truck, falling in step with the group as they walked toward the porch.

She and her friends.

Going into the place she designed. A job she found all by herself in spite of what some people tried to claim.

In the town she decided to make her own.

Most of the visitors were out for the day. Riding horses and exploring the mountains in the distance. A few lounged around the pool.

Nora, Clara, Mae, and Liza went straight to the open kitchen where Camille almost always was.

But this time Camille wasn't alone.

Maryann stood next to her, smiling wide as she chatted with another woman.

A woman Nora knew well.

Maryann's eyes lit up when she saw them. "Girls." She came straight for Nora, wrapping one arm around her shoulders as she turned to face Esmerelda Remington. "This is the designer I've been raving about." She squeezed Nora closer. "She is working with my son now on a house he's renovating."

The pride in Maryann's voice was clear.

But it wasn't loud enough to make it past the ringing in Nora's ears.

The disbelief tunneling her vision. Pinpointing it on the woman who tried to ruin her life as punishment for daring to think she was good enough for her son.

"Nora, this is Esmerelda Remington. She owns a design firm and saw our feature in Rustic Design and wanted to come see the place for herself." Maryann held her tight enough to keep her from falling over in shock.

But Maryann wasn't the only woman close at her side.

Liza stood on her left, standing tall and intimidating in a way Nora had never noticed before. "Where is your design firm located, Esmerelda?"

Esmerelda's lips spread in a slow smile. "Are you looking for a decorator?"

Liza's smile was just as slow and ten times scarier. "Something like that."

"I would think if Nora was so talented you would be happy to use her." Esmerelda was clearly loving the thought that these people were dissatisfied with what she'd done.

"I would think you'd be happy to tell us where you're located." Mae didn't hide the snark in her tone.

And Maryann didn't miss it.

Her hands gripped Nora tighter as she pulled her closer. "Esmerelda's company is in..." Maryann's voice made it impossible to know if she fully realized what was going on. "I know you told me and I'm so sorry, but I seem to have forgotten."

Esmerelda's nostrils flared the tiniest bit.

No doubt she'd added something besides money to the list of things she hoped to gain in her trip to Moss Creek.

"Seattle."

Maryann's smile held. "That's right." She turned to Nora. "Isn't that where you used to live, Nora?"

"Used to live?" Esmerelda's icy gaze fixed on Nora. "You moved?"

Clara edged in at Mae's side, forming a full line of women staring Esmerelda down. Even Camille edged away from the woman who'd done everything in her power to keep Nora where she was.

Hiding.

Stunted.

Alone.

Liza crossed her arms. "Cut the shit, Esmerelda."

"We know who you are." Mae looked down her nose at the woman who designed homes that most people would consider palaces.

The woman who had connections and wealth most people would kill for.

None of that mattered to the women at Nora's side.

"And we know what you're trying to do." Clara put her arm across Mae's chest as she tried to step toward the glass jar of kitchen utensils sitting on the counter.

Esmerelda didn't react at all to the revelation that her identity was a known one. "Ms. Levitt's contract with Remington Designery clearly states that we are entitled to half the fee charged for any jobs secured outside our direct pipeline."

"You'd already fired me when I found this job."

"Impossible." Esmerelda smirked. "Your date of termination is listed as less than a month ago."

"You packed my things up and set them outside the office doors over three months ago." She'd spent a month fighting for what few belongings she had and moving them into a storage unit. Then it was four more weeks before Maryann reached out to her after finding her resume on a freelance design website. "There was no overlap."

Esmerelda's smile was slick and snide. "Prove it."

"She doesn't have to prove it." Maryann's tone was short and sharp. "Because our agreement didn't involve payment of actual money." Maryann's smile matched Esmerelda's.

That of a woman who knows she has the upper hand.

"I had magazine features lined up. Nora agreed to take the job as a way to gain exposure."

Esmerelda scoffed. "I don't believe that for a second." She tipped her chin higher. "You paid her for her services."

Maryann's smile turned sweet enough to rot a tooth. "Prove it."

CHAPTER TWENTY-TWO

"THAT WAS A pain in the ass." Brody rode up to Brooks' side, slowing his horse to match Shadow's pace.

"It definitely wasn't as smooth as I was hopin' it would be." They'd just finished moving a herd to a new pasture. A task they'd accomplished a thousand times before.

But today everything seemed more difficult than normal.

"Maybe it's a full moon." Brody eyed him. "You doin' okay?"

"I'll be sore tomorrow." He'd taken a few hits trying to wrestle a cow loose from a section of fence. "I don't know what in the hell spooked her."

Whatever it was, the animal was scared even before she got tied up in the barbed wire. Once it had her she started fighting and didn't stop until he managed to work her free.

"Who knows what it was." Brody glanced up as Brett came riding their way, moving faster across the spotty grass than the situation required. "What's wrong with him now?"

"Probably the same thing that's always wrong with him."

Brett was the youngest brother, but he'd been ready to get married and have kids since he graduated high school. Unfortunately for him, the woman he wanted was fresh out of a bad marriage and had no intention of finding her way back into another.

Brooks tipped his head back as Brett closed in, coming to a quick stop in front of them. "What's wrong?"

"Just got word something's going on at The Inn." Brett's words were choppy and a little breathless.

"Go on back then. We're done here anyway." Brody squinted toward the late afternoon sun. "We'll handle whatever else needs done out here."

Brett's horse shifted on its feet, ready to keep moving. "Sounds like I'm not the only one who should be headin' in." His eyes went to Brody before landing on Brooks.

"Nora?"

Brett's mouth flattened to a thin line as he shook his head. "It's all of 'em."

Brody pulled his hat off and raked one hand through his hair before settling it back into place. "Shit." He whistled between his teeth toward where Boone was latching the gate on the new pasture.

Their brother immediately turned.

Brody used his whole arm to beckon him their way. "We're goin'!"

Boone immediately ran to where his horse waited, mounting up before racing to catch up with them as they rode toward The Inn.

It was one more thing they'd done countless times in their lives.

Gone to handle what needed handling.

There were never any questions asked. Never any hesitation involved.

But lately they'd been showing up late to the game. Finding out the hard way they weren't the only Paces people should think twice before fucking with.

There were plenty of cars parked at The Inn when they rode up. A few of them familiar enough to confirm Brooks' suspicions.

Nora's car was right next to Liza Cross's truck. Next to that was Mae's SUV and the new hybrid Clara drove.

It looked like they were late to the party again.

Brooks was off Shadow in a flash and running toward the door with his brothers right behind him. They hit the entrance louder than the herd of cattle they'd just moved.

His boots skidded on the hardwood as he came face to face with a line of women who looked ready to earn themselves a visit with Officer Grady Haynes.

And his mother was leading the pack. "If you think for one second you can come to my ranch and call me a liar then you are sorely mistaken."

Brooks edged in, trying to get a look at whoever his mother was staring down with the most deadly glare he'd ever seen.

The woman staring his mother down was definitely not from Moss Creek. Her skin looked plastic. Her hair was flattened within an inch of its life, sitting stick straight against the sides of her painted-on face.

But it was the expression she wore that almost made him take a step back.

It was cold and calculating. Devoid of any emotion that might make her look human.

Maybe this was what spooked the cow.

"I never called you a liar, Ms. Pace." The woman's lips barely moved when she spoke, and the pitch of her brows held their slashed-on position. "I simply asked for proof that you hadn't paid Ms. Levitt."

"You know she can't prove that." Liza was tight to Nora's side, glaring down the woman with spiky brows and stretched skin.

The woman lifted one shoulder. "Then she will simply have to pay me half the fee my company would charge for a job of this magnitude."

Brooks took a step closer. This could only be one woman.

And Nora wasn't giving her a dime.

"I'm not giving you anything, Esmerelda." Nora's voice was solid and strong.

Esmerelda looked as surprised as her frozen face could manage. "Do you think we're on a first name basis now, Ms. Levitt?"

He could see the instant the comment hit Nora. The way it threatened to take her down.

Brooks started toward her side, intending to make it clear as hell that Nora wasn't giving up a dime of the money she'd earned all on her own.

But any chance he had of getting close to Nora was cut off as his mother and Liza moved in tighter, arms around Nora as they offered her the support he wanted to give.

"I think we're on whatever basis I want us to be on." Nora stood a little taller, her spine straightening more and more with each passing second. "I owe you nothing. You will get nothing else from me."

Esmerelda smirked. "Nothing I took ever belonged to you, Nora. Not the job. Not the car. Not the man."

"You're right." Nora's head barely tipped. "None of it was mine." Her voice lowered. "But this is, and I will fight you for it."

Esmerelda's cool gaze moved around, slowly sweeping the space before landing on him. "This is the kind of place you belong." Her eyes dragged down his front, disdain curling her lip. "It's filthy."

Figuring out who lunged first was impossible. It was between Nora and his mother.

And the look on Esmerelda's face was priceless. Turned out that face could move at least a little under the right circumstances.

Luckily Liza and the rest of the girls were fast enough to grab both women before they could get their hands on the woman backing away as fast as she possibly could.

Esmerelda rushed around the large island and made for the door, the high heels of her shoes clicking like gunshots as she practically ran away. "You'll be hearing from my attorney, Ms. Levitt."

Mae held tight to his mother, managing to keep Maryann from making it to the open door before Esmerelda tore down the driveway in a sleek two-door.

His mother stood on the porch, her middle finger held high in the air until Esmerelda's retreating vehicle was out of sight, the only hint of her visit the cloud of dust she left in her wake.

Maryann spun around to face the group behind her, hands going to her hips. "Damn it, Mae. I could have taken her."

Mae held up her hands. "I don't know what happened. Usually I'm the one being held back."

"It's easier to stop someone else than it is to stop yourself." Liza stared down the driveway, but her eyes were far away. Like they were looking at a different place.

Maybe a different time.

"You think she's really going to take you to court?" Clara stood at Nora's side in the doorway, frowning out at the haze of dusty air.

Nora nodded. "Definitely."

Mae crossed her arms, her expression a cross between a frown and a scowl. "What a bitch."

"The biggest one I've ever met." Nora turned in the doorway, her dark eyes sweeping The Inn's entryway like she was looking for something.

They stopped when they landed on where he stood at the end of the main hall.

"You okay, Buttercup?"

Her nostrils flared and her eyes narrowed. "She called you filthy."

He almost smiled at the confirmation that the insult was the reason she finally tried to take Esmerelda down. "She's not wrong."

"Ew." Mae shook her head. "No one wants to hear that."

Nora's lips lifted a little. "You are kind of dirty."

Brooks smacked at the dirt clinging to the front of his jeans. "I had to fight a heifer that ended up somewhere she shouldn't be."

Nora's smile peeked out a little more. "I tried to do the same thing, but she got away."

His mother snorted out a bark of laughter. "You'll still get to fight her, Honey. Don't worry."

Nora's smile bloomed, wide and real as she stood in the middle of her friends.

Her family.

The people who would make sure she never spent another day alone.

Her eyes held his. "I'm ready."

She didn't have to tell him twice.

If this was what she wanted.

Where she wanted it.

Then that was what he wanted too.

Brooks dug into his pocket, fishing out the velvet bag that went into it every morning and came out every night when he offered her what was inside.

The ring made its last trip out of the bag as he dropped to one knee on the floor of The Inn's main hall, watched by all the people that mattered to him.

All the people who helped him convince the woman he loved to stay with them.

He held out the ring. "Marry me."

Nora nodded, her head bobbing faster as she raced his way, lunging at him right as he made it to his feet, almost managing to take them both down in the process.

He caught her, using the momentum to spin her around as she held onto his neck.

Loud applause echoed around them, but none of it came from their family or friends.

A group of visitors had made their way in from outside and were standing with them, faces bright, smiles wide.

One of them even had their phone out, recording the whole thing.

Nora grabbed his face, planting her lips on his as everyone cheered.

Maybe that was his mistake. Thinking Nora would want him to do this in private.

Alone.

He should have known better.

He should have known this would be what she wanted. What she needed.

He set her down on her feet, taking another kiss before working the yellow diamond down her finger.

Or not.

"Damn it."

Nora lifted her hand up and started to laugh, completely unbothered that the ring he thought was perfect wasn't quite. The gold band was stuck halfway down, wedged on her finger like a too-tight belt.

"I love it." She beamed at him.

"It doesn't fit." He was more than a little disappointed.

"It will." She worked the ring off, twisting back and forth. "Just because it doesn't fit now doesn't mean it never will." She held it up between them. "She just needs a little adjustment."

CHAPTER TWENTY-THREE

"YOU'VE GOT THIS." Brooks squeezed her hand with his.

"I know." Nora forced in a deep breath as she stared at the sleek office building in front of them. "I just really don't want to see her face."

"No one does, Buttercup." His mouth turned to a pondering frown. "Maybe her plastic surgeon."

Any other time she might have laughed, but right now all she wanted to do was throw up. "I thought it would be easier than this."

"Doesn't have to be easy." He took the first step leading to the location of her meeting with Esmerelda and their attorneys. "It's just got to be done." He gently pulled on her hand. "And you're ready for this."

Ready might be a stretch.

She was just as ready as she was going to get.

"She's awful."

"That's why it's time for us to be done with her." Brooks kept moving up the steps, leading her along. "We've got too much else going on to keep wasting our time dealing with her bullshit."

He wasn't wrong.

Clara and Brody's wedding was in two days.

They'd just started the heavy demo on the little house Brooks bought from Camille.

And Brooks' realtor friend found another property he thought they might be interested in renovating.

Any energy that went to Esmerelda, robbed it from something important.

And it was time for that to stop.

Nora held tight to Brooks' hand as she climbed the steps, each one taking her a tiny bit closer to throwing up, but also closer to the end of a chapter she couldn't wait to finish.

The office they were headed to was on the third floor, giving her heart plenty of time to start the marathon it clearly intended to run.

They stepped into the elevator and Brooks pulled her close, one hand cradling the back of her head as he leaned into her ear. "We've got this, Buttercup."

Nora started to relax a little.

But someone else stepped into the space.

She didn't need to see to know who it was.

She could smell him.

The cologne was one she used to love, but now it made her want to gag.

Brooks' eyes moved over her face, the line of his hat shielding her from whoever stood just behind him.

His whole demeanor shifted in an instant, taking him from soft and caring to something she'd never really seen before.

But had heard plenty of stories about.

His arm banded tight around her back as he straightened away from her, keeping her tucked tight to his side, still blocked from being able to see Dean where he stood on Brooks' other side.

Brooks didn't fully turn to face Dean, just tipped his head in that direction. It was impossible to see his expression, but she could feel the tension radiating off his body.

And she definitely wasn't the only one.

The second the doors opened Dean was out of the elevator, fast-walking in the direction of the same office they were headed for. He turned as he got near the door, looking back at Brooks with a hint of panic in his eyes.

He didn't even seem to notice Nora, instead quickly turning away to push his way into the office.

Brooks slowly smiled. "This should be interesting."

Seeing Esmerelda made her want to barf, but watching Dean run from Brooks took the edge off a little.

Brooks pushed open the door to the office, holding it wide as Nora went in first.

The waiting room was already empty. No sign of Dean or his panicked expression anywhere.

She went to the frosted window, waiting as it slid open. The woman on the other side gave her a wide smile. "Do you have an appointment?"

"I'm Nora Levitt."

The woman's smile froze on her face. "I'll let them know you're here." She glanced to one side before leaning forward. "Can I get you anything to drink?"

Nora shook her head. "I'm okay, thank you."

The woman glanced in the same direction she had a second before. "You sure? I've got some whiskey I can sneak into it."

"It's tempting."

The woman's eyes went wide. "I can imagine."

Looked like Esmerelda was already making friends. "I think I'm okay." Nora accomplished a genuine smile. "I might take you up on it when we're done, though."

"Deal." The woman suddenly straightened. "They'll be out for you in a minute, Ms. Levitt."

"Thank you." Nora turned as the window slid back into place.

Brooks reached out to snag the tie on the yellow dress she wore, using it to pull her closer. "Have I told you how much I like this dress?"

"Only four or five hundred times." She smoothed down the ruffles framing the deep V of the wrap dress's neckline. "But you could tell me again."

His lips lifted in a slow smile that made her insides heat in spite of the situation. "I love this dress."

"Ms. Levitt?"

Brooks' eyes lifted over her head toward the voice behind her.

Nora took a deep breath before spinning to face the older, trim man with a thick mustache and kind eyes. He reached a hand toward her. "I'm Albert Levy."

She immediately relaxed, taking his hand for a firm shake. "It's so nice to finally meet you face-to-face."

It turned out Maryann was still on friendly terms with the attorney she took to the rodeo the night she met Bill, and he was happy to refer her to a colleague licensed in Washington.

Albert's warm gaze turned to the man at her side. "You must be Brooks." He shook Brooks' hand. "Thanks for coming over." He stepped a little deeper into the room. "I don't expect this to take long, but it will be easier and cheaper to just shut this down right now, outside of court."

"Okay." Nora tried to inhale as slowly as possible, hoping the race of her heart would follow suit.

"You don't have to say a thing." Albert's voice was calm and his demeanor was relaxed. "If I need any information I will ask you myself. Remember not to answer any questions I don't ask you."

They'd been over this more than a few times on the phone. Albert was familiar with Esmerelda's attorney, and apparently they guy had a reputation for twisting people around until they didn't know which way was up.

Luckily, the best way to deal with it was exactly what she wanted to do anyway.

Keep her mouth shut.

Albert lifted his brows. "Ready?"

"I'm ready." It was a lie. She would never be ready for something like this.

And that was okay.

The important thing was that she was doing it anyway.

Brooks' hand spread across her back, the heat sinking into her skin as they followed Albert down the hall. The last door was open and Esmerelda's voice carried out into the hall.

"I don't care what she says. She worked for us at the time the contract was signed. Half that money belongs to me. Get it."

Nice to hear she talked to everyone the same way. Even the attorney she expected to work miracles.

Because, according to Albert, that's what it would take for Esmerelda to win this. A miracle.

Albert went in first and the room immediately fell silent. He went directly to a set of three chairs and pulled the middle one out. "Here you are, Ms. Levitt."

Nora smoothed down the back of her dress as she sat. "Thank you."

Albert took the seat on her left as Brooks sat to her right in the chair across from Dean.

Albert set his briefcase on the table, flipping the clasps before lifting the top. "I understand your client believes she is entitled to earnings Ms. Levitt has received."

"It's not a belief. It's a fact." The opposing attorney stared over the table from his spot across from her. "Ms. Levitt is withholding funds that contractually belong to my client." He pulled a copy of the contract Nora signed when she went to work for Esmerelda from the file in front of him and slid it across the table. "It is clearly stated in the contract Ms. Levitt signed that any work obtained while employed by Remington Designery was subject to the terms of her compensatory agreement."

"We are not debating the fact that Ms. Levitt was bound by those terms while she was employed by Remington Designery." Albert pulled out a file of his own, this one at least twice the size of the one Esmerelda's attorney had. "What we do disagree with is the date her employment was terminated."

"You can disagree all you want. The facts are that Ms. Levitt was employed by my client well after she began work on the account in question."

"I don't believe you and I have the same opinion of what determines the factuality of a statement." Albert flipped open the file. "For me, labeling something as factual requires a certain amount of proof."

"Do you agree with that, Ms. Levitt? Is proof required for something to be deemed factual?" The other attorney stared at her, waiting for an answer.

One she wasn't going to give him.

Albert went on without pausing. "Ms. Levitt's opinion is irrelevant here. What matters is the law." Albert sent his first bit of evidence across the table. "And the law will require you to prove your accusation. Which you cannot do."

The other attorney didn't even look at the paper. "I have more than enough evidence that Ms. Levitt was on the payroll until very recently."

"Fraud isn't something I would be willing to commit over a case that honestly belongs in small claims court." Albert sent over another paper, this one containing the email Esmerelda sent telling Nora to get her 'trash' out of the offices of Remington Designery. "I can keep going like this all day if you want." Next came text messages from Esmerelda, detailing what a mistake it had been to employ her and how she couldn't believe it had taken her so long to fire her. "But," Albert sent the most damning piece of evidence across the table, "considering I have video evidence of Ms. Levitt's belongings being left in a box outside the offices of Remington Designery weeks before her first contact with the client in Montana, I would say you should cut your losses."

The other attorney's eyes finally dropped to the line of papers in front of him, scanning each one as he turned toward Esmerelda.

"This is bullshit." Esmerelda stood. "I don't have time for this." She smacked Dean's shoulder as she passed. "This is your fault. You just had to have the little tramp come work for me."

Brooks was out of his seat in a second, knocking it down as he stood.

Albert was up almost as fast, rushing behind her to find his way in front of Brooks. It was clear he was positive things were about to get physical between Brooks and Dean.

He shouldn't have worried.

Dean might have moved faster than both Brooks and Albert put together, managing to get on his feet and halfway toward the door before Brooks could so much as breathe his direction, leaving his mother to fend for herself.

She smirked Brooks' direction. "You do look like the kind of man who would hit a lady."

"I'd never put my hands on a lady." Brooks' voice was deadly deep and his drawl was almost nonexistent. "But I'm happy to take out a snake when I see one."

Esmerelda's eyes widened and her mouth dropped open.

"Would you like me to show you out, Ms. Remington?" The woman from the front desk stood at the open door, her face perfectly straight.

But there was no hiding the amusement in her eyes.

"I'm fine." Esmerelda snarled at the pretty red-head as she stormed out of the room, slamming the door to the waiting area as she left.

Albert turned to Esmerelda's attorney. "I assume this matter is closed?"

The other man was busy collecting the papers Albert piled in front of him. "It appears that way."

"There's no *appearing* to it." Albert stood as tall as his five-foot-five frame would allow, but managed to seem like the biggest man in the room. "She has no case, and I won't allow her to waste any more of my or my client's time."

The attorney met Albert's gaze. "If there is another case filed, I won't be the one doing it."

"Good." Albert went to his briefcase and collected his file, stacking it in before closing the lid and turning to Nora and Brooks. "I will walk you out."

As soon as they were outside, Nora turned to Albert. "Do you think she'll just go get another attorney and try to sue me again?"

"I would hope not, but there was ample evidence she had no grounds to sue you in the first place, so who knows what she will try to do." Albert reached out to pat her shoulder. "If she does, we will handle it exactly like we did today. Eventually she will give up."

It wasn't the ending Nora was hoping for. The clean break she wanted.

But it was good enough.

Which meant it was time to put all of this where it belonged.

Behind her.

****

"YOU READY TO get the hell out of here?" Brooks was already switching the truck into drive.

"Absolutely." Every second they'd been here was one second too many.

How had she ever thought coming back to Seattle was the only option she had?

Who cared what anyone here thought of her?

Not her.

Not anymore.

They could think they won.

They could think she ran away.

They could think whatever they wanted.

It didn't matter.

Brooks reached for her as the truck and the trailer they hauled merged onto the highway that would take her back where she belonged.

To her home.

Her family.

He grabbed her hand and lifted it to his lips, brushing a kiss across her knuckles before letting their intertwined fingers rest on the console. His thumb worked the ring on her finger, idly moving the yellow diamond as they put more and more distance between her and the past she almost made her future.

"Will we be back by dinner?" They'd gotten up early and gone straight to the storage unit that held all her belongings, packing everything into the trailer they brought from Montana in less than two hours.

"I'm sure we'll make it in plenty of time."

His math seemed a little off. The drive was almost eleven hours, not counting stops for gas and bathroom breaks, and it was already after eight. No way would they be back before dinner.

The time she used to dread most.

Back when she was doing her best to pretend Moss Creek could never be her home and the people there could never be her family.

Nora stretched her legs out as much as possible and relaxed back in her seat, settling in for the long drive.

The long drive home.

They pulled into the driveway at Red Cedar Ranch at eight o'clock on the dot. Way past dinner, but still before the sun went down, so maybe she could sneak in and see Maryann before they went back to where their camper was parked beside the line of small cabins where the hands stayed.

As they pulled around the curve leading to the main house Nora sat up a little straighter in her seat, eyes glued to the porch.

A wide *Welcome Home* banner hung across the roofline and yellow balloons were tied to all the posts, drifting in the breeze easing across the pastures.

Her throat went tight at the sight of everyone lined down the porch. Maryann and Bill stood in the center, watching out at where history was repeating itself.

Just from a very different perspective.

"They waited for us." She couldn't stop the smile or the tears edging her eyes.

"No, Buttercup." Brooks parked the truck and turned to face her. "They waited for *you*."

EPILOGUE

“MAE, THIS IS so good.” Nora fell back in her seat, both hands resting against her stomach. “I probably should have bought this dress in a larger size.”

“Me too.” Clara grinned from her spot across from Mae as she scooped in another bite of wedding pie.

“That’s got nothing to do with my pie.” Mae wiggled her brows Clara’s way.

“I still think you’re crazy.” Liza tipped back the last of the champagne remaining in her flute. “One seems like too many, let alone five.”

Clara shook her head. “I only agreed to one more.”

“You know Brody will take that as a challenge.” Liza poured a little more bubbly into her glass. “He probably only makes twins.”

Clara’s eyes widened. “The odds of that happening are—”

“Still higher than I’d be willing to gamble.” Liza smiled. “But I’m sure as hell gonna love getting to play with yours.”

“No.” Clara pressed her lips together. “No. I’m sure that won’t happen.”

“Definitely not.” Mae snagged the bottle of champagne from Liza and filled her own glass to the top.

"That would be crazy." Clara turned to Nora. "Right? There's no way that could happen."

"Probably not." It was the best she could offer considering there was a family with two sets of twins in her neighborhood growing up. "But, if it does you won't be alone. You have a ton of people to help."

Clara frowned at them from her side of the table. "I'm going to tell the construction crew to accidentally build your houses closer to mine."

"Suckers." Liza laughed an evil sounding sort of laugh. "Can't make me live closer."

Clara pointed across the table. "You're watching the girls. I'm just gonna drop them off and drive away."

Liza grinned. "You sure you want me to influence them at such a young age?"

"Yes." Everyone at the table said it at the same time.

Michaela ran across the dance floor, blonde hair bouncing around as she raced Liza's way. "Auntie Liza, come dance with us!" She grabbed Liza with both hands and dragged her away.

"I think it's too late for her to worry about influencing them." Mae watched her best friend shimmy around with the twins. "They adore her."

"They should." Nora understood the twins' adoration. "She's awesome."

Mae leaned Nora's way. "She can be a little dense."

"I don't think that's the issue." It would be difficult to be a woman in charge of a herd of men. Even more so if certain lines were crossed.

"I know." Mae sighed. "Why does shit have to be so difficult sometimes?"

Nora watched as Brett worked his way to where Camille's son Calvin stood all by himself, watching the happy family celebrate around him. "I wish I knew." She pushed up from her seat. “I need to use the bathroom. I’ll be right back.”

The Inn was quiet when she went in. The weekend guests were all packed up and gone well before the Sunday evening wedding began.

Which meant there was no reason for Camille not to be out there with everyone else.

Nora moved through the open space of the main floor, checking the kitchen and each of the three half baths for any sign of her. All of it was spotless, which meant Camille had definitely been there.

She took her dedication to The Inn to an almost unhealthy level. One that probably helped distract her from the difficulties she’d recently faced.

But there might be another reason Camille spent every waking minute working, and it was time for that to end.

The upstairs of the large building was equally quiet, just the muffled sound of the music outside cutting the silence.

But the door to one of the rooms was open.

Nora made her way down the hall to peek inside.

Like she expected, Camille was stripping the bed, stacking the sheets into a rolling hamper.

“I don’t know if you realize this,” Nora smiled when Camille’s eyes jumped in her direction, “but there’s a party going on outside.”

Camille dropped the pillow cases on top of the pile in her hamper. “Do you guys need something? More ice? Should I bring out extra trash bags?”

“Uh,” Nora snagged the hamper and rolled it behind her, “no. You should come out with us.”

Camille smoothed one hand down the front of her sundress. “I don’t—”

Nora stepped closer to her friend. “It’s okay if it’s not what you want to do.” She smiled, hoping to soften what she was about to say. "I'm not here to pressure you into doing something you're not comfortable with." She'd been there and would never want to do it to Camille.

But Camille needed to know that the only reason not to be at that party was because she didn't want to be.

"You're one of us, Camille." A surprising amount of emotion threatened to clog her throat.

Dampen her eyes.

But Camille wouldn't understand the response wasn't pity. Sadness for all her friend had been through.

It was happiness for what they'd both found.

Hopefully Camille realized all she had to do was be brave enough to reach out and take it.

Camille cleared her throat, eyes dipping to the floor between them. "I just have a lot to do here."

"Do you need help?"

Camille's gaze lifted to hers, holding for a second.

Like she was surprised at the offer.

"No. I've got it." She barely smiled. "Thank you, though."

"Anytime." Nora grabbed the rolling cart. "I'll take this with me as I go." She pushed the hamper down the hall, sliding it into the laundry room as she passed on her way back downstairs.

Back outside to her family.

Brooks caught her just as she stepped out onto the patio surrounding the pool. "I've been looking for you." He slid one hand into hers. "Our song is on." He pulled her toward the dance floor.

"Our song?" She lifted a brow at him. "I didn't know we had one."

"You don't remember?" Brooks swung her around catching her as she spun into his chest. "It's the first song we danced to."

"I was busy trying not to trample you." Nora wrapped one arm around his neck as they fell into the same two-step pattern he'd taught her that night not so long ago. "Or fall on my ass."

"I would never let you fall, Buttercup."

Her chest went tight. "I know."

Brooks could spin her around, dance her through life.

And never once would she have to worry about falling.

****

"GET YOUR FOLDER and let's go."

Nora glared at him across the barn. "You're kidding."

"You've known me long enough to know I don't kid, Buttercup." Brooks led Shadow down the center aisle. "I've got shit to do."

She turned as he passed her, glare holding. "Last time you said that you didn't have anything to do. You just wanted to get me on the back of a horse."

"That was the shit I had to do." He shot her a grin as he walked out into the warm sun of the crisp fall day.

Nora stayed put a few seconds longer before letting out a long sigh and stomping her way after him. "If we lose something important out here it's your fault."

"Only important thing I got is you." He snagged the file from her hand. "And I don't plan on loosin' you." He tipped his head toward Shadow's back. "Get on up there."

She huffed out a breath, but didn't waste any time getting up in the saddle.

Nora could complain as much as she wanted, but she loved riding.

"Why am I riding Shadow?" She took the file as he passed it back to her.

"Because I've got a horse I need to ride." Brooks went back into the barn for the second horse they'd be taking out today.

This was why they needed to do this on horseback. They had someone in need of a real calm horse who could pretty much handle itself.

Brooks saddled up, settling down on the mare's back. She'd been on the ranch since she was born, but up until now had only had skilled riders on her back.

"Brett made me promise I'd get her out today so here we are." He resisted the urge to give the horse any direction at all.

"Where are we going?" Nora looked in the direction of the tree house.

"Anywhere you want."

He knew exactly where she'd go. It was the other reason she was showing him her plans for a house on horseback.

Again.

"You lead." Brooks crossed his arms, letting the reins lay slack. "Pumpernickel here is just gonna go wherever you go."

Nora gave him a little smile. One that said she'd finally figured out what was going on. "She's such a sweet horse."

"That's why we're doin' this." Brooks tipped his head Nora's way. "But you gotta get goin' or we're just gonna sit here all day."

She continued to smile as she gave Shadow the gentle nudge he needed to get going. Pumpernickel immediately fell in line, following behind the larger horse.

It wasn't a perfect ride. Without any direction the mare kept a little distance between them, which meant Nora couldn't show him any of her plans for their second project together.

A sweet little two-story Tanner found a few months back.

It was already bought and paid for, ready and waiting. They'd completed the work on Camille's old house the week before, and sold it before Nora could even finish staging it to be listed.

Word traveled fast, and one of the hands from Cross Creek was looking for a more permanent place than the bunk house at the ranch. He'd snapped it up within five minutes of walking in the place.

Which meant Nora spent the weekend finalizing her plans for the two-story.

Shadow slowed down as the line of trees came into view.

Looking a little trimmer than they used to.

Nora turned his way, eyeing him a second before looking back toward the project he'd worked on for years.

And finally finished a few weeks ago.

It was time to call it done. There were much bigger projects on the horizon.

Houses.

Homes.

Weddings.

Kids.

Not necessarily in that order.

The closer they got the slower Shadow went, dragging out the last little bit. Nora's spot in front of him meant he didn't get any hint at her reaction to what she saw.

Shadow finally stopped, coming to a halt in his normal spot, leaving Nora staring up through the trees.

Pumpernickel stopped right next to Shadow, exactly like she was supposed to.

"There's lights on the outside."

"There are." Brooks swung to the ground.

Nora didn't move. "How are there lights on the outside?"

"Got electricity back here now." They'd been so busy working on the little house that it was easy to get the power run without Nora finding out.

Her gaze dropped to the ground, following the line of flags marking the underground lines so they would be easy to avoid in the coming weeks. "When did you do that?"

"Little while ago." He held his hands up, wiggling his fingers. "Come on down."

Nora turned his way but her eyes went over his head. "What's that?"

"Come down here and I'll tell you."

She frowned at him. "You know what they say about secrets."

"What's that?"

"I don't like them."

"That's what they say about secrets?"

"Someone says that." She lifted a brow.

He grinned. "Get your ass down here."

Nora huffed out a breath. "You're turning out to be a real sneaky man."

He caught her as she dropped to the ground. "Does that mean you want to stay in the main house this winter?"

"Are my options the main house or the treehouse?"

"I'm tryin' to get you a third option, but you seem awful grumpy about it."

Nora poked him with one finger. "Stop giving me a hard time or I'll tell you I want an open floor plan in the two story." Her lips pressed down on a smile. "One that would remove a bunch of load-bearing walls."

"You might be evil."

Her head tipped back as she laughed. "And you love me so what does that say about you?"

"All you need to know." He pulled her tight to his side. "Now quit being a pain in the ass so I can show you where our barn's goin'."

BONUS BITS ONE

Mae

"YOU WARM ENOUGH?" Boone settled down beside her in the two-seater folding camp chair they brought to the bonfire blazing just outside the new barn Brooks and Nora built on their spot at the ranch.

It was a little late in the year to brave a bonfire, but there was a bunch of brush to get rid of and the day was unseasonably warm.

At least it was until the sun went down.

"We're good." Leah sat on her lap, cuddled under the thick blanket wrapped tight around both of them. "Can I have another s'more, Uncle Boone?" She batted her big blue eyes at him.

"How many have you had?"

Leah's lips smashed together. "I don't know."

"Liar." Boone called across the fire to where Brody and Clara sat, huddled together with Michaela. "Can this one have another s'more?"

Clara shook her head. "Absolutely not. She's already conned her way to four. If she eats another one she'll puke."

Boone's eyes were wide as they went back to Leah. "Four?"

Mae leaned into Leah's ear. "He's only worried because if you puke he'll puke too."

"At least it won't be in my bushes this time." Maryann sat in one of the single chairs eating a s'more of her own.

"Is that all we're going to remember from that day?" Boone pointed Michaela's way. "I saved her life."

Michaela sucked a line of melted chocolate from her fingers. "Then you threw up."

Leah wiggled around, breaking loose from the blanket. "See you later."

Boone draped one arm across Mae's shoulders and leaned close. "I think we were being used."

"Definitely." Mae relaxed into him as Leah went to where Brett sat alone on the other side of the fire and climbed up in his lap. "But it looks like she found a new mark."

"Don't give her any more chocolate." Clara nipped it in the bud immediately. "No matter how hungry she swears she is."

"What about you? You get enough to eat?" Boone's voice was low in her ear.

"I did." Mae lifted her eyes to the stars filling the chilly night sky. "Did everything get cleaned up?"

She and Maryann spent the afternoon making chili and cornbread for the evening that might almost be called a party.

There was so much to celebrate.

Nora and Brooks would have a warm place to park the camper they were living in. The twins were going to be big sisters to two new little Paces. The Inn was fully booked for the winter and most of the spring.

Life was back to normal at The Wooden Spoon.

Everything was as good as it could get.

For her anyway.

Her gaze trailed to where Calvin sat with Wyatt, both boys wearing the cowboy hats that never left their heads.

Seeing Calvin loved and safe and happy made the temporary loss of her home and business more than worth it.

Maybe if she found Junior and smacked him in the face again Camille would feel the same way her son did.

"You look a little pissed." Boone tucked the blanket tighter around her.

"I wish Camille would have come tonight." It didn't feel right all of them being out here while Camille stayed at The Inn. Working.

Like she always did.

"You can't make her figure it out." Boone slid one hand between the layers of blanket to find hers. "She's gotta do it on her own."

"I know." Mae huffed out a breath. "It's just taking so damn long."

"Imagine how my mother felt seein' you every week."

"That was your fault." She smiled.

It was amazing how quickly things could change. One year ago she hated Boone.

Would have hit *him* in the face with a sheet pan if she had the chance.

Now the ten years they spent apart almost made sense.

Almost felt like that was the way it was always supposed to be.

"And I suffered for it." He nosed along her neck. "Slept in that bed you broke until it damn near killed me."

"And now look at you." She laced her fingers with his. "You have a standing breakfast reservation at the best restaurant in town."

"Only until our house is finished." His thumb stroked her skin. "Course I've got to figure out how to tell my mother we already got married at some point. We might end up back in the cabins after that."

"Good point."

There was so much going on around them. Weddings and engagements and pregnancies and houses.

And as beautiful as Clara and Brody's wedding was, it wasn't what she and Boone were looking for.

Wasn't what they wanted.

"Maybe we can have a reception." Mae kept her voice low. "Something small."

It'd been nearly a month since they snuck to the county courthouse, not really thinking through the process of how to tell the people they loved what they'd done.

So they didn't.

And now it was starting to get a little stressful.

"Maybe we could get pregnant real quick. That would help."

She gave him her most serious look. "No."

Boone was more than ready to get the ball rolling with kids while she still wanted to wait a little bit.

But in all honesty he was wearing her down a little.

At least he was until they all found out Clara was pregnant with twins.

Now she was terrified it was genetic.

"What are you two talking about?" Maryann stretched her legs out. "It looks serious."

Boone lifted his brows in question.

Like he was asking permission.

Oh no.

Before she could stop him, Boone leaned to look at where Maryann sat. "Mae and I got married last month."

All conversation stopped and every eye came their way.

Maryann's jaw was slack as she stared their way. "Last month?"

Boone tipped his head in a nod. "Last month."

Maryann's eyes went to Mae, the silence dragging out.

Finally she snorted out a laugh, shaking her head as she went back to her s'more. "I can't believe it took you that long."

BONUS BITS TWO

Brett

"BRETT."

The quiet voice behind him was one he'd learned to listen for.

Calvin stood just outside the tack room of the barn behind The Inn, holding one receiver of a set of long-range walkie-talkies.

"Hey, buddy." Brett set down what he was working on. "What's going on?"

"I think I broke it." The little boy looked terrified and it cut into him in a way that was all too familiar.

"Everything's fixable." Brett was slow as he walked toward Camille's son.

He'd learned early on that moving too quick was a bad idea.

One that made him want to hunt down the son of a bitch that caused this kid so much pain.

Not to mention what he'd done to his mother.

"Can I see it?" He slowly lifted his hand, palm up, fingers relaxed.

Calvin passed the receiver, but didn't jerk his hands back like normal. "I tried to call you on it, but it didn't work."

Brett flipped the unit over and popped off the back. "Did you need something?"

Calvin shook his head, eyes locked onto every move Brett made. "My mom did."

Brett's hands stilled. "Your mom?"

"Yeah." Calvin came a little closer. "She dropped a plate and it broke." His eyes came to Brett's. "She cried." He was quiet for a second. "I thought maybe you could help make her feel better."

He'd love to.

Been waiting for the chance.

But Camille would want him to make sure Cal was okay first.

"I can try." He slid the battery cover off. "As soon as we figure out what's going on here."

It was important Calvin always knew he came first. Always knew everything Brett did was because he cared about him.

Not because he also cared about his mother.

"Looks like our battery's leaking." Brett pulled out the crusty battery. "I'll clean it out and get a fresh battery and it will be good as new."

"Okay." Calvin's relief was clear.

"We should check mine too, just in case." Brett pulled out the walkie always in his back pocket. It was how he knew that woman was causing problems with Nora at The Inn last summer.

Calvin called him anytime he was scared or upset.

Sometimes he called him just because.

Camille's son needed to know he was never on his own. That there was always someone besides his mom he could count on.

"Shoot." Brett held up his receiver. "Mine's corroded too." He popped the other battery out. "Looks like we got a bad batch."

"But you can fix them, right?"

"If I can't fix them then I'll get us another set." He rested one hand on Calvin's shoulder as they walked out into the main hall of the barn. "I'll test them out as soon as I make sure your momma's okay."

Calvin's head bobbed in a nod. "Okay."

"Hey, Cal." Brooks walked into the barn with a bale of hay. "You want to help me give this to the horses?"

"Yeah." Calvin rushed Brooks' way. He was one hell of a good kid. Eager to do anything he could around the ranch.

He was even going out with them for short jobs. He wasn't the best rider yet, but Pumpernickel was as perfect as Brett knew she would be, taking Calvin where he needed to go no matter what happened.

Brett watched as Calvin listened intently to Brooks' directions, ready to do the best he could.

A swell of pride warmed his chest. Pride at how far Calvin had already come.

How much less held him back these days.

If only he could help Camille get to the same place.

Brett ducked out of the barn and headed for The Inn. It was quiet when he went in.

Quiet enough he could hear her.

The soft sniffle stoked the anger always simmering under his skin.

Anger that a man could act the way Junior Shepard did.

Anger that he couldn't go back in time and make what happened to Camille and Cal right.

But Camille didn't need his anger any more than Cal did.

Brett walked toward the kitchen, following the soft sounds of Camille's choppy breathing.

As soon as he stepped into view she jumped. The same way she always did. She immediately turned away, wiping at her eyes.

But only with one hand.

"I didn't hear you come in."

The urge to help her was strong, but he had to be careful. "What happened to your hand?"

"It's just a little scrape." Camille tucked the hand in question behind her as she turned to face him, plastering on a perfectly professional smile.

Normally he didn't mind.

Normally he understood.

She needed time.

Space.

Room to find her footing after too many years of suffering and pain.

But right now the pain was here.

Running down her palm and dripping onto the floor.

And she was still smiling at him.

Like she owed it to him.

Brett dropped the walkie-talkies onto the counter and held his hand out. "Let me see it."

"It's fine."

"Then let me see it."

Her smile faltered. "I can take care of it."

"I know you can." He moved closer. "I want to see it anyway."

Her eyes held his, the uncertainty there so much better than the fear that usually tinted them.

Uncertainty he could work with. "Please let me see your hand, Camille."

She slowly pulled the hand from behind her back. It was loosely wrapped in a dish towel that did nothing to slow the steady drip of blood.

"What happened?" Brett carefully opened the towel. A thin slice ran down the side of her middle finger.

"There was a broken plate in the sink when I reached into the water." Her lip wavered. "I can pay for it."

"I'm not worried about that right now." He wouldn't worry about it ever. "What I'm worried about is you." Brett reached for a clean towel and went to work wrapping it tightly around the cut. "Come on." He held her hand, keeping pressure on the injury as they walked to the bathroom where his mother kept the first aid kit.

Camille was quiet as he went to work on her hand, washing it to rinse away the blood before using the wound glue to seal up the oozing slice. He blew across the repair, keeping her hand in his while it dried.

Once it was dry he fished out a Band-Aid and wrapped it around for an added layer of protection.

When he was finished Camille pulled her hand away, holding it against her chest. "Thank you."

Brett packed up the kit and slid it back into place. "You're welcome." He glanced up to find her watching him.

Her eyes immediately darted away. "I should get back to work." She turned.

"No dishes for a day or two. The glue will fail." It was a white lie.

One he didn't feel even a little bit bad about telling.

Camille's head snapped his way. "I can't go two days without doing dishes." She turned to the line of pots and pans that didn't fit in the dishwasher.

"You're gonna have to." Brett went to the sink, carefully pushing the suds to one side so he could see what was waiting for him under the water. "I'm sure we can find someone else to wash the dishes." He pulled out the broken plate, stacking the pieces on the counter.

"Actually, I have some free time the next few days. I can come help you out."

"You don't have to do—"

"And you don't have to work every hour you're not in bed." He glanced Camille's way. "But you do."

Her lips pressed together. She wanted to say something. He could see it in her eyes.

But she'd spent years hearing that her voice didn't matter.

So he went to work, draining the sink and rinsing out any remaining bits of broken ceramic before running fresh water and going to work on the pans left from breakfast.

Camille didn't move from where she stood, silently watching as he finished one of the many chores she claimed as hers and hers alone.

As if she had to earn her job every day.

He was on the last pot before she seemed to relax a little, one of her hips finally tipping to lean against the counter. Her eyes fell to the set of walkie-talkies at her side. "Is this the walkie-talkie Calvin always has?"

Brett nodded, watching as she picked it up, her brows coming together as she stared at the second one. It was a little dirtier and the finish was scuffed in more than a few places. "Who usually has that one?"

Brett waited for Camille's eyes to come to his. "I do."

****

Made in the USA
Monee, IL
25 March 2023

30540959R00173